AF492326

Whispers of Hope

PAT NICHOLS

Whispers of Hope by Pat Nichols
Published by Armchair Press
ISBN: 979-8-9912411-4-4
Copyright © 2025 by Pat Nichols
Cover Design by Elaina Lee
Edited by Sherri Stewart

Available in print from your local bookstore or online.
For more information on this book or the author visit:
https://patnicholsauthor.blog
Printed in the United States of America
Whispers of Hope is a work of fiction. Names, characters, and incidents are all products of the author's imagination or are used for fictional purposes. Any mentioned brand names, places, and trademarks remain the property of their respective owners, bear no association with the author or publisher, and are used for fictional purposes only.
Library of Congress Cataloging-in Publication Data
Nichols, Pat.
Whispers of Hope/ Pat Nichols

All rights reserved. No portion of this book may be reproduced in any form, stored in a retrieval system, or transmitted in any form by any means—electronic, photocopy, recording, or otherwise—without written permission from the publisher or author, except as permitted by U.S. copyright law.

Books by
Pat Nichols
Women's Fiction

Blue Ridge Series

Blizzard at Blue Ridge Inn
The Inheritance
The Wedding
Christmas at Hilltop Inn
The Promise
Summer of Second Chances
Whispers of Hope
Fragile Hearts

Willow Falls Series

The Secret of Willow Inn
Trouble in Willow Falls
Starstruck in Willow Falls
Bridges, Books, and Bones

Butler Family LegacySeries

Big Secrets, Little Lies
Truth and Forgiveness
New Beginnings

Dedicated to my dear friend, Dana Turpin, who opens her home to members of Word Weavers and shares words of wisdom.

Chapter 1

Four and a half hours after backing out of their garage, Chris Armstrong turned off the two-lane road onto a gravel driveway winding up a steep hill. Wendy lowered her window to breathe in the fresh mountain air. A six-foot-long rectangular boulder speckled with bronze streaks conjured up images of an old, abandoned coffin. She squeezed her eyes shut, willing the image to disappear. "What if this is the last time we see my mother before..." Swallowing the dreaded word seconds before it could roll off her tongue, Wendy splayed her fingers across her seven-and-a-half-month baby bulge in a feeble attempt to ease the swarming-butterflies sensation. "I hope she has enough strength to hold on for six more weeks." Wendy opened her eyes. Her voice faltered. "Every time we talk Mom seems a little weaker."

Chris stopped halfway up the driveway then turned toward her. "Spending Labor Day weekend with you and her grandson will give your mother the boost she needs to continue fighting her illness."

Wendy gazed into her husband's brown eyes. "After all those years Mom and I were apart, we've had so little time to become reacquainted."

Chris stroked her cheek. "You're making every minute count, angel."

"I'm glad you're with us on this trip, darling."

"So am I. Besides, there's no way I'd let my pregnant wife drive two-hundred-plus miles alone."

"You also chauffeured me to Hilton Head to confront my father when I was eight-months pregnant with Ryan. Of course, you know how that turned out. He had no idea I even existed. " Wendy laid her hand on Chris's thigh. "One good thing came out of that trip. You proposed on a hotel balcony overlooking the Atlantic."

His face lit with a smile. "Lucky for me, you said yes." At the sound of their son's babble, Chris glanced over his shoulder. "Our little guy agrees."

"When Ryan's old enough to understand, we'll tell him you loved him so much you adopted him."

"You, our little guy in the back seat—" Chris pressed his hand to Wendy's belly. "—and our little gal make me the happiest man in the world."

"Hmm." Wendy squeezed his thigh. "What do you say we park here for a while and pretend we're love-struck teenagers."

Chris winked. "Tonight, if we have a private bedroom."

"Oh my goodness." Wendy playfully fanned her face while summoning her best Southern accent. "Making your hormone-charged lover wait until dark. Such torture."

Chris leaned close, whispering. "You, my dear, are the sexiest blue-eyed, blonde, seven-and-a-half-month pregnant woman on the planet."

"You're not so bad yourself."

"What do you think? Should we head on up the driveway before our hosts become suspicious?"

Wendy brushed her fingers through Chris's thick brown hair. "Thank you for helping me deal with my anxiety."

"Still jittery?"

"A lot less than I was three minutes ago."

"Mission accomplished." Chris gripped the wheel then drove forward. Gravel crunched beneath the tires as they eased up the driveway to the parking pad fronting an impressive A-frame house. He parked beside the Gilmores' SUV. "One fact is undeniable. Your mother's friend owns an expensive vacation house."

"Now I know why Mom wanted to spend this weekend here instead of at their home in Nashville." Wendy peered at the windows stretching to the top of the slanted roof. "Peace and quiet plus luxury. The perfect place to create new memories—before it's too late."

Nine-year-old Riley rushed out the front door and down the porch steps followed by sixteen-year-old Kayla. Wendy climbed out and embraced the half-sisters she hadn't known existed until months after she moved to Blue Ridge.

Riley pulled away. "Me and Kayla baked three dozen chocolate-chip cookies." She headed straight to the open driver's side and peered up at Chris. "Can I hold Ryan's hand and walk him inside?"

"Of course, you can." Chris lifted his son from his car seat. "Aunt Riley's gonna take good care of you."

Riley gripped her nephew's hand while leading him toward the porch. "You're gonna love the baby rocking horse we bought for you."

Wendy slid her arm around Kayla's shoulders. "How's our mother doing?"

Kayla stared straight ahead. "When I first learned Mom had cancer, I was angry at her for refusing treatment. But now...during the past three months, Mom has spent more time with me and Riley than she did during the last three years. I still don't like her decision, but now at least I understand it."

"You mentioned you and your sister spending time with our mother. What about Zach?"

"Lots of days my little brother goes straight from school to some friend's house. When he is home, he hides out in his room and barely talks to any of us, especially Mom." Kayla plucked a rock off the concrete and hurled it away from the driveway. "If you ask me, he's acting like a jerk. At least he's here, but only because Dad made him come."

Kayla turned toward Chris. "You're a lawyer. Maybe you can straighten him out like you did me when you caught me smoking weed at your house."

"I'll talk to Zach if and when either of your parents ask for my help." Chris lifted two suitcases from the back of the SUV then followed Wendy and Kayla to the front porch.

Brent, Kayla and Riley's father, pulled the front door open. His smile failed to mask his drawn features. "We're all glad you're here."

Wendy stepped inside, breathing in the chocolate aroma sweetening the air. "The cookies smell delicious."

"Mom's favorite. Dad and I brought some of the food she likes best, so maybe she'll gain a few pounds." Kayla pulled away. She took two steps then stopped and turned back toward Wendy. "Riley wants to challenge all of us to a game of Monopoly."

"Sounds like fun."

Kayla pointed to a spiral staircase. "Us kids are bunking in the loft. You and Chris are staying in one of the downstairs bedrooms." She turned and headed straight to the French doors leading out back.

Brent nodded toward an open door beside the kitchen area. "That's your bedroom. Cynthia and I are staying in the other downstairs suite. When you two are ready, come on out to the deck. The beer's cold and the steaks are marinating."

"We won't be long." Wendy followed Chris into their bedroom. "A private room with a bath."

"Perfect for a romantic weekend." Chris lifted Wendy's suitcase onto the bed. "Do you want to unpack now or later?"

"Later, except for one thing." Wendy unzipped her suitcase and removed a gift-wrapped box. "I want to have this ready the right time." She tucked the box under her arm then ambled to the great room. A tan sofa, a leather ottoman serving as a coffee table, and two recliners completed a cozy arrangement in front of a television anchored to the brick fireplace. Wendy ran her hand along the polished-wood dining room table separating the living area from the open kitchen.

Chris laced his fingers with Wendy's. "Everyone's waiting for us."

"I know." She swallowed the lump rising in her throat while fixing her eyes on the French doors. "Okay, I'm ready." They walked out to the deck.

Sitting on the second rocking chair in a row of four, Cynthia held out her hand while peering up through dark sunglasses. "Come sit beside me, Wendy darling."

Choking back tears, Wendy nestled her mother's frail hand in hers then bent down to kiss her cheek.

"How sweet." Cynthia fingered Wendy's wrist. "You're wearing one of the matching bracelets I bought for me and my beautiful daughters when we visited Blue Ridge."

Kayla held up her wrist. "So am I, Mom."

"I know you are, honey."

Surprised her mother wasn't loving on her grandson, Wendy settled beside her and set the gift on the floor. "Perfect place for another family get-together."

"This is the first time I've shared my friend's vacation getaway with anyone." Cynthia set her rocking chair in motion. "Tell me everything that's going on back in Blue Ridge."

"Well…" Matching her mother's rhythm, Wendy brought Cynthia up to speed while Riley and Kayla entertained their nephew.

When Wendy finished, Cynthia leaned her head back. "I still find it fascinating how you, Amanda, and Erica were strangers nineteen months ago and are now closer than a lot of families. Especially after you discovered you were all married to the same con man."

Wendy folded her hands across her belly. "The three of us refused to become victims then risked everything to turn our lives around."

"I'm beyond proud of the amazing woman you've become. Not only are you the chief financial officer for the company you three ladies started, but you're also studying to earn a college degree." Cynthia nodded toward Chris. "You married a successful attorney who's also a good man..." She paused for a long moment. "After leaving you all those years ago, I'm blessed to have you back in my life."

Wendy broke eye contact. Memories of the eighteen years between the day her mother abandoned her and the day she and Amanda showed up unannounced at Cynthia's Nashville home raced through her mind at warp speed.

"You're remembering, aren't you?"

Startled, Wendy blinked. Did her mother understand the depth of her pain? Their eyes met. "For a moment. Now, I'm cherishing every minute we have together."

"Funny how one's hopes and dreams change when time is suddenly cut short." Cynthia leaned her head back. "During the past few months, I've discovered so many special qualities about my children. Including Zach, even though he barely speaks to me. Can't say I blame him, considering how little attention I've given him, or any of my children for that matter."

Wendy stole a sideways glance at her mother's downcast eyes. "The happy memories we're making now will diminish those from the past and remain in our hearts forever."

Pushing her sunglasses up, Cynthia stopped rocking and turned to face Wendy. "If I had time, I'd do my best to become more like you."

Choking back tears, Wendy placed her hand on her heart. Their eyes met.

There wasn't a flicker of doubt in her mother's gaze—only calm, steady faith. "In the years ahead, I want you to tell my grandchildren how much their Glamma Cynthia loves them, and that I'll always watch over them."

Wendy pressed her hand to her belly the moment her little gal moved. The perfect time for the gift. "Even better than telling them—" Smiling, she lifted it off the deck and handed it to her mother.

Cynthia peeled off the wrapping paper then opened the box and removed a framed photo of her and Ryan.

"After you sign the picture, we'll take it home so our little guy will always remember his Glamma."

Cynthia held the gift to her chest while fingering the empty frame remaining in the box. "Is this for..." Her voice faltered.

"A signed picture of you and your granddaughter."

Cynthia's smile burst forth, lighting up her face as tears streamed down her cheeks. "This is the most precious gift you could ever give me." Her eyes met Wendy's. "Nothing will keep me from living long enough to welcome my granddaughter into this world."

Chapter 2

Erica Nelson settled on a stool while splaying her fingers on the island in Hilltop Inn's kitchen. Her two-carat diamond engagement ring sparkled under the overhead light bringing a smile to her lips. "Before November I need to order two new business cards. One with the name Erica Barkley, Awesam Chief Executive Officer, and the other with Erica Barkley, Massage Therapist."

Chef Millie Cunningham, the seventy-plus-year-old who hiked from her home next door five mornings a week to prepare breakfast for guests, closed the dishwasher and pushed the start button. "Marrying Brad will prove that old saying— 'Third time's a charm.'"

"Especially after I was married to an abusive cop and later to a bigamist con man."

"Wendy was the first of Gunter's illegal wives to marry a good guy, and you're the second." Millie draped the dishtowel over the oven's handle. "Now we need to ensure SAGA pays off."

Erica pressed her lips tight. No one other than her knew that her business partner was on to the 'snag a guy for Amanda' ploy. "Our little company's president believes her first husband was her soulmate—"

"Yeah, well." Millie planted her hands on her hips. "A soulmate who died in a car crash more than thirteen years ago can't warm her bed on cold nights."

"Amanda and Gary Redding are partners in a political campaign, and they've become good friends."

"Don't you know that friends make the best lovers?" Millie dropped her hands to her sides. "Besides, a handsome bank president is a doggone good catch. Especially in a town as small as Blue Ridge."

"Amanda claims she's not interested in fishing for a guy."

"She's forty-five-years-old, for goodness sakes. How much longer is she willing to stay single?" A chime sent, Millie heading toward the door. "Saved by the bell. I'll find out if we have an early check-in or if someone forgot their key."

"Be my guest." Erica slid off her stool then ambled into the elegant dining room. Transforming the mansion that had stood vacant for more than two decades into a first-class inn had been a labor of love for her and her partners. Now they were reaping the rewards.

Millie escorted a woman with shoulder-length dark hair into the dining room. "Erica Nelson, meet Ms. Wellington—Sierra's mother."

Words refused to form. Erica gripped the back of a chair and gawked at the woman who had obviously spent a lifetime indulging in far too many desserts. After Sierra and her once-abandoned son moved into the ranch house, they hadn't heard a peep from her mother. Why did she suddenly show up?

"My daughter says she works in this fancy place Mondays and Tuesdays." Ms. Wellington peered around the room, her eyes wide, as if ticking off the value of every item. "How come she ain't here?"

Erica pried her fingers off the chair. "She's home with a cold, which is why I'm filling in for her."

The woman thrust her thumb over her shoulder. "Home's next door, right?"

Millie folded her arms across her chest. "Why are you asking?"

"'Cause I done drove all the way from Chattanooga, and I aim to talk to my daughter."

Knowing full well Millie would tag along, Erica moved closer to the stranger who reeked of cheap cologne. "We'll take you to her." She led the way out to the front porch, down the steps, and across the sidewalk.

Ms. Wellington paused to peer up at the three-story mansion. "How many guest rooms you got?"

"One on the first floor," Millie spoke with authority. "Six on the second. The third floor is unfinished."

"Bet it costs a pretty penny to stay the night here."

Millie stared at the woman as if she'd asked the most ridiculous question imaginable. "My friend Eleanor Harrington and her husband owned this place before my business partners and I turned it into a first-class bed-and-breakfast."

Unsure what Millie would say next, Erica jumped in. "Did Sierra tell you she's studying to earn her high school equivalency?"

"You mean her GED? Yeah, she told me. Big waste of time, if you ask me." She stepped up her pace while they headed across the driveway and side yard to the sidewalk fronting the ranch house. She pointed to the ramp leading to the front door. "What's that for?"

Erica stepped onto the porch. During the past few days had anyone noticed that her normally optimistic child seemed glum? She blinked. "My daughter was injured in a car accident last year. Abby's still in a wheelchair."

"I hope you sued the pants off whoever caused the wreck."

Erica cringed. No way she'd tell this stranger that the son of the man she was weeks from marrying had crashed into her daughter's car.

Millie tapped her foot while glaring at Sierra's mother. "For your information, no one sued anyone. The accident happened because an overgrown bush hid a newly installed stop sign. Besides, my partners don't sue people they care about."

"Wouldn't of stopped me."

Erica unlocked the front door then stood aside. "Come in."

Ms. Wellington stepped across the threshold.

Abby's golden retriever, Dusty, padded over and sniffed the newcomer, then sneezed.

Erica stifled a laugh. So much for cheap perfume.

Ms. Wellington pointed to the office set up in the living room. "You running a business out of here?"

Erica raised a brow. *What's with this woman?* "A little company called Awesam—after our names, Amanda, Wendy, Erica, plus my daughter Abby and Amanda's daughter Morgan. We added the S to create a real word."

Their uninvited guest jabbed a finger toward Millie. "How come she didn't say your name?"

"Because Millie became a partner later." Erica gripped the woman's arm and steered her into the paneled den.

Ms. Wellington ran her fingers along the back of the sofa facing the brick fireplace. "This place ain't nearly as fancy as next door."

Millie scoffed. "Because we spent all our money fixing up the inn. Why don't you and I have a seat while Erica tells Sierra you're here."

"Might as well."

Erica shot Millie her best 'behave yourself' expression then moved to the hall and tapped on Sierra's bedroom door.

"Come in."

Erica stepped inside. "How are you feeling?"

Sierra sat on a chair with an ankle tucked under her knee while her seven-month-old son sat in his crib clutching a teething ring. "Better than yesterday." She grabbed a tissue and blew her nose. "Thanks for covering for me at the inn."

"You're welcome. I have something to tell you." Erica sat on the edge of the bed. "A few minutes ago, your mother showed up at the inn."

Her mouth agape, Sierra stared at Erica, her eyes as round as silver dollars. "Is she alone? Did she say what she wants?"

Erica nodded. "She wants to talk to you."

"The whole time I was pregnant and living with Grandma, my mother never called me. Not one time. Since I moved in here, the only time we talked is when I called her." Sierra lowered her foot to the floor then stood and lifted her baby into her arms. "She drove all this way because she wants something from me."

"It's your decision whether or not you see her."

"She's my mother. I owe her a couple of minutes. At least when she sees my baby, she'll know I'm taking good care of him."

Erica stood. "We'll keep her company until you're ready to join us." She walked out, closing the door behind her before returning to the den. "Sierra will be out shortly."

Ms. Wellington sat on the sofa with her fingers laced, twiddling her thumbs. Millie had chosen a club chair—her back ramrod straight as if she'd assumed the role of a judge facing a defendant.

"Would you like a glass of water or lemonade, Ms. Wellington?"

"Lemonade if that's all you got that's sweet."

"All right." Resisting an eyeroll, Erica headed to the kitchen, returned moments later, and handed her the glass.

Their guest swallowed a long drink before setting the glass on the end table. At least she knew enough to use the coaster. Erica lowered onto the other club chair. Dusty sprawled on the floor between her and Millie. "Is this your first trip to Blue Ridge?"

"I ain't had no reason to come here before today."

Millie tapped her finger on her chair arm. "What reason do you have now?"

"That's between me and my daughter."

"I'm surprised to see you here." Sierra's tone came across as flat, devoid of any trace of emotion. She settled on the opposite end of the sofa from her mother with her son on her lap. "This is my baby, Theo."

"Bet he wasn't so cute before the doctors fixed his cleft lip."

Erica stared at the woman. Did she know her daughter had left her newborn in a gym bag on the crisis center front stoop? Did she also know that she and Abby had rescued the infant? "Sierra's taking excellent care of her baby."

"The kid looks healthy enough. That don't erase the fact that a boy needs a father to raise him right."

Sierra's eyes narrowed to a slit. "What's the real reason you showed up?"

"To take you and Theo back to where you belong—"

Erica leaned forward. "She belongs here with us, Ms. Wellington."

Millie waggled her finger at the woman, her eyes sharp as knife blades. "Those Hackett brothers put you up to this, didn't they?"

"Dereck has legal rights to his son—"

Sierra pulled Theo close to her chest. "All Jay and Dereck want is the money left in Theo's GoFundMe account."

Her mother folded her arms tight across her chest. "I don't know nothing about that."

Sierra stared at her mother. "Did Jay promise you half?"

"No matter what you think, Dereck wants to do what's right."

Millie scoffed. "He should've thought about that when he broke the law and got a seventeen-year-old girl pregnant."

Ms. Wellington's forehead furrowed, her head tilted. "What law you talking about?"

"Tennessee's consensual consent law."

"Jay didn't say nothing about his brother breaking no law." Ms. Wellington unfolded her arms and turned toward her daughter. "Forget those boys. Come home with me and sign up to get your check from Uncle Sam."

"She's not—"

"Please—" Sierra aimed her palm toward Millie. "Let me handle this." She drew in a deep breath then faced her mother. "I made a big mistake the day Theo was born, but now that I have him back, there's no way I'll let him grow up as a poor welfare kid."

"What are you gonna do? Get some minimum wage job?"

"Maybe, at least to start. Then I'll work my way up to something better."

"Your daughter is a smart young woman with a bright future." Erica moved to the sofa and settled beside Sierra. "She and Theo are welcome to stay here with us until she has the means to live on her own."

"I know what you're up to." Her mother sneered. "You wanna keep that money for yourself."

"Aha." Millie scooted to the edge of her chair. "You do know about Theo's fund, don't you?"

Ms. Wellington shrugged. "Jay might've mentioned something 'bout it."

"I'll bet he did." Millie waggled her finger at the woman. "When you return to Chattanooga, tell Jay and his brother that sending you here was a colossal waste of your time."

She stared at Millie for a long moment before facing Sierra. "Dereck ain't a bad kid. Jay's the one that got 'em both sent to juvenile detention."

"Doesn't matter, Mom. I'm not going with you."

"Maybe not today." Ms. Wellington lifted her girth off the sofa. "Jay's gas tank's running low, and I ain't got enough cash to fill it up."

Of course she doesn't. Erica stood. "How much money do you need?"

"I dunno. Maybe fifty?"

"Wait here." Erica headed to her bedroom then returned and handed over the cash.

Sierra's mother stared at the bills. "You got any more?'

"No, Mom." Sierra's voice was laced with embarrassment. "She doesn't. Why don't you let Millie walk you out?"

"Good idea." Millie rose, closing the distance to Sierra's mother.

"You wanna make sure I don't go stealing nothing from your fancy inn, don't you?"

"I'm just being courteous, Ms. Wellington. Same way we are to all of our guests." Millie linked arms with the woman while steering her through the foyer and out the front door.

Sierra released a heavy sigh. "My mother's not a bad person; she was just raised wrong."

Erica slid her arm around the young woman's shoulders. "I'm proud of you for breaking free from her lifestyle."

"Know what? For the first time in my life, I'm kinda proud of myself as well." Sierra's lips curled into a smile before she carried her yawning son back to her room.

Millie returned, scowling. "Odds are we haven't seen the last of that woman or the Hackett brothers."

Chapter 3

The stillness of the early Labor Day morning remained unbroken while Wendy donned her robe then tiptoed to the door, leaving Chris and Ryan sleeping in the guest bedroom. She eased into the great room that smelled of freshly brewed coffee and stopped beside the unfinished Monopoly game spread out on the dining room table. Riley had halted the competition last night when her mother's energy gave out, insisting they continue playing through the holiday. Everyone had joined in the fun except Zach, who made a brief appearance to gobble down his meal before hightailing it back to his room. Wendy stepped out to the back deck and breathed in the fresh mountain air. Light spilling from an outdoor lantern cast a soft glow against the predawn sky.

"Trouble sleeping?" Brent Gilmore's voice drifted from the far end of the deck where he sat in a rocker.

Wrapping her robe tightly around her, Wendy joined him. "A little. What about you?"

He cradled a coffee mug in both hands. "I haven't slept much since learning about my wife's cancer."

"Understandable." Wendy settled on the rocking chair beside Brent. "You have a lot to deal with."

He remained silent for a long moment. "Things haven't been the same between us since...Did Cynthia tell you what happened after Riley was born?"

Unsure, Wendy focused on a moth flitting in the lamp light. Maybe her silence would answer his question.

"She told you about her affair, didn't she?"

Wendy nodded. "She also told me that you forgave her."

"Forgiving didn't erase the pain." Brent took a sip of coffee then lifted off his rocker and ambled to the railing.

Wendy hesitated, then followed him. "After I forgave Cynthia for abandoning me all those years ago, I continued to struggle with anger."

"Even though I'm a small-time performer, you'd be surprised how many women throw themselves at me. I never crossed the line...until my wife cheated on me."

Wendy glanced at his profile. "Does Cynthia know?"

"I've never told anyone...until now. They say confession is good for the soul. If I'd told Cynthia back then—" He shook his head. "—but I didn't, and I'm not about to burden her now." He took a sip of coffee before dumping the remaining liquid over the railing. "If I'd spent more time at home, instead of at Gilmore's Bar and Restaurant..." His lips drew into a thin line, his head tilted down.

Would learning why his wife cheated help ease his guilt? "There's something you need to know." Wendy peered at the first hint of dawn turning the inky black sky to dark gray. "Cynthia's affair wasn't your fault. It happened when she realized her dream to become a famous singer would never become a reality."

Brent exhaled deeply, his shoulders slumped as if a heavy weight had been lifted off his back. "Thank you for telling me." He lumbered back to the rocking chair. "Riley still believes Cynthia will beat her illness.

Kayla's had to grow up fast, taking on the role of her little sister's substitute mother."

Wendy followed him.

"I'm worried most about Zach. Puberty is difficult enough for a thirteen-year-old boy to navigate without the added burden of a dying mother. He ignores Cynthia and refuses to talk to me."

Wendy set her rocker in motion. "Kayla believes it might help if Chris talks to him."

"Maybe she's right. Is he willing?"

"If you approve."

"At this point, I'm ready to try anything." Brent matched Wendy's rocking rhythm. "Go ahead and tell your husband to give it his best shot."

"I will."

They fell silent, each lost in their own thoughts while the morning sun crept over the horizon. What would happen to the Gilmore family in the months ahead? Wendy closed her eyes while tuning into the melody of chirping birds. Whatever happened, she'd be there for them.

Five hours after sunrise, Brent laid burgers on the grill as Zach trudged out to the deck, his earbuds inserted, his phone in his hand. Ignoring the rest of the family, he dropped onto a rocker. His thumbs tapped the screen.

Chris leaned close to Wendy. "Time to put my parenting skills to the test." He headed to the chair beside the teenager and nudged his arm. "Bet that requires a lot of skill."

"I guess."

"What's the objective?"

Zach stopped tapping. "Why do you wanna know?"

"No particular reason, except keeping up with the latest games."

Zach hesitated for a moment, his eyes focused on his phone. "This one deals with alien creatures." He spent the next few minutes explaining the game and his strategy to win.

"Impressive. Do you mind if I upload the app and give it a try?"

Zach shrugged. "Suit yourself."

While Brent tended to the burgers, Wendy's focus volleyed between her sisters playing with Ryan, her chat with her mother, and the Chris and Zach drama. Would her brilliant husband manage to breakthrough to her half-brother?

When the burgers were ready to serve, Zach pocketed his phone then traipsed behind Chris to the glass-top table. Although the teenager didn't utter a word during lunch, at least he seemed to tune into the conversation.

After swallowing her last bite of burger, Riley raced inside, returning with a plate of chocolate chip cookies. "After dessert, can we finish our Monopoly game?"

Cynthia pushed her half-eaten meal aside. "Great idea."

"Tell you what—" Chris stood. "You guys go ahead while Zach and I continue fighting off the aliens."

Riley tilted her head. "If you don't play, you lose."

"We'll take the loss, right, Zach?"

"Whatever." Zach followed Chris back to the rocking chairs.

A smile tugged at Wendy's lips. Her babies' daddy had skillfully connected with a troubled boy.

While Brent, Kayla, and Riley carried the dishes inside, Cynthia scooted close to Wendy. "Chris knows how to connect with kids."

"Successful attorneys understand how to deal with people of all ages."

"Based on Zach's behavior, one of these days he might need a good lawyer."

Wendy stared wide-eyed at her mother. "Meaning what?"

"Kids these days are exposed to a lot of bad influences. Neither Brent nor I have been what you'd call model parents. Running Gilmore's Bar and Restaurant plus performing with his band six nights a week take most of his time." Cynthia paused. "Same for me until I learned how little time I have." A flicker of pain clouded her eyes. "I'm doing my best to make up for all those years of neglect."

Wendy swallowed the fist-sized lump forming in her throat. "Your children love you more than you realize."

Cynthia's eyes met hers. "Will you promise to stay close to my...I mean *our* family...after I'm gone?"

Wendy's heart ached. Why hadn't she attempted to find her mother years ago? "I promise."

Tears pooled in Cynthia's eyes. "I love you so much, my darling Wendy."

She touched her mother's arm. "I love you, Mom."

Riley dashed out. "Come on, you two. We're ready to play."

Cynthia cleared her throat while dabbing her cheeks.

Wendy pulled her hand away from her mother's arm. "Seems my youngest sister is eager to prove her Monopoly skills." Wendy stood. "Maybe she'll grow up and become a real estate tycoon."

Riley peered up at Wendy, her head tilted. "What's a tycoon?"

"A successful businessperson."

"Oh."

Cynthia lifted off her chair then clung to Wendy's arm while they followed Riley into the great room.

Throughout the afternoon and early evening while Riley sailed to a win, Cynthia put up a valiant fight to ward off waning energy. By the time they ended the game and enjoyed dinner on the deck, she had lost the battle. "Why don't y'all watch one of the movies we brought while I take a hot bath then turn in for the night."

Riley rushed to her mother's side and touched her cheek. "I love you, Mommy."

Cynthia pulled her youngest child close, her lips curled into a trembling smile. "I'll love you forever, my sweet girl."

Had her little sister finally started to accept the inevitable? Struggling to keep tears at bay, Wendy gathered plates and carried them inside. Kayla followed her to the kitchen area while Brent escorted his wife through the great room and into their bedroom. Zach brought in the last of the plates while Chris carried Ryan inside. Riley dashed to the hearth. The moment Brent returned she handed him a DVD. "Can we watch *Home Alone*?"

He nodded. "Good choice."

Zach rolled his eyes. "How many times have you watched that movie?"

"I dunno. I didn't count."

Kayla knuckle thumped her brother's arm. "Don't pretend it's not one of your favorites, Mr. Smarty Pants."

"Maybe when I was ten."

"Know what?" Chris lowered his son onto a play mat. "It's been a long time since I've watched Kevin outsmart those dumb-as-rock robbers."

Wendy set the last plate in the dishwasher. "I don't remember ever seeing that movie."

"How's that possible?" Zach stared at her as if she'd been raised in a cave by Neanderthals. At least he was talking.

Riley rushed over and grabbed Wendy's hand. "Will you sit by me?"

"Absolutely." Wendy settled on the sofa with Riley on one side and Kayla on the other. Chris dropped onto a club chair while Zach sprawled on the floor with his back propped against the coffee table ottoman. After inserting the DVD into the player and pressing play, Brent sat in the other club chair. For two hours Wendy managed to escape reality while laughing along with the rest of the family.

When the movie ended, Brent stood and stretched. "Good choice, Riley."

"Can we watch another movie, Daddy?"

"You go ahead, honey. I'm turning in for the night."

"So am I." Chris lifted his sleeping son from the play mat and carried him to their bedroom while Zach climbed up to the loft.

Eager to spend time alone with Chris, Wendy lifted off the sofa, yawning. "Seems all of us old folks have run out of energy."

Kayla scooted close to her little sister. "I'll watch another movie with you."

"Yay." Riley rushed to the stack of DVD's.

Wendy mouthed a thank you to Kayla before slipping away. Inside the bedroom, she closed the door. "I've been waiting all night to find out what you've learned about Zach."

"Up to this point, all I know is he's dealing with a lot of pain and anger." Chris lowered Ryan into his portable playpen. "At least we've begun establishing a relationship and opening lines of communication."

Desperate for strength to sustain her during the difficult weeks ahead, Wendy melted into her husband's arms. "The Gilmore family needs both of us now more than ever."

Chris held her tight. "I know."

Chapter 4

Preparing for the one o'clock board meeting, Amanda Smith assumed the role of Awesam's president while settling across from Erica at the dining room table in the den. She booted her laptop. "How many minutes after Millie arrives do you suppose she'll bring up her ridiculous bet?"

Sierra wandered in from the kitchen. "What bet are you talking about?"

Erica peered up from her laptop. "That she'll end up with a man in her life before Amanda."

Sierra's brows shot up. "Isn't Millie kinda old and cranky to have a boyfriend?"

Amanda laughed. "Too old? No. Too cranky? Maybe."

"What's the prize for the winner?"

Erica leaned back. "A sexy nightie from Victoria's Secret or Walmart, depending on who wins."

Sierra giggled. "Can I guess how long before Millie talks about the bet?"

"Absolutely."

"Hmm. I'd say five minutes."

Wendy rushed in from the carport. "Five minutes until the meeting starts?"

"Nope." Amanda explained while Wendy settled between her and Erica. "I'll guess three minutes."

"Seven for me." Erica eyed Wendy. "What's your guess?"

"If no one cheats and asks Millie a question, I'd say ten. One of us has to keep track."

Sierra raised her hand. "How about me?"

"Perfect. Have a seat." Wendy pointed to the empty chair beside Amanda. "Millie will never suspect a thing."

The back door flew open followed by brown sugar, cinnamon, and vanilla aromas wafting around Hilltop Inn's chef. Millie set the cookies and her iPad on the table then pulled out a chair. She eyed Sierra. "Is she staying for our meeting?"

Amanda nodded. "You don't mind, do you?"

"As long as she understands that everything we talk about is private Awesam business."

Amanda faced Sierra. "You understand, don't you?"

The young woman glanced at her phone. "You know I can hear everything you talk about from my room."

"Good point. Why don't we begin with a financial update—"

"Not so fast." Millie peeled foil off the cookie plate. "Before we delve into the boring details, how about an update on Keith Armstrong's campaign?"

Stifling a grin, Amanda folded her arms across the table. "We have two meet and greets scheduled. One at Keith and Linda's neighbors' house. The other at the Armstrong law office." Time to go for the win. "Gary is confident we'll attract more than a hundred voters."

"Well—" Millie tapped her finger on the table. "If you ask me, he needs to spend more time figuring out how to attract his campaign partner."

Sierra cocked her head. "Are you talking about Amanda?"

Millie raised a brow. "Who else would I be talking about?"

"That's what I thought." Sierra tapped her phone.

Amanda leaned toward her. "What's the verdict?"

Sierra's eyes darted from Amanda to Millie, then back to Amanda. "Is it okay to say?"

"By all means."

"Two minutes and fifty-three seconds makes you the winner."

Erica laughed. "Slick move, Ms. President."

"You know—" Wendy snickered. "We could accuse you of setting this whole thing up."

Millie glanced around the table, her eyes narrowed. "What sort of mischief are you four up to?"

Amanda reached for a cookie. "We wagered how long it would take you to bring up your 'who snags a man first' bet."

Millie scoffed. "In case you didn't notice, I didn't say diddly about the bet."

"You didn't need to. Sierra knew what you meant."

"Hmph. Given my partners plus one are in the mood to gossip, how about an update on the Douglas Hewitt drama?" Millie jabbed her thumb toward Sierra. "Unless you don't want her to know your business."

"Actually, I've heard you talking about him during your board meetings." Sierra twirled a lock of hair around her finger. "Douglas Hewitt's Wendy's rich father who lives in Hilton Head. He didn't know he had a daughter until Wendy and Chris showed up at his house. Now he says it's her fault his wife, Donna, is divorcing him, even though he's cheated on her lots of times."

Amanda shot an incredulous look at the young woman. "You really do hear everything, don't you?"

Sierra shrugged. "When y'all get going, you talk kinda loud."

Millie turned toward Wendy. "Now that Miss Big Ears has given us a summary, you might as well bring us up-to-date."

"There's not much to tell, other than Donna hasn't told her two sons about the divorce, and Douglas is moving ahead with the lawsuit suing us for breaking up his marriage."

"Seems it's time to help Chris win."

Wendy glared at Millie. "You're not suggesting you and your Mystery Book Club members investigate my father, are you?"

"How many times have I told everyone that the word 'book' isn't in our name. Besides, with Gordon as a member—"

Amanda nudged Sierra. "Gordon is the reason Millie will win the sexy nightie bet."

"Does he drive that funny-looking three-wheel whatever it is I've seen parked in Millie's driveway?"

Millie huffed. "It's a Polaris Slingshot, and its owner's a retired cop, not my boyfriend. That's beside the point. Our Mystery Club—minus the word 'book'—did Sierra a big favor when we dug up all those details about the Hackett brothers. Why not do the same for you, Wendy?"

"Because wasting your time when Chris's law firm has their own investigator doesn't make sense."

"Even if we uncover details Chris's guy misses?"

Wendy raised a brow. "You've already started snooping around, haven't you?"

Millie lifted a shoulder. "Last night."

"I suppose expecting you and your cronies to stop would be a big waste of energy."

"You mean six seasoned senior citizens dedicated to truth, justice, and the American way?"

Sierra giggled.

"You have no idea that I just quoted Superman, do you?"

"I mean no disrespect—" Sierra's head tilted. "But aren't you kinda—you know—too old to watch cartoons?"

Amanda swallowed the laugh itching to escape. "Good question."

Millie waggled her finger at Amanda. "Don't encourage her, and I don't watch cartoons. Although I could if I wanted to." Her eyes shifted to Sierra. "The reason I know that phrase is because back in the day, *Superman* was my son's favorite movie."

"Oh."

"Now that we've discussed topics totally unrelated to Awesam—" Amanda tapped her keyboard. "I suggest we focus on business, beginning with our CFO's financial update." While Wendy shared details, Amanda's thoughts drifted to the campaign. With only two months before the election, she remained frustratingly confused about Gary's feelings for her. Not that it mattered all that much, given she wasn't looking for a romantic relationship. Although it would be reassuring to know she could still attract a man. An involuntary smile curled the corners of her lips. Especially given a man as intelligent and good-looking as Keith's campaign finance manager.

"We need your vote, Amanda."

Wendy's voice broke through her musings. "On what?"

"Fifteen percent raise for all of us."

Amanda's eyes widened. "Can we afford that much?"

"You didn't hear a word I said, did you?"

Hoping Millie hadn't drawn any conclusions, Amanda squared her shoulders. "You obviously wouldn't have suggested that much if we didn't have the revenue. So I vote yes."

"Which makes it unanimous, beginning with our next paychecks."

"Good." Hoping the grin tugging at the corners of Millie's mouth wouldn't lead to a cunning remark about her mental lapse, Amanda tapped her arm. "You need to give us an update on our private dinner reservations, beginning with the one scheduled for tonight."

"You mean with the old guy and the hot young chick less than half his age Erica checked in this morning. I'm telling you either she's after his money, or he left a wife at home while he's cavorting with his honey."

Amanda jeered. "I'm surprised you and your little band of detectives aren't investigating them."

"Even though I'm Awesam's CIO—"

"What's a CIO?" Sierra faced Millie, her eyes wide.

"Chief Information Officer, who normally manages a company's information and computer technology systems. Since the only technology Awesam has is a website, I keep a close eye on guests and report any alarming behavior to my partners. Other than that, what goes on at Hilltop stays at Hilltop. Anyway, today is Bernie's day off, which means either Amanda or Erica needs to fill in for her tonight."

"I hope you don't mind taking on dinner duty, Amanda. Brad and I are meeting with a contractor."

"Not a problem. What time do you need me, Millie?"

"Six will work."

Responding to Theo's cry, Sierra lifted off her chair. "My baby's calling me. Thank you for letting me sit in on your meeting."

Erica smiled at her. "You're welcome to join us anytime."

The moment Sierra returned to her bedroom, Millie leaned forward, her eyes locked on Erica. "Please tell me you're not planning to make her a partner." Her voice rose barely above a whisper.

"Of course, not. However, since she hears everything anyway, why not let her sit in on our meetings?"

Wendy nodded. "Erica's right. Besides, our success might inspire her to do something important with her life."

Millie leaned back, her arms crossed. "As long as her mother or those Hackett boys don't come around again."

Amanda plucked her buzzing phone off the table then stood while peering at the screen. No way she'd tell them Gary was calling. "I need to take this." She swiped her finger across the screen then headed straight to her room.

Responding to footsteps striking the inn's dining room floor, Millie spun away from the kitchen counter the moment Amanda walked in. "About time you showed up."

"Eight minutes past six, and you're already complaining?"

"Observing, not complaining." Time to exercise her role as chief snoop and information gatherer. "Must've been an important phone call to keep you from returning to our meeting this afternoon."

"Every phone call I answer is important. Since you're itching to know who called, yes, it was Gary, and no he didn't invite me to dinner. Any more questions disguised by clever comments?"

"Hmph."

"All right then, time for me to go to work."

Stifling a satisfied grin, Millie focused on finalizing the gourmet meal while Amanda set the table for two beside the dining room window. At seven, she greeted her guests. "Welcome. You didn't mention celebrating a special occasion on your reservation."

The too-young-for-the-old-guy honey wearing a ridiculously low-cut black dress, peered up at her escort. "You could say we're celebrating falling in love."

"You've chosen the perfect place." Millie swept her arm toward the table. "Have a seat, and my assistant will bring you the wine you selected." Millie lifted her chin and returned to the kitchen. "They're ready for you."

"Hmm." Amanda leaned close. "Maybe I should tell our guests that your *assistant* owns this inn and approves your paychecks."

"I could call you my sous chef, except plating the salad doesn't qualify you for such a prestigious position."

"You're a trip." Shaking her head, Amanda lifted the wine off the island then carried it into the dining room.

Following three courses during which nothing suspicious happened, the front doorbell rang.

"One of our guests must have forgotten their key." Amanda headed out the door leading to the den.

Should she wait or follow? Definitely follow. Millie caught up with Amanda the moment she pulled the front door open. A woman dressed to the nines stepped inside without an invitation, her eyes blazing with the icy edge of controlled fury.

Amanda backed up. "How may we help you?"

"I'm here to talk to one of your guests. His name's George Snyder."

Aha. Millie's pulse accelerated. The old guy in the dining room.

"I'm sorry." Amanda raised a brow. "Who are you?"

"His wife."

Before Amanda could resist, Millie jumped in, her gaze darting toward the living room. "Your husband is enjoying a private meal in our dining room with his daughter."

Mrs. Snyder's eyes narrowed. "He doesn't have a daughter."

"Oh dear, I misspoke."

The woman pointed toward the pocket doors separating the living room from the dining room. "He's on the other side of those doors, isn't he?"

Amanda responded before Millie could. "Yes. However, I don't think it's wise—"

"Look, I appreciate you protecting your guests' privacy, but I don't intend to leave without confronting him. You don't have to worry about me killing the bum. He isn't worth the effort."

"I'm Hilltop's chef." Millie eyed Amanda's clenched jaw while looping her arm around the woman's elbow. "Do you mind if I take our guest to the dining room?"

Amanda shot her a do-I-have-a-choice glance. "We'll both go."

After escorting the woman through the living room, Millie slid the pocket doors open. "Mr. Snyder, you have a visitor."

He turned toward Millie, his eyes wide. "Who?"

His wife stepped inside. "I'm the last person you expected to interrupt your little tryst, aren't I?"

Mr. Snyder's fork slipped from his hand clanking onto his plate.

The other woman's eyes darted from the intruder to her date. "Who is she?"

His neck reddened.

The wife sidled toward the table. "What's your name, honey?"

"Tiffany."

"He didn't tell you he was married, did he?"

Tiffany's eyebrows shot up. "You're his wife?"

"For the past thirty-two years."

"Doesn't matter. He wants to marry me." Tiffany tucked her long dark hair behind her right ear revealing a diamond stud. "He gave me these before dinner."

"To create the illusion that he's rich and committed to you?" Stepping behind her husband, Mrs. Snyder placed her hands on his shoulders.

"When you go back home, have those earrings evaluated, sweetie. The results might shock you."

Tiffany peered up at her. "Are you saying he's not rich?"

"In a sense, yes, but only because he's married to money. In case you're wondering, his little fling is nothing more than a pathetic attempt to deal with a mid-life crisis. Believe me, he won't abandon the comfortable lifestyle my family money affords him. Which is why he's coming home with me before he makes a bigger fool of himself."

Tiffany glared at her lover. "What is she saying, Georgie pie?'

Millie choked back a laugh.

He fingered his collar. "You're a sweet girl, Tiffy, and I never meant to hurt you."

"Are you breaking up with me?"

Mr. Snyder lifted off his chair. "It's best for both of us."

Tiffany looked up at him, her eyes blazing. "What am I supposed to do now? How do you expect me to get home?"

Mrs. Snyder moved from behind her husband. "Stay here for the rest of the reservation, then drive his cute little sportscar to wherever you're going. Consider it your consolation prize." With her shoulders squared and her chin lifted, she strode out of the dining room.

After leaning down and whispering something to Tiffany, Mr. Snyder followed his wife through the living room and out the front door.

Amanda settled on the vacated chair across from the jilted lover. "Are you okay, honey?"

"Guess I shouldn't be surprised he has a wife—especially the way we were always sneaking around."

"Believe me, you're better off without him."

Millie ambled over. "What did he whisper to you?"

Tiffany fingered her earlobe. "These are real."

"I'd call diamond earrings and a sportscar well-deserved rewards." Millie lifted Mr. Snyder's plate off the table. "What do you say the three of us enjoy dessert while we take bets on what's about to happen to poor old Georgie Pie."

Tiffany's face crumpled for a brief moment before the hint of a smile appeared. "Might as well."

Chapter 5

After her only client scheduled for the day handed over a generous tip, Erica locked the massage room door and headed back to the ranch house.

Sierra dashed in from the den carrying Theo, her face beaming. "Good news."

"Let me guess." Erica tossed the key in a bowl on the kitchen counter. "The GED test results came in."

"Uh-huh, and I passed every test." Sierra's eyes appeared to brighten from within. "Now I'm a high school graduate."

"Congratulations." Erica slid her arm around Sierra's shoulders. "A well-deserved achievement we'll celebrate tonight after your hearing."

"Is Amanda going with us?"

"She'll leave her planning meeting and join us at the courthouse. Are you ready to face the judge?"

Sierra shrugged. "I guess so."

Fifteen minutes after grabbing Abby's car keys, Erica walked beside Sierra while she pushed her baby's stroller up the ramp and into the county courthouse—which for Erica was familiar territory after observing three cases and sitting on a jury.

Jillian Abernathy, their child services caseworker, who had failed to convince Sierra to wait a few more months before requesting a hearing, met them outside the courtroom. "Based on your smile, I assume you passed your tests."

Sierra nodded. "Every single one of them."

"Good for you. Although there are no guarantees, your accomplishment could work in your favor." Jillian glanced at her watch. "It's time." Moments after three people filed out, she escorted Sierra into the courtroom then on to the front row.

Relieved Theo was distracted by the toys attached to his stroller, Erica assumed stroller duty then followed Jillian and settled in the back row. Only two other observers, a court recorder, a bailiff, and the judge occupied the space.

Amanda strode in and slid onto the seat beside Erica. "How's Sierra doing?"

"At least for now, she's floating on a cloud. Other than going through with her pregnancy, earning a high school equivalency is the most meaningful achievement in her young life."

Amanda hiked one leg over the other. "I hope the good news will be enough to soften the blow if this hearing doesn't go her way."

"So do I." Erica glanced sideways at Amanda. "I've been wondering...have you noticed a change in Abby?"

"If you mean that she's sullen and spends more time alone in her room than she did a month ago, yes, I noticed."

Erica released a sigh. "At least I'm not imagining it."

"Probably something going on at the crisis center. After all, Abby deals with a lot of tough situations." Amanda nodded toward the front of the courtroom the moment the bailiff announced Sierra's custody case. "Here goes."

Jillian escorted Sierra to a defense table on the other side of the railing.

The judge peered down from her bench. "I'm surprised you requested another hearing, given it's only been a few months since I granted Ms. Wellington visitation rights with her son."

"We understand, Your Honor." Jillian spoke with authority. "However, Ms. Wellington has been living in Theo's foster home and has taken full responsibility for his daily care."

"I'm well aware of her living arrangements, Ms. Abernathy. Who's assuming the financial responsibility of caring for the child?"

"Her foster parents, Amanda Smith and Erica Nelson."

"Ms. Nelson is engaged to be married in November, which I assume means she'll move out of the home."

"That is correct."

Erica leaned close to Amanda. "Does the whole town know about our engagement?"

"What do you expect in a town where everyone knows everyone?" Amanda whispered. "Especially since you're marrying a popular high school principal and former award-winning football coach."

"Good point."

The judge leaned forward. "Do you have a job, Ms. Wellington?"

"Yes ma'am. I work two days a week as a housekeeper at Hilltop Inn."

"How much do you earn a week?"

"Depends on how many rooms I clean."

"On average."

"About eighty dollars. I pay for all of Theo's food and his diapers, plus I'm saving up money."

"Have you calculated the amount of monthly income you would need to raise your son on your own?"

"No..." Sierra seemed to hesitate. "I know it's more than I'm making now."

"Do you have a car, Ms. Wellington?"

"No ma'am. I mean, Your Honor. But I passed my GED today, and I'm taking good care of Theo." Sierra aimed her thumb over her shoulder. "He's back there with Erica and Amanda."

"You've clearly taken steps toward becoming a responsible parent." The judge paused, folding her arms across her desk. "I have two important assignments for you, Ms. Wellington. First, budget the amount of monthly income you'll need to raise a child." She rattled off a list of expenses to include. "When you finish, take the steps needed to meet that budget. After you prove you are capable of taking full responsibility for your son's care for at least six months, I will consider granting you custody. Until that time, Theo will remain in foster care."

The judge's words hung heavy as the weight of reality settled in on Erica. She was two months away from thrusting the full responsibility for Theo and his mother on Amanda and Abby.

Amanda nudged her. "Are you okay?"

"Even though it was a long shot, I'd hoped for a different outcome."

After thanking the judge, Jillian escorted Sierra to the back of the courtroom.

Amanda and Erica followed Sierra who pushed the stroller out to the hall. "I hope you're not too disappointed," Amanda said.

Sierra halted. "I kinda didn't expect the judge to approve custody. At least now I know what I need to do to make everything go my way."

Amanda slid her arm around Sierra's shoulders. "Do you want Erica and me to help you create a budget?"

Sierra shook her head. "I need to figure everything out on my own. When I'm finished I'll show you my plan."

"Good for you. I'll see you at home in a couple of hours. Right now I'm heading back to a campaign planning meeting." Amanda pulled her arm away then waved over her shoulder while heading toward the exit.

Jillian bent down to pat Theo's head. "Your mother is an extraordinary young woman." After the baby responded with a heartwarming smile, Jillian straightened and faced Sierra. "You've come a long way during the past few months. Chances are good that by this time next year, you'll be granted custody. You have a lot to accomplish between now and then."

"You can count on me."

"I know. Which is why I'll no longer require weekly reports and will reduce home visits to once every six weeks. For now, I'm off to take on a new case." Jillian shouldered her oversized purse then hastened down the hall.

Controlling her conflicting emotions the best she could, Erica forced a smile. "It's such a lovely day. Why don't we take a walk and buy some cupcakes?"

"Sounds like fun." After heading outside and making their way down the ramp, they turned toward Depot Street. "Do you know why Abby's been kinda down the past couple of weeks?"

Erica stole a quick glance at Sierra. Had everyone noticed? "Probably work-related stress." They turned right and walked across the railroad track. At the light they crossed the street to the sidewalk fronting East Main. Three doors down, Erica breathed in the mouthwatering aromas the moment they stepped into the Sweet Shoppe.

Sierra's eyes widened when she peered into the glass case displaying rows of cupcakes. "There are so many yummy flavors to choose from."

"Indulging on cupcakes is one of our favorite ways to celebrate." By the time they reached the end of the case, Sierra had selected eight assorted cupcakes and four cookies. Erica carried the goodies outside then turned left.

While heading back toward the courthouse, conflicting thoughts played havoc with her emotions. Why hadn't she postponed her wedding until the new year? Especially since Amanda already had a full plate. Assuming full responsibility for Sierra and Theo didn't seem fair, although Millie would help out. Plus, Brad and her new home was only a short distance from the ranch house. By the time they arrived at Abby's car, Erica had muddled through and come to one important decision. No matter how long it took, she would continue to share the responsibility until Sierra was granted full custody.

Back home, Sierra lifted her sleeping baby from his car seat and carried him to her room. She closed the door, making it clear she wanted time alone.

Before Erica had a chance to relax, Millie rushed in. "What did the judge say?"

"Pretty much what Jillian expected." Erica explained.

"Good thing I've taught Sierra how to show up to work on time." Millie pointed to the Sweet Shoppe box sitting on the dining room table. "Given the judge denied custody, what in the dickens are we celebrating?"

"Sierra passed all her tests and earned her GED."

"Well now, that accomplishment calls for Chef Millie's secret mac and cheese recipe. I'll be back at six with dinner." She pivoted then rushed back through the kitchen and out to the carport.

Responding to Brad's ringtone, Erica pulled her phone from her purse then stepped out to the backyard patio and activated FaceTime. Dusty padded over and sprawled at her feet while she relayed the day's events. "Can you join us for tonight's celebration?"

"Wouldn't miss it. Are you available to play golf with Jimmy and Ashley Saturday afternoon? We could have a friendly competition, the guys against the gals."

Erica laughed. "Is that the only way you and your son have a shot at beating his amateur golf-champion girlfriend?"

Brad winked. "Definitely. Although your game has improved a lot over the summer."

"Which means Ashley and I have a decent chance of beating you."

"I'd say that's a distinct possibility."

Dusty peered up at Erica, her tail slapping the concrete as if rooting for Erica to win.

Chapter 6

Eight minutes after leaving the courthouse, Amanda pulled onto Linda and Keith Armstrong's driveway and parked behind Gary's car. Eager to return to the meeting, she climbed out of the truck, headed to the front door, and rang the bell.

Linda greeted her. "How'd the hearing go?"

"As expected, the judge didn't grant custody." Amanda followed Linda into the cozy great room and kitchen. "Anything exciting happen while I was gone?"

"Only if you call our guys taking a break to compete for pool-shark bragging rights exciting."

The way she referred to her husband and Gary as 'our guys' made it clear Linda hadn't abandoned her mission to spur a romance between her and Keith's finance manager. "Who's winning?"

"Last time I checked, my sweet husband." Linda removed a pitcher of tea from the fridge. After pouring two glasses, she climbed onto a stool beside Amanda. "When Keith first told me he wanted to run for district attorney, I supported him even though I secretly hoped he'd change his mind."

"Because he'd had a heart attack a while back?"

"His doctor gave him a clean bill of health, and I make sure he eats healthy and gets plenty of exercise. So I'm not worried about his physical condition." She paused, wrapping her fingers around her glass. "After spending his entire career defending clients, Keith is a couple months away from taking on the role of prosecutor. All because he believes the citizens in our district deserve an honest district attorney."

"For good reason."

"I'm not questioning his motive. The emotional impact this drastic change will have on him is another story. Especially when he ends up arguing against someone represented by the three-generation law firm founded by his father."

"How does Keith's mother feel about him leaving the law firm?"

"As a parent, Susan understands and believes Keith's dad would have done the same thing. On the other hand, she's a retired nurse, which is why she's also concerned about the emotional impact on him. Neither one of us have or will share our concerns with Keith. At least the attorney he and Chris hired this week could take the lead when he attempts to convict one of Armstrong Law Firm's clients." Linda took a sip of tea. "Ironic how after serving thirty years as an assistant DA in Chattanooga, she's leaving public service for the private sector."

"Have you met her?"

"Not yet, but according to Keith she comes with great credentials. We've invited her along with Chris and Wendy to dinner Saturday night. You and Gary should join us."

Could she be any more obvious? As much as she'd enjoy meeting the new attorney, no way she'd give in to Linda's matchmaking ploy. "Thanks for the invitation, but I already have plans." *Relaxing with a glass of wine and a good book.*

"Maybe next time." Linda's tone failed to mask her disappointment.

Keith called up from the terrace level, "We need you ladies down here."

Linda slid off her stool. "Seems we've been summoned."

Amanda followed her down the stairs to the high-ceiling paneled room. Keith sat across from Gary at the round pedestal table. Pool balls scattered on the table confirmed they'd stopped playing mid-game. "What's going on?"

"Nancy Campbell texted to give us a heads-up about her podcast that's about to start with Richard Watson and his campaign manager. Gary has her tuned in."

"This should be interesting." Linda settled on a high-back leather chair closest to the window offering a view of the patio beneath the deck.

Amanda sat across from her, eyeing Gary. "Do you believe his campaign manager will try to pull some sort of dirty trick against you?"

"Depends on how big a grudge she's holding on to."

All eyes focused on Gary's phone at the sound of Nancy Campbell's cheery voice. "Good afternoon, friends, and welcome to Nancy's Nuggets. Today I'm talking with Richard Watson, and his campaign manager, Melissa Grovner. Tell us how long you've served as district attorney and why you're running for another term."

Watson responded by rattling off a long list of accomplishments. "My experience putting lawbreakers behind bars is why I'm far more qualified to hold this position than my opponent who has spent his entire career defending criminals."

Linda glared at the phone, her eyes filled with fury. "How dare he."

Nancy responded to Watson's comment. "You were a defense attorney before you served in your current position, so I assume like your opponent, you were committed to proving your clients' innocence."

Keith snapped his fingers. "Good going, Nancy."

"My qualifications are far superior to his." Watson's tone screamed of irritation while he expanded on his list of so-called achievements.

"Thank you, DA Watson. Ms. Grovner, you're a real estate professional. What prompted you to become involved in a political campaign?"

"First, because I believe in my candidate and the job he's doing. Second, because it's important for your listeners to know that the staff a candidate selects speaks volumes about their integrity." She came across as arrogant. "For example, take Gary Redding, our opponent's choice of finance manager—"

"Who's a respected bank president," added Nancy.

"That's his professional persona, not who he is as a man. The fact is I dated Gary during high school and college. When I realized he was dishonest and self-absorbed, I ended the relationship. Even more telling, years later his wife divorced him."

Amanda stared at the phone, her jaw clenched. How would Nancy respond?

"Earlier this year when I interviewed your opponent and his campaign team, Mr. Redding told our listeners that he had discovered his wife was involved in an affair with his assistant manager."

Following a long moment of dead air, Melissa found her voice. "And I'm telling your listeners that a married woman doesn't become involved with another man unless she discovers she's married to a loser."

Watson jumped in as if he had suddenly realized that his campaign manager came across as a bitter rejected lover. "I asked Ms. Grovner to manage my campaign based on her integrity and business experience." During the remainder of the interview he shared stories about his childhood and college days, shutting Melissa out of the conversation.

When the podcast ended, Gary leaned back, fingering his neatly trimmed, salt-and-pepper beard. "If I'm not mistaken, our inept opponent has discovered that his new campaign manager is as much a liability as the one he fired."

Keith drummed his fingers. "Up to this point, we've overcome all of Watson's attempts to undermine our reputations."

Linda reached across the table and patted her husband's arm. "You're a good man with a sterling reputation, darling. Doesn't matter what Watson has in his little bag of dirty tricks. Most people won't fall for his deceptions."

"Hopefully, he's run out of ammunition. Enough talk about politics. Time for the guys to finish our game before I treat the four of us to a victory dinner." Keith lifted off his chair then ambled to the pool table.

Gary followed Keith, clapping his hand on his friend's shoulder. "Victory as a pool shark or political figure?"

"Both."

Amanda peered at Gary leaning on his pool cue while Keith took the first shot. She had to admit he was confident, and as Millie had described him, movie-star handsome. What would it be like to kiss a man with a beard? Tickly? Gary's eyes met hers. He winked. Resisting the sudden urge to crawl under the table, Amanda forced a half smile before breaking eye contact.

Linda watched her from across the table, grinning. "While the guys finish their game, why don't you and I enjoy a glass of wine upstairs?"

Sensing the heat creeping up her neck was seconds from turning her cheeks as red as her hair, Amanda blinked. At least this time Linda hadn't called Keith and Gary 'our guys.' "Perfect way to end the meeting." *And escape more embarrassment.*

Amanda followed Linda while mentally debating whether or not to comment about what had just happened. By the time she'd reached the top step, she'd come to the only conclusion that made sense. Pretend she hadn't noticed while talking about anything other than Gary Redding.

Chapter 7

Millie cracked the door open and peered into Hilltop's dining room. Three hours after she and Bernie had begun serving breakfast, four guests refused to leave. Scowling, she spun away from the door. "Don't they have something better to do than sitting around shooting the breeze?"

"We want our guests to feel like they're staying in a home away from home." Bernie placed plates in the dishwasher before facing her friend. "No one's checking out today, which means I'm off the hook for housekeeping duties. Why don't I finish cleaning up while you go do whatever you need to do to get ready."

Millie propped her hands on her hips. "What makes you think I'm not ready to go now?"

"Oh, I don't know. Maybe the nine times you've peeked into the dining room followed by incessant grumbling?"

Millie dropped her hands to her side. "I don't want to show up late, that's all."

"We have plenty of time, so scoot on out of here. I'll pick you up and drive us both over in an hour."

"What? Now you don't trust me to drive myself?"

"Given your eagerness, you'd likely break every speed limit in the book and land us both in jail."

Millie rolled her eyes. "Good thing you have a day job, or you'd starve if you tried earning a living doing standup comedy." She tossed her apron onto the island then scurried through the den to the back patio. Millie waved at a couple sitting on the wrought iron bench facing the five-foot-tall, three-tier bronze fountain. At least those guests had sense enough to leave the dining room.

She headed straight across the backyard to her kitchen door. Inside, she fed her two cats before heading down the hall to her bedroom. After hesitating, Millie slid her closet door open and pulled her high school freshman yearbook off the top shelf. For the second time since she'd met the newest Mystery Club member, Millie sat on the edge of her bed and opened the book. After turning to the junior section and tracing her finger over Gordon's photo, she flipped back to the C's and stared at Rupert's picture. The man she ended up marrying was a decent-looking guy, but he couldn't hold a candle to Gordon Davenport. Millie continued leafing through the yearbook stopping every time she came across a picture of the ex-cop.

Curiosity led her to the freshman section where she found the one and only picture of herself. She could turn a few heads back then. Especially the older man who had traveled to Blue Ridge every week on business. Struggling with a moment of guilt, Millie closed the yearbook and set it back on the shelf.

Mittens slinked in from the hall and curled around Millie's leg. She lifted the kitty into her arms. "What do you suppose a woman my age should wear to a barbeque hosted by a guy who dated a cheerleader before he left for college? Hmm. How about jeans, my fancy new top, and white sneakers?" Mittens purred before springing from her arms. "I'll take your reaction as a yes."

After changing, Millie meandered to her living room bookcase and peered at Eleanor's journals Wendy had found while transforming the Harringtons' vacation home into Hilltop Inn. She carried one of the journals to her recliner then flipped to the last pages and began reading what Eleanor had written.

This afternoon while Millie and I were preparing food for our last dinner party before Warren and I leave tomorrow, she began shaking as tears rolled down her cheeks. Since I've never seen her sniffle, much less cry, I feared she was experiencing some sort of medical emergency. When I suggested driving her to the hospital, she blurted that the love of her life had passed away. Needless to say, I was shocked to discover that years ago Millie had a secret affair with an older man who traveled to Blue Ridge every week for business."

Millie closed her eyes trying to picture his face. Nothing had changed since the last time she'd read the journal. The man's image had faded from her memory a long time ago. She opened her eyes and continued reading.

When she met him, she had no idea he was married until five months into the affair, when one of Millie's friends saw him in Chattanooga holding hands with another woman. When Millie confronted him, he admitted the truth and promised to leave his wife and marry her. Desperate to believe his promise, she continued seeing him. Seven months later, after they'd spent a romantic weekend in Atlanta, he called and ended the affair.

Brokenhearted, she began dating a high-school friend. Six months later, she became Mrs. Mildred Cunningham. For years, she held onto the belief that her lover would return and take her away. By the time she accepted the truth, she'd damaged her marriage beyond repair. At first, she and her husband stayed together for their son. When he grew up and left home, neither parent had the will or desire to start over. Millie had wasted all those years waiting for a cheater who had no intention of leaving his wife.

Millie snapped the journal shut. What had prompted her to read about the affair today of all days? A guilty conscience? Or proof she had once been a desirable young woman who attracted a married man? At least no one other than her Awesam family knew about the affair.

Thirty minutes after returning the journal to the bookcase, Millie carried a cake carrier out to the driveway and climbed into Bernie's passenger seat. "Everything okay at the inn?"

"The kitchen and dining room are all cleaned up and ready for tomorrow. You look spiffy."

Millie set the cake on her lap. "At least my jeans aren't full of holes."

"You know that's the style, don't you?"

"Back in the day, people would never pay good money for pants we tossed out with the trash."

"I bet some designer who knew kids would buy anything with a high enough price tag came up with the ripped jeans trend."

"Or some broke designer who couldn't return a bolt of damaged denim."

"Whatever the story, the fad continues." Bernie backed down to the street. At the stop sign, she turned toward town. Shortly after leaving Millie's, Bernie parked in the driveway behind Susan Armstrong's car. "Nice house. Wonder what it's like inside?"

Millie peered at the manicured lawn fronting the single-story brick house. "He's a retired cop. Probably a lot of leather."

Bernie opened her door. "By the way, Eileen's grandchildren are visiting her, so it's just the five of us." She climbed out. Millie followed her to the front porch.

Susan responded before they rang the bell. "Come on in. The guys are out back."

Millie entered the small foyer, her eyes wide.

Susan swept her arm toward the combination living and dining room. "Not the decor you'd expect for a police officer."

"Hardly." Millie gawked at the large landscape painting on the wall above a dark blue upholstered sofa. Two patterned blue and white easy chairs anchored each end of a glass and chrome coffee table. Another traditional painting hung above a sideboard beside the dark wood dining room table. "Not a stitch of leather anywhere."

"At least not in here. Come on." Susan led the way to a combo kitchen and den. Two dark red leather recliners faced a large flatscreen TV anchored to a brick fireplace. "Our three-wheeled motorcycle riding host obviously has excellent taste."

"Indeed he does." Millie peered at five framed photos displayed on the bookcase built along a wall. She turned toward the glass door sliding open. "Are those pictures of your family?"

Gordon ambled over, nodding. "Everyone except my ex."

"Good-looking family." Millie held up the cake carrier. "Double chocolate fudge."

"Perfect addition to a barbeque. You ladies come on out back with me and Stanley."

After following their host, Millie set the cake on a glass-top table while eyeing the outdoor kitchen anchoring one end of the patio. "Impressive setup."

"One of the reasons I bought this place."

Bernie raised a brow. "Are we to assume you're a good cook?"

"For a single guy, I'm not too bad."

"Don't let him kid you." Stanley nodded toward the grill. "His barbeque ribs are the best I've ever tasted."

Susan sat at the table across from Stanley. "Maybe we should rename our little group to the Mystery and Gourmet Cooking Club."

Stanley chuckled. "I'd be disqualified."

"In that case, we'll keep our Mystery Club title. Speaking of which—" Millie settled between Susan and Bernie. "How much dirt have you guys dug up on Wendy's father?"

Gordon sat across from her, crossing his arms on the table. "On the surface, Douglas Hewitt appears to be one of Hilton Head's upstanding citizens and a successful real estate developer. He has a lot of family money and belongs to all the right clubs."

Millie scowled. "He also cheats on his wife."

"Discreetly. Except for a picture posted on a young woman's social media page—"

"A photo of the two of them?"

Gordon shook his head. "He's too smart to allow himself to be photographed with one of his honeys. Other than her calling him a pig who treated women like playthings before discarding them, the guy's record is clean. He's never even had a traffic ticket."

Millie slumped back in her chair, her posture sagging as if all the air had escaped her lungs. "So much for helping Wendy and Chris."

Gordon smiled at her. "In my experience, the good guys almost always win."

Millie's brow furrowed. "It's that 'almost' part I'm worried about."

"There's no need to fret, Millie." Susan's tone radiated confidence. "Chris is not only my grandson, he's also an excellent attorney. Believe me, he'll win the case."

"You're right." Millie's brow unfurrowed. Her eyes shifted from Susan to Gordon. "Even though 'book' isn't in our title, we should select a nail-biting thriller to discuss at our next meeting, at least until another mystery needing our expert sleuthing skills pops up."

"Works for me." Gordon tapped the cake carrier. "For now I suggest we sample your dessert."

"Before our meal?"

Gordon's eyes twinkled as a sly grin tugged at the corner of his mouth. "Why not start with dessert, especially one prepared by an award-winning chef."

Millie tilted her head. "Are you flirting with me?"

"You are one interesting woman." Gordon chuckled. "Do you remember what you wrote in my yearbook?"

Surprised he'd taken the time to look her up, Millie leaned forward, lacing her fingers on the table. "Something clever, I suppose."

"You wrote, 'good luck to the best-looking guy in Blue Ridge.' You added a little heart over your name."

"Well now." Bernie thumped Millie's arm. "You just might win the little bet you have with Amanda."

Sensing her cheeks were seconds from turning multiple shades of pink, Millie cleared her throat while lifting the lid off the cake. "Dessert before the main course is a great idea."

During the remainder of the afternoon and into the early evening, the mystery club members chatted and laughed as if they'd been life-long friends. By the time Bernie drove her home, Millie had begun to wonder if she might actually lose the bet with Amanda.

Chapter 8

Hoping to cheer her daughter up before Tommy arrived to drive her to work, Erica carried a platter of crisp bacon and chocolate chip pancakes to the dining room table. "I fixed your favorite breakfast, sweetheart."

"Thanks, but you didn't have to go to all that trouble." Abby wheeled her chair up to the table.

Yesterday and again this morning, her child had abandoned maneuvering from her wheelchair onto a regular seat. Erica's brows pinched then released while she sat beside her daughter. "How's everything going at the crisis center?"

Abby shrugged. "Same as always. Some battered women coming in, others leaving." She placed a slice of bacon and two pancakes on her plate then drenched the pancakes with maple syrup.

Keeping a close eye on Abby's expression, Erica reached for her coffee mug. "How'd your therapy session go yesterday?"

Abby hesitated, seemingly deciding how to answer. "I...um...didn't go."

Alarmed, Erica tightened her fingers around her mug. Had her child missed more than one session? "Did your therapist cancel?"

Abby shook her head, her eyes focused on her plate. "I was too busy at work to take time off."

Desperate to understand the real reason she'd skipped, yet respecting her daughter's privacy, Erica swallowed the question begging to roll off her tongue.

Amanda ambled in from the hall. "Good morning." She headed to the kitchen before returning with her coffee mug and settling across from Abby. "Our favorite Saturday morning indulgence. Are we celebrating a special occasion?"

Abby shrugged. "Not as far as I know." She shot a questioning look at Erica. "Why aren't you eating?"

"No reason." Erica peeled her fingers off her mug. She transferred two pancakes before passing the platter to Amanda.

Abby swallowed a bite of bacon. "I've been doing a lot of thinking, and um...I don't want to continue counting on you and Tommy to drive me to and from work every day."

Erica eyed her daughter. "I enjoy spending time with you, sweetheart."

"I know, Mom. But you're busy. Besides, in a few weeks you and Brad will move into your new home." Abby paused. "Which is one reason why Monday I'm having my car retrofitted with a hand-operated accelerator and brakes."

Erica halted her fork halfway to her mouth. Desperate to silence the alarm bells clanging in her head, she inhaled through her nose, exhaling slowly. "Even when you're able to drive, someone will have to help you move your wheelchair in and out of your trunk—"

"Which only takes a couple of minutes, not half an hour."

Amanda flashed a smile at Abby. "Good for you. Being independent is important, right, Erica?"

Amanda had painted her into a corner, making it impossible either to agree or disagree. Erica's jaw tensed as she set her fork down. "You'll still need me to drive you to your doctor's appointment next week, sweetheart."

"I know."

Sierra bounced in and lowered Theo into his playpen. "I have good news." Failing to read the room, she dropped onto the chair beside Abby then laid a pad of paper on the table. "Yummy breakfast."

"Good morning to you." Amanda passed Sierra the platter. "Are you going to fill us in, or make us guess?"

"I have a budget all figured out." After loading her plate, Sierra tapped her finger on the pad. "Take a look."

Amanda read the list aloud. "Well done, Ms. Wellington."

"Thanks." Sierra swallowed a bite. "Now all I need is a good paying job."

"About that." Amanda stole a quick glance at Erica before setting the pad aside. "The three of us talked it over, and decided to help out—"

Sierra's brows raised. "By giving me a good recommendation?"

"Yes, but even better. We'll release a portion of the money in Theo's GoFundMe account so you can buy a car."

Sierra stared at Amanda for a heartbeat, seemingly frozen in disbelief before her face lit up. "For real?"

"It's too far to walk to town, and hitchhiking is out of the question. Besides, we already have a couple of options for you to check out."

"I've never owned a car or even a bicycle. If it's okay with you and Erica, I want Abby to help me pick out the car."

Amanda nodded. "Fine with me. What do you think, Erica?"

"Considering how well Abby negotiated a deal on her car, I'd say my daughter is the perfect car-buying partner. If she's willing."

Anticipation lit Sierra's face as she turned toward Abby. "You're willing, aren't you?"

"Sure. We can go today after I finish work."

"Yay."

"Tell you what." Amanda wiped her mouth with a napkin. "I'll watch Theo to give you gals plenty of time to negotiate a great deal."

"Just think." Sierra pressed her palms together. "This time next week I'll be a working woman and one step closer to the judge giving me custody."

Erica fell silent while Sierra continued to keep the conversation focused on cars and jobs. Moments after Abby left with Tommy, she delegated cleanup duty to Sierra and Amanda then escaped to the bathroom hoping a hot shower would ease her growing anxiety.

At ten o'clock, Erica carried her golf bag out the front door to Brad's SUV. "I heard you drive up."

"Good morning. Perfect weather for a friendly competition." He kissed her cheek then held the passenger door open.

"Sorry, I was a bit distracted." Erica forced a smile then climbed in and buckled her seatbelt while Brad carried her clubs to the back. After stashing the bag, he slid onto the driver's seat. Erica gripped the dashboard while peering through the windshield at Abby's car.

Brad reached across the console, placing his hand on her thigh. "Do you want to talk about whatever's bothering you?"

Erica flinched. "When Abby bought her car, she refused even to consider having it altered." She relayed the breakfast conversation. "Why now, and why did she skip therapy?"

"To answer the first question, because she's ready to get back behind the wheel."

"I suppose that makes sense, although it wouldn't hurt to wait another month. Unless—" Erica's eyes met Brad's. "What if she's losing hope?"

"Have you ever heard Abby utter the slightest doubt about a full recovery?"

"No, but during the past few weeks, she's seemed moody, even a little depressed. We've always been close. Lately...she's brushed me off both times I tried to talk to her."

"Maybe something's going on at the crisis center she doesn't want to talk about."

Erica ran her fingers along her seatbelt. "I understand she has a stressful job—"

"There you go, a logical explanation." Brad squeezed her thigh then started the engine and backed down to the street.

"There is one bit of good news. This afternoon Abby will help Sierra find a car so she can begin looking for a job. She'll need a decent income to win the judge over."

Brad braked at the stop sign then turned toward the country club. "I might have a solution." He explained. "What do you think?"

"What's important is what Sierra thinks."

"When I bring you back to the ranch house tonight after dinner, I'll run the idea by her. Until then, there's a lot at stake in today's friendly competition."

"Hmm." Erica eyed his grin. "What's the prize for the winning team?"

"A round of drinks and dinner paid for by the losers."

"If Ashley and I win, a three-course gourmet meal accompanied by an expensive bottle of wine. Paid for by the high school principal and one of Blue Ridge's finest firefighters."

"Fancy. What if you lose?"

"Beer and hotdogs."

Brad laughed. "Are you trying to motivate me to lose, or are you admitting you're cheap."

"Is the motivation factor working?"

Brad pulled into the country club parking lot. "I'll let you know at the end of the first nine."

Nearly four hours after joining Jimmy and Ashley at the first tee, Brad birdied the sixteenth green placing the guys one stroke behind. On the way back to their cart, Ashley linked arms with Erica. "You've been playing exceptionally well. Now all you need to do is keep your ball in the fairway and two-putt each green. I'll do the rest."

"You're a good coach."

"Only because you're a great partner and an excellent student."

Erica drove the ball relatively straight down the seventeenth hole, only to blow their lead with three putts. By the time they reached the eighteenth green, she knew she had to sink the putt with one stroke. Erica stared at her ball lying twelve feet from the hole, mentally rehearsing everything Ashley had told her about aim and speed. Tuning out the chirping birds, Erica took one practice swing, then lined up her putter. *I can do this.* She swung. Her pulse accelerated as the ball slowly followed the exact path Ashley had described. At the last second it veered left and dropped into the hole.

Ashley let out a loud yelp before rushing to embrace Erica. "You keep playing like you did today and soon you'll be able to compete in a club championship game."

"She's right." Brad slid his arm around Erica's waist as they ambled off the green. "Now, about that steak and lobster dinner..."

Following an afternoon hanging out in the clubhouse, then dinner at Grace Prime Steakhouse, Brad drove back to the ranch house. Erica released her seatbelt. "Do you suppose they found Sierra a car?"

"Only one way to find out." Brad grabbed the door handle, then circled to the passenger side and pulled the door open.

After climbing out, Erica headed toward the kitchen, stopping beside her daughter's car. "Abby and I have struggled through so much together—always as a team." She swallowed the lump rising in her throat. "Now...it's as if she's drifting away."

Brad slid his arm around her shoulders. "Is it possible my fiancée is experiencing empty-nest syndrome?"

"Except I'm the one who's weeks away from fleeing the nest, not my daughter."

"Another reason Abby is flexing her independence."

"Know what?" Erica patted his cheek. "You're going to be a great step-dad."

Brad winked, squeezing her shoulder. "Yeah, I know."

"Hmm." Erica tilted her head. "Are all former football high school coaches as self-assured as you are?"

"Only those who have winning records. What do you say we go talk to two bright young high school grads who are stretching their wings?"

"Lead the way, Coach Barkley." Inside, they followed voices drifting from the den. Abby and Sierra sat on the sofa facing each other. Erica ambled over. "Based on your smile, I'm guessing you found the perfect car."

Sierra nodded. "A little white Toyota. Perfect size for me and Theo. Even better, Abby negotiated a good price."

Abby peered up at Erica. "We gave the owner a deposit. Now all we need is cash from Theo's fund."

"We'll transfer the money to Sierra's bank account tomorrow." Erica settled on one club chair, Brad on the other. "There's something else to talk about." She nodded toward Brad.

He faced Sierra. "In a couple of weeks, the high school's office assistant is retiring." Brad leaned forward, folding his arms across his knees. "How would you like to interview for the job?"

Her eyebrows shot up. "For real?"

Brad nodded. "There are no guarantees you'll land the job, but yes, for real."

"Except—" Sierra blinked, her brows pinched. "I've never interviewed for a job."

"Not a problem." Erica crossed one leg over the other. "Abby and I will coach you, right, sweetheart?"

"Of course."

"All right then, it's settled. Time for me to head home." Brad stood, motioning to Erica.

She followed him out the front door, second thoughts hounding her. "Are you sure you want to take a chance on hiring an inexperienced teenager?"

"A lot depends on how Sierra handles the interview with me as well as the woman she'd replace. Which means you and Abby have a big coaching job ahead of you."

Erica linked arms with Brad. "Any pointers, Coach?"

"Ask tough questions. Correct her when she messes up and compliment her when warranted. Then leave the rest up to her."

"No wonder your students love their principal. You're brilliant."

"Comes from years of experience." Brad pulled her into his arms and kissed her, sending a tingling sensation racing through her limbs. "Sleep well, my love."

Chapter 9

Saturday afternoon Wendy peered out the French doors at dark clouds hanging low over their deck and wooded backyard. "I'm looking forward to meeting Armstrong Law Firm's new partner, who's old enough to be your mother."

Chris sidled beside her, chuckling. "Are you admitting you'd be jealous if we hired a gorgeous young female lawyer?"

Wendy laced her fingers around his neck. "Only because she would have a hard time resisting my handsome, sexy husband."

"I see." Chris encircled her waist. "And what happens the next time I defend a good-looking thirty-something, single female client?"

"I'll sit in the row behind the defense table so she'll know she doesn't have a chance against his brilliant, blue-eyed, blonde wife."

"Clever, except you left out the word beautiful."

Wendy tilted her head. "Too many B's." Her mother's ringtone sounded from the kitchen.

"Just like a mother." Chris playfully clucked his tongue. "Wrenching her daughter from the arms of a man who has a gorgeous blonde a few yards away from the bedroom."

"A blonde who looks as if she'd swallowed a ginormous watermelon." Wendy unlaced her fingers then dashed to the kitchen. She slid her finger across her phone, activating the speaker and FaceTime. "Hey, Mom. How are you feeling?"

Cynthia smiled. "Better, now that I'm looking at your beautiful face."

"You know everyone says you and I could pass as sisters."

"I wasn't fishing for a compliment, but I'll take it. Where's my grandson?"

"Taking a nap. Do you want me to wake him?"

"No, let him rest."

"I'll let you know if he wakes up." Wendy carried her phone to the sofa. "How are Kayla and Riley holding up?"

"Every day they rely more and more on each other." Her mother's smile faded. "Brent and Zach are the two I'm worried most about."

Chris sat beside Wendy. She aimed the phone toward him. He smiled at her mother. "Hi, Cynthia. I hope you don't mind me listening in."

"Of course, I don't. You're my only son-in-law, and a doggone good one."

"Your daughter brings out the best in me. About Zach, what's going on?"

"He's moodier than ever. Unfortunately, Brent's having a hard time dealing with reality. Holding my family together is taking more energy every day."

"I haven't talked to Zach in a couple of days. Do you mind if I call him now?"

"You're welcome to try, if he bothers to answer."

"I'll give it my best shot." Chris lifted off the sofa then headed downstairs.

"You married a good man, Wendy. Hold on." Cynthia looked away from the screen for a moment. "Your sisters just came home. They'll want to talk to you."

Five minutes into chatting with Kayla and Riley, Wendy responded to Duke, bounding in, his tail setting his backside in motion. "Our canine baby monitor is announcing the end of our little guy's nap."

Riley's face lit. "Can I talk to my nephew?"

"Of course." After Wendy hastened to her son's room and carried him to the den, Cynthia's eyes sparkled. Ryan's babbles peppered their conversation until her mother's waning energy prompted Kayla to end the call.

Chris returned from the basement, dropping beside Wendy. "How'd your mom hold up?"

She released a shaky breath. "She's fading fast." Responding to a kick, Wendy placed both hands on her baby bulge. "She promised to hold on long enough to meet her granddaughter." Tears pooled and tracked down Wendy's cheeks. "I'm afraid she won't find the strength to keep her promise."

"Believe me—" Chris wrapped his arm around Wendy's shoulders, pulling her close. "Your mother's desire to meet our little gal will give her the will to fight."

Drawing on her husband's words, Wendy swiped her fingers across her cheeks. "I need to call her every day and give her a big dose of Ryan charm." She snuggled with Chris while Ryan climbed off the sofa then toddled to his toy basket. Duke followed, sprawling on the floor beside him. "Any luck reaching Zach?"

"Afraid not. If he fails to respond to my message, I'll keep calling until he answers or returns my call."

Wendy's gaze swept to the photo displayed on the end table; her mother holding Ryan in her arms. "At least for the foreseeable future, Mom needs both of us to love on the Gilmore side of our family."

Chris brushed a lock of hair away from her cheek. "Reuniting with your mother eighteen years after you last saw her was divinely guided."

His words rang true. Despite the pain that losing her mother would inflict, a peace washed over Wendy. She closed her eyes and silently prayed for the strength to be the Gilmore family's number one comforter and cheerleader.

Two hours after the phone call with Cynthia ended, Wendy and Chris left Ryan at the ranch house with Nana Amanda before driving to his parents' home. When they arrived, he scurried to the passenger side, opened the door, and helped her to her feet. "Are you ready to size up my new law partner?"

"Are you looking for my honest opinion or approval?"

"Yup to both." Chris gripped her elbow and escorted her to the front porch then into the foyer. Garlic and tomato aromas drifted from the back of the house. They followed voices to the den. "We're here."

A tall, attractive brunette whose face was free of makeup except for a hint of lipstick set a glass of wine on the island then approached with her hand extended. "It's a pleasure to finally meet Chris's better half. I'm Regina Reeves."

Wendy smiled at the woman whose handshake was firm. "Pleasure's all mine."

"Chris tells me you're a partner and chief financial officer of a successful company."

"Yes ma'am."

"Please call me Regina."

Intrigued by the woman's take-charge approach, Wendy maintained eye contact. "I understand you're switching sides, so to speak—from prosecuting to defending."

"Exact opposite of your father-in-law." Regina released Wendy's hand. "After negotiating traffic and dealing with big-city crime, I'm looking forward to working in a two-lawyer firm and experiencing small town life."

Wendy blinked. Should she ask the real reason a high-powered assistant district attorney ditched a career to start over in a strange town? Too soon. "You've definitely chosen a small town which on any given day has more tourists than residents. Are you moving here alone?"

Regina lifted her glass off the island. "Clever way to ask about my marital status. Years ago, I was married for a short time until my husband and I discovered that our demanding careers were incompatible with marriage. And no, I don't have children or cats."

Keith chuckled. "We've hired a no-nonsense professional with a sense of humor."

Regina aimed her glass toward him. "Helps keep opposing attorneys off-balance."

Keith clicked his glass to Regina's. "I'll remember, should we ever face off in a courtroom."

"I look forward to the day. For now, what's the scoop on the DA you're about to unseat?"

Keith handed a glass of ginger ale to Wendy then a glass of wine to Chris. "I'll let my son do the honors."

Chris pointed to the stool beside Wendy. "You might as well take a seat. This will take a while." He spent twenty minutes relaying information and answering questions.

When he finished, Regina shook her head. "Talk about a serious cleanup needed on aisle five. Men like Richard Watson are the reason why lawyer jokes are rampant—although I admit some are freaking hilarious."

Linda removed lasagna from the oven. "Now that you're up-to-date on local politics, how about a Georgia-style Italian dinner?"

"Everything smells delicious." Regina slid off her stool. "What can I do to help?"

"Chris and Wendy will escort you to our dining room while Keith and I serve."

After Keith blessed the meal, he refilled the wine glasses. "Since you have a captive audience, what do you want to know about this little town you're choosing to call home?"

"First, what should I expect as a newcomer?"

"As the only newcomer sitting here, I'll give you the inside scoop." Wendy shared her experiences with the locals beginning with the first week she moved to Blue Ridge. "Believe me, before long you'll feel as if you've lived here for years instead of weeks. Although—" Wendy patted Chris's arm. "I can't guarantee you'll end up marrying the man of your dreams."

Regina laughed. "It would take one heck of a man to make me abandon my independence and begin doing laundry for two." She swallowed a sip of wine. "Although now that I'm buying a house with a yard, I might consider adopting a dog—if it's housebroken."

Chris unclipped his phone and peered at the screen. "I apologize, but I need to take this call." He aimed his phone toward Wendy before pushing his chair away from the table.

All eyes focused on Wendy as Chris answered the call while walking out. "That's my brother returning Chris's call. Watching our mother lose the battle to stage-four cancer is a lot for a thirteen-year-old to deal with."

"Losing a parent is difficult, especially for one so young." Regina's soft tone conveyed understanding.

Wendy eyed Regina, sensing an unspoken connection with the woman, who an hour ago had been a stranger, Wendy's eyes met hers. "Before I moved to Blue Ridge, I hadn't had any contact with my mother since I was five years old." The story spilled out of being raised in a series of foster homes then meeting Erica and Amanda before locating her mother,

Cynthia. "In two short years I've gone from having no family to being blessed with three."

The hint of a smile tugged at Regina's lips. "Sometimes blessings come in unexpected ways."

Wendy spread her fingers across her baby bulge. "Especially bringing new life into this world."

Chris returned and settled beside Wendy. Breaking eye contact with Regina, she faced her husband. "Is Zach okay?"

"For now. What did I miss?"

Regina's lips bloomed into a full smile. "Your wife's incredible story."

"She's an amazing woman." Chris reached for Wendy's hand as their eyes met, warming her heart at the depth of the love and respect they had for each other.

Chapter 10

Amanda closed her laptop then ambled from the living room serving as Awesam's office to the ranch house dining room. "Are you certain Abby doesn't want us to wait for her to come home?"

Erica looked up from the papers lying on the table. "Two more women—one with two children, the other with three—checked into the crisis center this afternoon. Which means Abby will need to stay well past dinnertime, leaving Sierra's final coaching session up to you and me."

Amanda pulled out a chair. "Fortunately, I have a few hours before meeting Gary and Keith for our first meet and greet."

"Are you expecting a big turnout?"

"If everyone who's been invited shows up."

Sierra wandered in with Theo propped on her hip. "Is Abby on her way home?"

Erica shook her head. "Since your interviews are tomorrow morning, Amanda's filling in for her."

"Okay." Sierra lowered her child into his playpen before settling between her coaches. "I'm ready."

"All right." Erica handed Amanda a sheet of paper, keeping a copy for herself. "We'll ask a series of questions, followed by our feedback on your reactions and responses."

Sierra picked at a cuticle. "Isn't this kind of like cheating?"

"Preparing is what smart people do." Amanda folded her arms on the table. "The first time I interviewed for a job as a New Orleans tour guide, a friend who'd had the same job for a year took me through two practice interviews. Without her help, I wouldn't have had a clue how to answer the questions."

Sierra's head tilted. "You and Erica know a lot about a lot of things, don't you?"

Amanda smiled. "So it seems. Are you ready to begin?"

Sierra squared her shoulders. "I'm ready."

Nearly two hours after Amanda asked the first question, Erica offered the final bit of feedback before leaning back. "Well done, Ms. Wellington. In our expert opinion, you're more than ready to shine."

Sierra held her head high, her eyes bright. "I'm gonna make Theo proud of his mother."

"You already are." Amanda touched Sierra's arm. "We're all proud of how far you've come during the past few months, honey."

"Because you and Erica, Abby, and even Millie believed in me when no one else did." Sierra scooted away from the table then lifted her son into her arms. "You and me—I mean you and I—have a real good family now. One that loves and cares about both of us."

After Sierra carried Theo to the kitchen, Amanda shared a knowing glance with Erica. Their little non-traditional family definitely had two new members.

Wearing a new royal blue suit and four-inch heels, Amanda walked into Mountain Mama's Coffee Lounge ten minutes before the meet and greet was scheduled to begin. Keith and Gary appeared deep in conversation at the far end of the room.

Linda approached Erica. "You look stunning. That shade of blue is perfect for a redhead."

"Thanks for the compliment, and I love your outfit." Amanda stole a quick glance at their candidate and his finance manager, still deep in conversation. "What are you expecting from tonight?"

Linda fingered her earring. "Given our invitation list, we'll likely raise enough money to pay for a series of ads while ensuring everyone turns out to vote."

Amanda smiled at Linda. "You're a natural as a politician's wife."

"We both are."

"Except you're the only wife on this team."

"At least for now." Linda nodded toward a couple walking in. She linked arms with Amanda. "Come meet our longtime friends and neighbors."

Fifty minutes after welcoming their first guests, the room teemed with activity. Amanda had schmoozed with at least a dozen potential voters, secured hundreds in donations, and caught Gary smiling at her twice. An hour into the event, he ambled toward her. "Based on comments I've overheard, you're impressing all the right people."

"I've had a lot of practice as an innkeeper."

He leaned close. "Keith and Linda were wise to hire a campaign manager who's smart and gorgeous."

Should she tell him about Linda's matchmaking scheme, or had he figured it out on his own? Maybe a little subtle probing would provide the answer. "I suppose they had several reasons for choosing the two of us."

"The most important factor in selecting a campaign team is trust—something our opponent hasn't learned."

Based on his response, either Gary didn't know about Linda's primary motive, or he wasn't saying.

An impeccably dressed woman with stylish white hair approached. "How's life treating you, Gary?"

"Couldn't be better. Amanda Smith, meet Gladys Zander, one of our town's most distinguished residents."

"It's a pleasure." Amanda extended her hand.

Gladys sandwiched Amanda's hand. "Mine as well. Congratulations on Hilltop Inn's success."

"Thank you."

"You're welcome." After glancing around as if determining whether or not anyone was listening, Gladys faced Gary. "As you know, I've been involved in a prison ministry for years."

Gary nodded. "A noble cause."

She leaned close. "I've discovered a situation that could have major implications in Keith's campaign. If you two will meet me at Hook and Eye at nine, I'll give you all the details."

"We'll be there."

"Excellent." Gladys removed a check from her purse and handed it to Gary. "My contribution for our next district attorney." With a nod, she turned and walked away.

Amanda eyed the check. "Talk about generous."

"Gladys is a wealthy widow who owns dozens of rental properties and supports numerous charities."

"What revelation do you suppose she wants to share with us?"

"Whatever information she's uncovered, you can be assured it's a big deal." Gary pocketed the check. "I'll give Keith a heads-up."

While Gary made his way across the room, Amanda greeted another guest. By quarter to nine, the crowd had thinned to fewer than a dozen guests. Amanda's mind ran wild with speculation.

Gary eased beside her. "It's time to leave." He gripped her elbow then held the door open.

Amanda stepped out, breathing in the cool night air. Street lights cast a warm glow on the park across the street.

"Do you mind walking over?"

"Not at all. Especially since I need a few minutes to clear my head."

"That makes two of us."

They headed up East Main, turned left at Depot Street, then right on West Main. After passing Southern Charm Restaurant, Amanda's pace slowed as she glanced up the driveway leading to Blue Ridge Inn's back entrance. Nearly two years ago, she'd arrived at the inn expecting to celebrate her ninth anniversary with the man she'd known as Paul Sullivan. Soon she, along with Wendy and Erica, found out they were all illegally married to the same con man. The discovery been the most humiliating shock she'd ever experienced. At least Gunter Benson was in jail on the opposite end of the country.

Gary gripped her elbow. "Are you okay?"

Amanda blinked away the memory and stepped up her pace. "Maybe a little apprehensive."

"Understandable."

Minutes later they entered Hook and Eye bar and joined their informant at a corner table. After a waitress took orders for three glasses of white wine, Gladys removed her phone from her purse then tapped the screen and turned it toward them.

Amanda stared at an arrest photo of a middle-aged woman.

"Her name's Crystal Bullock. Twelve years ago Richard Watson convinced a jury she was guilty of second-degree murder in what could only be described as a sham trial."

Gary folded his arms on the table. "What are you suggesting?"

"I, along with three other volunteers, believe she's innocent."

"Has she asked for an appeal?"

"Numerous times. Watson always denies it. With his position in jeopardy, this is the perfect time to request a retrial."

The waitress arrived with their wine. Gary waited for the woman to walk away. "You're aware that Keith can't be involved."

"Absolutely. However, Armstrong Law Firm's new hire is the perfect person to take the case. Regina Reeves is a former prosecutor and as tough as nails."

Amanda's brows raised. "Do you know her?"

"Personally, no. Her reputation, yes. If she's willing to take the case and prove Watson convicted an innocent woman, he'd lose the election in a landslide."

Gary leaned back. "The election is fewer than two months away."

"Which is why I'm asking you two to take this on."

Gary turned to Amanda. "What do you think?"

"Watson tried to railroad Jimmy Barkley because Brad suspended his son years ago. Maybe there's a reason he did the same thing to Crystal."

"Good point." He faced Gladys. "Tell you what, we'll set up a meeting to discuss our next steps. If Keith and his partners approve, we'll move forward."

"I knew you'd understand." Gladys lifted her glass. "A toast to justice being served."

Chapter 11

Following her only scheduled massage for the day, Erica returned to the ranch house. In thirty minutes she would accompany Abby to what would likely become another routine neurology appointment. How many more weeks would pass before the months of therapy led to the results they'd prayed for every day since the accident? Erica tossed the spa keys on the kitchen counter then followed voices to the den.

Sierra strode in from her room wearing the new dress and heels Abby had helped her pick out. She turned in a slow circle. "What do you think?"

Abby wheeled away from the sofa. "Perfect."

Amanda lifted Theo from his playpen. "Do you see your mother over there? She's on her way to acing an interview for a very important job." Responding to Theo's babbled response, she carried him to Sierra. "You're right, she's an amazing young woman."

Sierra kissed her son's cheek. "Tomorrow I'll find the perfect daycare where you'll have fun while Mommy goes to work." She lifted her purse off the end table then waved over her shoulder. "I'm off to ace my interview."

The moment the back door closed, Amanda returned Theo to his playpen. "Sierra is almost unrecognizable from the frightened young woman we met the day of Theo's surgery. In large part thanks to your friendship, Abby."

She shrugged. "Mom suggesting she live with us had the biggest impact."

"We've all played a role," added Erica. "Are you ready to leave, sweetheart?"

"As ready as I'll ever be." Abby moved her wheelchair to the foyer then out the front door and on to her car parked beside the sidewalk.

After her daughter maneuvered onto the driver's seat, Erica stashed her wheelchair in the trunk then settled on the passenger seat. Still amazed at how quickly Abby had learned to drive using hand controls, she buckled her seatbelt.

Abby turned on the radio, hinting she preferred to drive in silence. During the short trip, Erica focused on the passing scenery while willing her shoulders to relax. Hopefully, today they'd hear good news, especially with her wedding fewer than two months away. Twelve minutes after backing down their driveway, they entered the neurologist's waiting room. Erica settled on a chair while Abby checked in.

After chatting with the receptionist, Abby wheeled beside Erica. "I have a huge favor to ask."

"All right."

"I know you've always gone into Dr. Kennedy's office with me..." Abby hesitated. "Today, I want to go in alone."

Caught off guard, Erica stared at her daughter's profile. Why the sudden request?

Abby turned toward her as if she'd read her mind. "It's time for me to become more independent, Mom."

Hoping to mask her disappointment riddled with concern, Erica forced a smile. "Good for you, sweetheart." She lifted a *People* magazine off an end table. Minutes passed. Was Abby flexing her independence, or was something else going on?

A door opened. The nurse called her name.

Abby reached across her chair and touched Erica's arm. "Thank you for understanding." She spun away, aiming her wheelchair toward the door.

Erica's eyes followed her daughter wheeling toward the door. The nurse, who had become a friend, flashed Erica a knowing smile, as if she understood the pain behind her stare. Abby disappeared down the hall seconds before the nurse closed the door, leaving Erica alone in the empty waiting room. Was Abby Dr. Kennedy's last patient for today? How would he react when he discovered she hadn't accompanied her daughter to the exam room?

Desperate to counter the anxiety holding her hostage, Erica leafed blindly through the magazine's first few pages. What was the real reason Abby skipped therapy and now insisted on seeing her doctor alone? She turned more pages. If she postponed her wedding until spring, would Abby have behaved differently?

A woman carrying a baby wearing a protective helmet walked in from the outside hall. After a conversation with the receptionist, she sat across from Erica. The child, who appeared to be the same age as Theo, gripped a ring of plastic keys.

Erica returned the woman's smile before diverting her eyes to the magazine. Was something seriously wrong with the helmeted child? Seconds gave way to minutes as she attempted to read an article about a celebrity she'd never heard of. Frustrated, she laid the magazine aside then removed her phone from her purse and opened Hilltop's website. Two new massage reservations; one for tomorrow morning, the other for next week. She closed the website then pulled up her personal emails. Nothing urgent. Had something happened during Abby's last therapy session to cause her to lose hope?

Responding to her name being called, the woman hiked her baby on her hip then followed the nurse into the hall. Moments later Abby returned, her expression neutral. Erica rushed to open the door. "How'd your appointment go?"

She shrugged while wheeling toward the exit. "Same routine as usual. Take off my shoes, wiggle my toes."

Erica followed her out to the main hall, then on to her car. After stashing her wheelchair in the trunk, she slid onto the passenger seat. "Are you going to work after you take me home?"

Abby nodded while cranking the engine. "I have a lot to do."

Erica pressed her lips tight to prevent the question sitting on the tip of her tongue from escaping.

A quick glance at her mother's expression hinted she suspected something was going on. As much as she disliked telling a fib while keeping her mother in the dark, Abby couldn't allow anyone to sway the decision she needed to make. Hoping to ease the tension hanging heavy in the air, she tapped her fingers on the steering wheel while humming along with the radio until she turned onto their street. She slowed using the handheld controls then eased up the ranch house driveway.

Gripping the door handle, her mom turned to face Abby. "Brad and I are going out to dinner….Maybe you and I can talk after I come home."

"If I'm still awake."

Her mother stared at her, knowing full well she never went to sleep before eleven.

"Okay, Mom, we'll talk. For now I need to head to work."

"All right, sweetheart."

Abby waited for her mother to climb out and head to the kitchen door before turning off the radio and backing down the driveway. During the drive, she teetered between following through with her decision now or wait until the end of the year. By the time she arrived back in town, she'd come to the only conclusion that seemed right.

After circling the block twice, she eased into an open space beside the park. Her fingers trembled as she pulled out her phone and tapped Tommy's name. One ring. Two. Three.

He answered. "Hey. How'd your appointment go?"

The sound of him—just his voice—sent a ripple through her chest. Her throat tightened. "I'm downtown by the park. Can you come meet me?"

A pause. "Right now?"

Don't hesitate. Don't you dare back down. "Yes. It's important."

Another pause, longer this time. "Give me twenty minutes."

The call ended with a soft click, but the air in her car thickened, heavy with everything she didn't know how to say. Abby closed her eyes, letting the memories roll in like a tide she couldn't stop. The first time she'd seen Tommy—sandy-haired, confident on the basketball court. Their first awkward-but-perfect date. The way he made her laugh while they hiked that muddy trail. Shooting hoops in his driveway. His hand wrapped around hers while she lay in a hospital bed, unable to move her legs.

A dog barked in the distance, yanking her back to the present. Her heart thudded as she glanced around, but the world outside kept moving. She tried the radio. A song about holding on and letting go filled the car. She shut it off fast. Too raw. Too close. Scrolling mindlessly through social media didn't help either. Then—a tap on the window. She jumped, her phone slipping from her fingers and falling onto the floor.

Tommy stood outside, his jeans covered with drywall dust. She unlocked the door.

He slid onto the passenger seat. "What's going on? Why are we meeting here?"

She stared through the windshield, past the row of cars and everything that still made sense in the world. "I've given this a lot of thought...and well..." Her voice trembled. "I think our relationship has run its course."

For a beat, the only sound was the breeze brushing past the car.

Tommy blinked. "Wait—what?" He leaned toward her, eyes wide. "Are you breaking up with me?"

Abby's chest tightened. "I think it's best."

"This is because of your accident, isn't it?"

"You don't deserve to be stuck with someone who can't be who she was when we met."

"Is this about what happened at today's appointment?"

"Nothing's happened. That's the problem." Her eyes met his, raw and honest. "Months of therapy, and all I've managed to do is wiggle my toes. That's it, Tommy. That's all."

His expression hardened. "So, you're just giving up and calling it quits?" He snapped his fingers. "Just like that?"

"I'm not giving up," she whispered. "I'm choosing to stop chasing something that seems impossible. I'm tired, Tommy. So tired of the struggle with nothing to show for it."

He shook his head, disbelief turning to anger. "What about me? I love you, Abby. I want to be here. I want to take care of you—"

"Don't you see?" Her voice cracked open like glass. "I'm not the same girl you fell in love with. I don't know if she's ever coming back."

"You're right." His jaw clenched. "You're not. That girl would never have pushed me away without a fight."

Abby flinched. "That's not fair—"

"Call me when you're ready to stop feeling sorry for yourself and return to being who you really are." Tommy reached for the door handle, his eyes glistening. "Call me when you understand that no matter how far you run, I will never stop loving you." He stepped out, shut the door gently—almost too gently—then strode away.

Abby sat there, trembling, her hands covering her face as the tears came fast and hard. Struggling to regain control, she swallowed the fist-sized lump in her throat. Had pushing Tommy away been the biggest mistake of her life?

Desperate to pull herself together, she swiped her fingers across her cheeks. Her eyes drifted to a young couple strolling along the sidewalk holding hands. Tommy would soon realize he was better off without her. Wouldn't he? How would her mother react to the breakup? Abby squared her shoulders then pulled out of the parking space. No one needed to know about her decision until she figured out how to share the news without breaking any more hearts.

Chapter 12

Amanda dashed into Armstrong Law Firm's conference room, settled beside Keith's finance manager, and set her purse on the floor before Gary had a chance to stand. Chris sat on one end of the table, the candidate on the other, Regina across from her. Amanda scooted her chair close while eyeing the thin folder lying on the table in front of Keith. "How much have you learned about Crystal Bullock's situation?"

Keith tapped his finger on the folder. "Enough to take Gladys Zander's claim seriously. To avoid appearing biased, Chris and I agree that we need to take a back seat on this one."

Regina leaned forward, her eyes focused on Amanda. "Leaving me to assume the role as Crystal's attorney, with you and Gary functioning as witnesses."

Amanda raised a brow. "Witnesses to what?"

"A conversation with the prisoner. I've arranged for the three of us to meet with Crystal—" Regina glanced at her watch. "In two hours. I'll drive, in order to give you and Gary time to review what we've discovered up to this point."

"I appreciate your confidence." Amanda twisted the cap off a water bottle. "However, becoming involved in a criminal case seems way beyond a campaign and finance manager's responsibilities"

"Our role is to ensure our candidate wins." Gary's eyes met Amanda's. "Including exposing our opponent's failures at his job."

"Gary's right," added Chris. "Especially considering every dirty trick DA Watson has attempted to use against us."

Amanda released a heavy sigh before taking a long sip of water.

Keith crossed his arms on the table, his eyes focused on Amanda. "You're not keen about walking into a prison, are you?"

"On a list of the top ten things I'd never want to do, that would be number two, right behind walking barefoot across a bed of hot coals."

"Visiting a client in prison isn't as bad as it might seem." Chris's tone came across as reassuring. "Good news is you won't have to interact with any prisoners other than Crystal."

"At least I'll never be forced to visit Gunter Benson in jail." Amanda blinked. Why had she uttered his name out loud? She stole a quick glance at the law firm's new attorney. Had anyone told her about the con man? If not would she ask?

Regina leaned forward. "Is Benson another one of DA Watson's innocent victims?"

"He's a con man who's serving twenty-five to life for killing a loan shark." Regretting her angry tone, Amanda eyed Regina. "On the flip side, he's also the reason I moved from New Orleans to Blue Ridge."

"I'm looking forward to hearing the rest of what sounds like an intriguing story. Which will have to wait until we're on our way back from visiting an inmate at least one person believes is a wrongfully imprisoned woman." Regina stood, scooping the folder off the table.

Hoping their mission would quash Regina's curiosity about Gunter, Amanda grabbed her purse off the floor then followed the take-charge attorney through the reception area and out to the parking lot.

"You sit up front with me, Amanda." Regina slid behind the wheel of her not-so-new luxury sedan while Gary climbed in behind her. "Which one of you wants to examine the documents first?"

Amanda glanced over her shoulder. "You do the honors."

"Works for me."

Regina passed the folder to Gary then secured her phone in a holder attached to her windshield and tapped the screen. "Next stop, Allendale State Prison."

Amanda's breath quickened as her mind drifted to a steamy hot day thirteen years earlier. A phone call from the New Orleans district attorney. The drunk driver who'd snuffed out Preston Smith's life had agreed to a plea deal. Thirty years behind bars. Was he still in prison, or had he been released on parole? Amanda ran her fingers along her seatbelt. The gut-wrenching anger she'd experienced the day she first learned the criminal's name had faded over the years. All that remained was deep sorrow for two destroyed lives—one innocent, the other guilty.

"There's not much in this file." Gary's voice pulled Amanda back to the present.

Regina glanced in her rearview mirror. "A good indication the case was poorly defended while being bulldozed by a DA desperate to win at all costs."

Gary passed the folder to Amanda. "Twelve years ago Richard Watson would have been smack dab in the middle of election season."

"My point exactly." Regina veered into the left lane to pass a slow-moving truck.

Amanda opened the folder, focusing on the first page. Crystal Bullock, a thirty-seven-year-old homeless woman living on the streets in a North Georgia town was arrested as the prime suspect two days after the murder of a local business owner. "I don't know much about the law, but forty-eight hours doesn't seem like enough time to conduct a thorough investigation."

Regina nodded. "Unless a suspect is caught standing over the victim with a murder weapon in hand, it isn't."

After leafing through the remaining documents, Amanda closed the folder then laid it on the dashboard.

Regina steered back into the right lane. "I want you both to tell me about DA Watson's behavior since Keith announced he's running against him."

Amanda stared out the windshield while Gary relayed their opponent's underhanded tactics. He told how the crooked DA had used his campaign manager to bribe a former juror to falsely accuse Keith of jury tampering; then fired the guy when caught. By the time they pulled onto the prison parking lot and stashed their watches and cellphones in the glove box, the dull pain at the base of Amanda's skull had exploded into a full-blown headache.

Regina retrieved the folder off the dashboard then climbed out and led the way to the small check-in building. A minute after pressing the door buzzer, Regina claimed Gary and Amanda as her assistants. The door swung open. Inside the tight space, they each walked through a metal detector.

After Regina turned over her keys and driver's license, a guard with an attitude examined the folder contents then led them through two gates in the double barbed-wire fencing and into a building. Another guard, her attitude slightly more tolerable, escorted them to a square room encased in unpainted concrete. A gray metal table bolted to the floor and three mismatched metal chairs—two on one side, one on the other—filled the tight space.

The guard pointed to the door opposite the one they'd walked through. "A guard will bring the prisoner in shortly."

After she left, Amanda pulled out a chair. "How long do you suppose we'll have to wait?"

"Depends on how long the guards intend to make us squirm." Regina sat beside Amanda, while Gary stood beside them with his back against the side wall. "We're on their turf, their rules."

Hoping to ease the pain, Amanda pressed her fingers to the base of her skull. "At least we weren't frisked."

"We would have been if any of us had set off the metal detector."

Amanda lowered her hands to her lap while squinting at the dull gray walls and overhead fluorescent light. "I can't imagine living in such a colorless environment."

Regina laid the folder on the table. "Especially for someone who's innocent."

A minute passed. Then two more.

Gary folded his arms across his chest.

Regina reviewed the documents.

Amanda fidgeted.

Another five minutes crept by.

The door clicked open. A burly male guard led a thin woman with shoulder-length hair graying at the temples to the single chair. After unlocking one side of her handcuffs and relocking it onto a metal bar bolted to the table, he walked out without uttering a word.

Armstrong Law Firm's newest lawyer scooted close to the table. "My name is Regina Reeves. I'm your new attorney."

Crystal's brows furrowed. "How'd you find out about me?"

"Gladys Zander filled us in."

A flicker of hope burned in Crystal's hazel eyes. "She's the only person who's ever come to visit me."

Amanda's heart ached for the woman who appeared far older than forty-five. Had eight years behind bars or living on the street prematurely aged her?

Regina leaned forward, her fingers laced on the table. "Ms. Zander believes you might have been wrongfully convicted."

Crystal's body sagged into her chair, as if strings manipulated by a puppeteer had been cut free. "I've sent more letters than I can count to the district attorney's office. No one's bothered to respond before now."

"I'm not a public defender. I represent a private law firm—"

"I don't got no money to pay you."

"If my associates and I believe you're innocent, my firm will take your case pro bono and work diligently to right a wrong." Regina's eyes remained laser focused on Crystal. "We want to hear your side of the story, beginning with your life before you were arrested all the way up to the moment a jury found you guilty."

Crystal raked her free hand through her hair. "How much time do I have?"

"As much as you need."

For nearly an hour, Crystal Bullock relayed details about her life before, during, and after the arrest, ending with evidence she believed proved her innocence. By the time she finished telling her story and answered all of Regina's questions, Amanda believed beyond a reasonable doubt that Richard Watson had railroaded an innocent woman straight to prison.

Crystal massaged her handcuffed wrist, her eyes wide with tenuous faith. "Are you gonna help me?"

"Not only will I help you—" Regina reached across the table and placed her hand on Crystal's arm. "I also won't stop fighting until justice is served."

Tears pooled then tracked down Crystal's cheeks. "Thank you for believing me."

"You're welcome." Regina stood, then knocked on the door, summoning the guard.

He entered then unshackled the prisoner and led her from the room.

Regina scooped the folder off the table. Her jaw clenched. "Victims like Crystal are the reason I switched sides." She strode out.

Amanda's mind raced with questions while she and Gary followed her. Had Regina discovered other innocent victims in her prior position? Had she wrongfully prosecuted someone?

After exiting the building and walking through the check-in building, Gary fell in step behind Regina. "What's our next move?"

She peered over her shoulder. "Convince a judge to hear Crystal's case."

Chapter 13

Two days after Abby's private meeting with her neurologist, Erica packed a lunch then drove the truck to the high school. Hoping spending an hour with Brad would help ease her growing anxiety, she carried the mini cooler to the main entrance, punched the intercom, and announced her arrival. The door buzzed open. Erica headed straight to the principal's office, knocked once, then stepped inside, closing the door behind her. She set the cooler down. "Chicken salad sandwiches and cookies, compliments of Chef Millie."

Brad rounded his desk and gathered her into his arms. "Perfect lunch. Even better company." He kissed her, sending waves of desire coursing through her limbs.

"Oh my," Erica whispered. "Being summoned to the principal's office has a whole new meaning."

"Keep looking drop-dead gorgeous, and I'll have to give you detention."

"Better yet—" Erica pulled away then patted his cheek. "Take the afternoon off and help me find a good used car."

"In a big city, I couldn't leave. This is a small town, so as long as I'm not more than ten minutes away, I'll risk playing hooky for an hour to help boost the local economy "

She raised a brow. "Are you agreeing to go with me?"

"How could I resist such an intriguing offer? Especially since you brought cookies."

"Are sweets and kisses all it takes to steal you away?"

"Only if delivered by one very special brunette." A knock on the door. "Uh-oh, we've been caught." He winked then released Erica and returned to his desk chair. "Come in."

The retiring office assistant stepped inside. "Sorry to interrupt. I called Sierra to let her know she'll become my replacement."

Erica leaned against Brad's desk. "I imagine she was excited."

"She's over the moon. I'll begin training her tomorrow morning. For now, I'll leave you two alone."

"Before you go—" Brad scooted his chair close to his desk. "—Inform the staff that after lunch I'm taking an hour long break. Call me if anything needing my attention comes up."

"We'll keep everything running smoothly. Nice to see you again, Erica."

"Likewise." The woman walked out, closing the door behind her.

Erica settled on a chair facing the desk then removed the sandwiches from the cooler. "You hiring Sierra means a lot."

"She earned the position, fair and square." Brad pulled two water bottles from his mini fridge. "Has Abby said anything about her neurology appointment?"

"Not a peep. She's worked late every day since. When she comes home, she goes straight to her room." Erica pushed a sandwich across the desk. "This morning when I tried to talk to her, she brushed me off, explaining she'd been extra busy at work. I know my daughter. Whatever's troubling her has nothing to do with the crisis center."

Three hours after arriving at the crisis center, Abby wheeled into her office with Lucky, the crisis center's golden retriever, plodding behind her. After she pushed the door closed, he plopped his head on her lap. She stroked his muzzle. "I knew I couldn't fool you." Her heart ached as her eyes shifted to the picture of her and Tommy on her desk. He hadn't reached out to her since the day she'd ended their relationship. Although deep down she'd expected him at least to text her asking if she was okay, who could blame him for ignoring her. She'd stabbed him in the heart without warning. Even though not telling anyone about the breakup tormented her, somehow she had to get a grip and learn to live with reality as it was, not as she hoped it would become.

Responding to a tap on her door, Abby spun away from her desk. "Come on in."

The door swung open. Sierra's face beamed as she pushed her son's stroller into the small space. Lucky padded to the stroller, welcoming Theo with a tongue bath, triggering a wince followed by a giggle.

"First thing I do when Theo and I move out on our own is buy him a puppy. Anyway, I wanted you to be the first to hear the good news."

"Oh my gosh." Abby pressed her palms together. "You got the job, didn't you?"

"Uh-huh, and I found the perfect daycare center for Theo." Sierra plopped onto the love seat. "A lot has happened since that day I left my baby on the doorstep out front." She paused while peering around the office. "After I rang the doorbell, I hid behind a tree, watching to make sure someone answered. When your mom carried him inside...I cried because I knew he'd be safe."

"You're a good mother."

"I wasn't back then." Sierra scooted forward and lifted Theo onto her lap. "But I am now. Anyway, I want to treat you and Tommy to dinner tonight to thank you for being more like my sister and brother than my best friends."

Abby stared at the young woman she'd grown to love. Maybe her showing up at this exact moment wasn't random. "I want to share something with you, but first I need you to promise not to tell anyone."

Sierra traced an X on her chest.

Abby wheeled closer. "Two days ago, I broke up with Tommy." Her words poured out ending with the revelation that had prompted her decision. She eyed Sierra's arched brows, her parted lips. "You understand, don't you?"

Sierra's brows lowered. "Do you want me to tell you the truth?"

Abby clasped her hands together. "I don't know, do I?"

"You tell me."

Maybe she should have chosen someone else to unload on. "Go ahead."

"Okay, here goes. I think you're making two ginormous mistakes. First, you ditched the guy who has stayed with you despite you being stuck in that chair. Second, you're giving up without a fight."

Abby recoiled. "I thought you of all people would understand."

"Not after everything I've learned living with you, your mother, and Amanda. Oh, have you told Erica what you just told me?"

Abby shook her head. "If I confide in Mom, she'll postpone her wedding—"

"Giving her the silent treatment is another big mistake." Sierra returned Theo to his stroller. "Even though you haven't asked for my advice, I'm gonna give it to you anyway." Her eyes met Abby's. "You've fought too hard to call it quits after one little setback. So either tell your mother what's going on, or go back to therapy and work harder than ever."

"Easy for you to say." Abby's tone screamed of sarcasm. "You haven't spent nearly a year working your butt off without any meaningful results."

"I can't pretend to know everything you've been going through, but I do know miracles happen when we don't give up hope." Sierra stood and pushed the stroller toward the door. "I'll postpone treating you to dinner until you and Tommy are back together." She yanked the door open then pushed Theo out to the hall and around the corner.

Abby spun away from the door then gripped her chair's arms. "How dare Sierra preach to me," she murmured. "What does she know about fighting a losing battle?" Lucky plunked his paw on her thigh while his tail slapped the floor. Abby slowly released her grip and brushed his paw away. "Who asked you, anyway?"

"Your friend rushed out in a hurry. Is everything all right?"

Abby rolled her eyes then spun toward Pamela Worthington standing in the doorway. The last thing she needed was her boss asking questions she wasn't willing to answer. Forcing a smile, she maneuvered her chair closer to her. One little white lie wouldn't hurt. "Everything's fine. Sierra left in a hurry because she's on her way to an appointment."

"Okay. Come on, Lucky, one of our new arrivals needs a friend."

Relieved the dog padded out behind Pamela, Abby closed the door then wheeled to her desk and stared at Tommy's photo. If she turned it face down or stashed it in a drawer, would someone notice and ask questions? Better to leave it in place until she figured out how to break the news to her mother. Determined to stay busy, Abby booted her laptop and pulled up a document she'd begun working on the day before.

Forty minutes passed, then an hour. Try as she might to stay focused on work, Sierra's comments kept creeping in. Maybe she needed a few days alone in her room, away from prying eyes. Besides, she had a couple of vacation days coming. Why not come up with a good excuse to take them now? An hour after closing her laptop and making her way to Pamela's office, Abby parked in the ranch house carport beside the empty space.

Relieved, Amanda had stepped out of the kitchen instead of her mother, Abby popped the trunk, then opened her door.

Amanda pushed the chair beside the driver's seat. "You're home early."

"I have a big exam coming up." Another little white lie. "I'm taking a couple of days off to study." Abby moved onto her chair then wheeled to the front sidewalk, up the ramp, and into the foyer. Dusty greeted her with an enthusiastic tail wag. "Did you miss me?" Her canine companion responded with a muffled bark. Relieved her mother wasn't home, she headed straight to her room with Dusty padding behind her. After pushing the door closed, her eyes drifted to the beanbag chair—her favorite study spot before the accident. Her lips trembled as she struggled to hold back the cry rising in her throat. The chair stood as a reminder of everything she had lost.

The moment Dusty plopped her front paw and head on Abby's lap, the mental anguish she'd hidden from everyone she loved rushed to the surface. She buried her face in her hands and wept until no tears remained.

Chapter 14

Watching Ryan play with one of his favorite toys warmed Wendy's heart. "You're such a smart little guy." His babbled response made her smile. "Are you ready to call Glamma Cynthia?"

Ryan toddled over and fingered the phone.

"You know who we're going to talk to, don't you?" Wendy stood from her place on the floor in front of the fireplace, wiped away the fingerprint smudge on the phone, then pressed her mother's number and activated FaceTime.

Cynthia answered before the second ring. A brave smile creased the skin around her tired eyes. At least she still had enough energy to apply makeup and fix her hair. "Hi."

No longer asking how she was feeling, Wendy mirrored her mother's expression. "Someone is eager to talk to you." She turned the phone toward Ryan.

"Hi, sweet boy. Glamma Cynthia loves you."

Wendy's emotions flickered between joy and heartbreak while listening to her mother carry on a conversation with her grandson. The hours she and Chris had spent coaching Ryan to say Glamma had yet to pay off. One of these days he'd master the word.

Ryan sneezed, spraying the screen with droplets.

She wiped the phone with her shirt sleeve before facing her mother. "Sorry about that."

Cynthia laughed. "My grandson can sneeze on me any day."

Eager to follow up on yesterday's conversation about her oldest sister, Wendy asked, "How'd Kayla's algebra test go?"

"She passed with a B minus."

"Pretty good for a teenager who considers math a useless skill. Anything new going on with Zach?"

"Chris's talk with him helped some." Cynthia fell silent for a long moment. "I'm especially worried about Brent. He's barely getting any sleep. Adding to his anxiety, his long-time guitar player quit to go on tour with Nashville's next superstar. Too much is happening too fast."

Reality weighed heavy on Wendy. The family she hadn't known existed a year earlier would be relying on her and Chris more than ever in the coming months. How would she be able to give them what they needed while taking care of a toddler and a newborn? Not to mention her responsibilities as a wife, a business partner, and a student.

"Are you okay, honey?"

Wendy blinked. "Sorry." Had her expression given her away? "Your grandson distracted me."

"Easy to understand; he's such a darling child. He reminds me a lot of Zach when he was a baby."

Their conversation continued for twenty more minutes before Cynthia's energy gave out. Wendy glanced at her watch, swallowing hard. Her mother had held on two fewer minutes than yesterday.

"Give my grandbaby a kiss for Glamma Cynthia."

"I will. We'll talk again tomorrow." Wendy placed her palm on her chest while lifting her chin toward the ceiling. "Please help my mother stay with us long enough to meet her granddaughter," she whispered. Peace filled her with hope that her prayer would be answered.

Ryan's jabbering curled Wendy's lips into a smile. She uncrossed her legs then gripped the coffee table and pushed up to her feet. "In a couple more weeks, Mommy won't be able to sit on the floor with you."

Ryan toddled over, peering up at her. "Mama."

She pocketed her phone before grasping her little guy's hand. "It's time for our walk down to the mailbox." Halfway to the front door, her step-mother's ringtone sounded. "Seems the mail will have to wait." Wendy released Ryan's hand then tapped her screen. "Good timing. I just ended a call with my mom."

"How's Cynthia doing?"

"She's a little weaker every day, but hanging in there. What's going on with you?"

A long moment of silence. "Two nights ago I found the courage to tell my boys about you."

"Oh my gosh." Wendy settled on the sofa, her eyes wide. "How did they take the news?"

"Better than I expected, especially Carter, my youngest. Tyler was harder to read. Can't say the same about their father. When I broke the news to him, he accused me of turning his sons against him." Donna's tone dripped with disgust. "Rich, considering his entire family is giving me the silent treatment. No telling what lies Douglas has told them about me. Anyway, as soon as Chris defeats my husband's bogus lawsuit, I want my sons to meet the rest of their family."

"I'm looking forward to that day." Wendy fingered her baby bulge. "Funny how after growing up without siblings, I now have three brothers and two sisters."

"Life is full of surprises. Some good. Others not so much."

The garage door opening sent Duke springing to his paws and scrambling to the kitchen. Ryan toddled after him.

"Chris is home early."

"I'll let you go. Promise to call me with any news about the lawsuit from your end."

"I promise. Now that your sons know I exist, tell them hi for me."

"Will do."

Wendy ended the call then laid her phone on an end table and headed to the kitchen.

Chris breezed in from the garage. He tossed a stack of mail on the counter and patted Duke's head then scooped Ryan into his arms. "How's my boy and his gorgeous mother?"

"We're glad you're home early. Is today a lemonade or beer sort of day?"

He kissed her cheek. "Lemonade will do."

She filled a glass then followed her guys to the sofa. "I was talking to Donna when you drove up. After all these months of keeping me a secret, she finally told my brothers they have a big sister."

"Bet that was an interesting conversation."

She handed Chris the glass, then sat beside him. "Douglas didn't take the news well."

He scoffed. "What a shocker."

"I can't help but feel sorry for his sons—their family splitting apart and their father suing their mother. Speaking of which—" Wendy tucked her ankle under her knee. "Any progress on Douglas's ridiculous lawsuit?"

"Nothing new." Chris took a long sip of lemonade. "How's your mom?"

"A little weaker than yesterday." Wendy relayed their conversation. "Ryan always cheers her up."

He patted Wendy's knee. "So do you."

"A year ago I never would have believed Mom and I would have a loving relationship."

"Proof that miracles happen."

"So it seems." Wendy faced Chris, her elbow propped on the back of the sofa, her chin resting on her fist. "How'd your meeting with Judge Davis go?"

"She cleared her calendar and scheduled a bench retrial for Crystal a week from Monday."

Wendy raised a brow. "Talk about fast. What are the chances of an acquittal?"

"Based on Judge Davis's reaction today, better than fifty-fifty." He took another sip of lemonade. "Regina will take the lead. I'll second chair."

"Your new partner's first big case as a defense attorney."

"With a woman's fate and a political campaign at stake."

"I can't imagine the anguish knowing you're locked up for a crime you didn't commit." Wendy lifted her arm off the sofa and leaned back. "You know Mom's mother served time for killing her husband."

"I do."

"When Mom was nine she visited her in jail." Wendy picked at her fingernail. "She never wanted to go back."

"Had to have been a traumatic experience for such a young child, knowing her mother killed her father."

Wendy's mind drifted to the days before Cynthia abandoned her. Riding two buses to visit her grandmother. The tubes in the old lady's nose. The way she smelled funny and coughed a lot. "I never liked my grandmother—the way she said mean things and made my mother cry. She was the worst kind of role model. Everything considered, Cynthia turned out to be a surprisingly good mom and grandmother."

Chris set his glass on the end table then slid his arm around Wendy's shoulders and pulled her close. "Thanks in large part to her renewed relationship with you."

A wistful smile tugged at the corners of her mouth, even as her eyes welled with emotion. "When I asked Vincent Adams to find Mom, I had no idea how much impact his discovery would have on our lives."

"Do you ever regret your decision?"

Wendy shook her head. "Only that I didn't make it sooner."

Chapter 15

Erica struggled to focus while updating her list of tasks for her and Brad's wedding. For the third day in a row, Abby had remained secluded in her room, only emerging to carry food from the kitchen back to her private space. Her explanation about needing extra time to study didn't pass the reasonable-excuse test. Something she didn't want to talk about made more sense. Hopefully, Abby would escape her cocoon long enough to join her and Amanda for supper.

Erica glanced at her watch. Time to head to the spa to prepare for her two o'clock client. She closed her laptop, grabbed a key off the kitchen counter, and headed out the back door. Dark clouds threatening rain hovered overhead. A gust of wind rustled leaves and tousled her hair as she rushed across the side yard to Hilltop's spa.

Inside the converted three-car garage, Erica exchanged a nod with a male guest running on the treadmill before unlocking the massage room. She stepped inside, headed straight to her private office, and set her laptop on the built-in desk. Her eyes drifted to the diploma from the Massage Institute of Cleveland displayed on the wall—her version of a college degree.

Erica returned to the massage room. After spreading sheets on the table, she moved to the waist-high cabinet anchored to the dark blue accent wall. She switched on the subtle overhead lights then lit a candle and breathed in the fresh scent. From the cabinet she selected a CD. Soothing background music drifting from the wall-mounted speakers along with her head roll helped ease the tension gripping her neck and shoulder muscles. Raindrops began trickling down the window facing the ranch house backyard. Hopefully her client was on the way over.

"My husband and I have different ideas about a relaxing vacation. He's working up a sweat out there while I prefer a relaxing massage."

Erica turned and smiled at the young woman. "I would have made the same choice, Mrs. Bennett."

"Please call me Kimberly. This is a lovely room. I love the blue wall, and the music is perfect."

She's definitely a chatty client. "Thank you, and I'm Erica. I'll be in my office. Let me know when you're ready."

"I will."

Erica slipped into her office as the rain escalated to a squall sending a sheet of water cascading down the glass. She removed her engagement ring, gazing at the diamond before setting it aside to select the massage oil.

"I'm ready," Kimberly called out.

"Okay." Maybe a talkative client was exactly what she needed to distract her from worrying about Abby, at least for a while. She entered her work space, breathing in the refreshing scents. During the following hour, she worked her magic while Kimberly talked a blue streak. By the time the session ended and her client gave her a generous tip, Erica was more than ready for a few minutes of uninterrupted quiet.

She returned to her office, washed her hands, then dropped onto her office chair and slipped her ring back on her finger. In a few weeks she and Brad would recite their vows and exchange matching wedding bands. Out of nowhere, a smidgen of doubt crept in. Was she about to make another huge relationship mistake? Impossible. Unlike Jack the abuser or Gunter the con man, Brad was one of the good guys.

Her eyes drifted to the rain-streaked window. If it rained on their wedding day, at least their guests would be protected by the ginormous white tent she'd rented along with outdoor heaters to keep guests warm if the temperature dipped below a comfortable level. Two big items she'd already checked off her to-do list. Erica remained in her private space reviewing the remaining tasks. When the rain ended, she stripped the sheets off the massage table, stuffed them in the laundry basket, and returned to the ranch house.

Sierra sat on the sofa reading a book to Theo. Amanda tapped her laptop keyboard at the dining room table. Abby was nowhere in sight.

Amanda looked up. "Chatty Cathy or quiet client?"

"A whole new version of chatty." Erica plopped onto a chair. "Has Abby come out of her room?"

"Not since I've been sitting here." Amanda leaned close. "You're still worried about her, aren't you?"

"The last time Abby hid in her bedroom and refused to talk to me was back in Asheville when her best friend abandoned her."

"Maybe she and Tommy had a fight."

Sierra carried Theo over and plopped on a chair between Erica and Amanda. "Me and Abby are BFF's. We talked last night after you two went to bed."

Erica shifted toward the teenage mother, dismissing any guilt over discussing Abby with the young woman who'd been a stranger not long ago. "What'd she tell you?"

"That she's dealing with a bunch of stuff."

"That's obvious." Erica regretted her snarky tone, but not enough to apologize or back off. "Did she tell you what stuff?"

"Only that she had some big decisions to make. I think maybe there's something going on with her and Tommy."

"Something she said, or are you guessing?"

"He hasn't been around for a couple of days, so I'm mostly guessing."

"Thanks for sharing your perspective, Sierra."

"No problem."

A simple you're welcome would've been a more appropriate response. Erica's chest tightened as she pushed away from the table then made her way toward the hall. With her hand on her bedroom doorknob, she halted. Light spilled beneath Abby's closed door. Should she knock on her child's door or walk right in? Abby was no longer a child; she was a woman who deserved privacy to work through her struggles. Reluctantly, Erica turned away from her daughter's room.

Amanda closed the distance toward her. "You made the right choice."

"Do you suppose we'll ever stop worrying about our daughters?"

"Not as long as we're on this side of heaven."

Abby leaned back against her headboard while Dusty sprawled across the foot of her bed. During the past three days, she'd talked more to her dog than any humans—including Sierra. Although Dusty couldn't judge her, she also couldn't offer any advice. Abby's eyes drifted to the photo of Tommy still sitting on her desk. Even though his silence spoke volumes, she missed him more than she'd imagined possible. Had she made the right decision?

Desperate to talk to someone, Abby grabbed her phone and typed a text. She hesitated for a moment before pressing send. Unsure how long she'd have to wait, Abby returned to studying.

The sky had turned an inky shade of gray by the time Morgan's ringtone cut through the silence. Abby hesitated a beat before swiping to answer the FaceTime call.

"Hey." She tried to sound steady.

Morgan's face appeared on screen, her eyes narrowed. "Hey back. What's going on?"

Abby exhaled slowly. Her fingers tightened around the phone. "I broke up with Tommy."

Morgan's expression didn't shift—she just waited without a word. Abby pressed her lips together before continuing. "I told him I wasn't the same person anymore. That he deserves someone who hasn't forgotten how to live."

Morgan blinked slowly. "You might look different on the outside, but have you really changed at your core?"

Abby frowned. "What do you mean?"

Morgan leaned in slightly, her voice soft but firm. "From the moment I met you, I recognized someone who refused to let life knock her down. You've fought your way through all sorts of challenges—and now you're... what? Calling it quits?"

Abby's throat tightened. "I'm not quitting. I'm accepting what is."

"Are you?" Morgan's gaze sharpened. "Or are you just tired or scared? Because it sounds less like acceptance and more like surrender."

"Holding on to faith is hard." Abby's voice wavered. "Especially when all I can do after months of therapy is wiggle my toes."

Morgan didn't flinch. "Has your therapist given up on you?"

Abby shook her head. "Anna's an optimist."

Morgan's expression was gentle but unrelenting. "That's not what I asked."

Abby stared past the screen, the silence thick between them. Finally, she whispered, "No. She hasn't."

"Then maybe it's time you stop giving up on yourself."

Abby's eyes welled. The truth of those words cracked something open inside her. "I don't know if I have any fight left."

"Trust me, you do." Morgan's tone came across as reassuring. "You just forgot how strong you are—and I'm here to remind you."

Abby brushed her fingers across her cheeks. "One part of me wants to shut the door and be done. The other part is telling me to stop letting life happen to me and take back control."

Morgan smiled. "Sounds as if you're ready to make some life-changing decisions."

"At least I'm a little closer than I was before you called."

"Glad I could help. Let me know what you decide."

Abby nodded. "We'll talk again soon." As much as Morgan helped, one fact remained—she had to summon enough courage to choose which path to take. She pushed away from the headboard then laid back and closed her eyes, hoping the morning would bring clarity.

Following a long night of mental gymnastics, Abby maneuvered into her private bath. After showering and dressing, she wheeled into the narrow kitchen. "Hey, Mom."

Her mother spun away from the fridge. "You're up bright and early."

"Vacation's over. I'm going back to work." Part one of her decision completed. Part two needed a lot more self-reflection.

Chapter 16

Voices drifting into Hilltop Inn's kitchen drew Millie to the dining room door. She peeked in then turned away. "Second morning our honeymooners show up twenty minutes before breakfast's official start time. How old do you suppose they are?"

Bernie slid a pan of Millie's homemade cinnamon buns into the oven. "I'm guessing they're both in their eighties." She glanced at Millie. "It's sweet how they're proving it's never too late to find romance."

Millie glared at her, an eyebrow raised, her voice low. "What are you implying?"

A sly grin tugged at the corner of Bernie's mouth. "Why are you assuming my comment is anything other than an innocent remark about two of our guests?"

"Hmph." Millie grabbed a coffeepot before rushing into the dining room. "Good morning, you two lovebirds."

Mr. Bishop pulled a chair out for his bride, then settled beside her. "Every morning we wake up is a good morning. Right, sweetheart?"

Mrs. Bishop patted her groom's deeply lined cheek. "Especially when I wake up beside you, Sweetums."

Sweetums? Millie stifled a giggle while filling their coffee mugs. "I'm curious. Why did you choose Hilltop Inn as your honeymoon destination?"

"The inn is only fifteen miles away from Ellijay." Mr. Bishop stirred sugar into his coffee. "At the spry young age of eighty-seven, I no longer drive long distances."

An eighty-seven-year-old newlywed must be some kind of record. Millie set the coffeepot on the sideboard. "Good for you."

"For staying close to home, or still driving at my age?"

"Both."

Bernie carried two glasses of orange juice in from the kitchen. "You're such a sweet couple. How'd you end up together?"

The groom's eyes twinkled. "The day this pretty lady moved into Oaks—"

"That's a senior living facility—"

"For old folks like us." Mr. Bishop slid his arm around his bride's shoulders. "She smiled at me—"

"Because you're sexier than Paul Newman was back in the day, sweetums."

"Your beautiful smile made my heart beat so loud I could have sworn you'd heard."

"All I could hear was my own heart pitter-pattering in my ears."

Millie struggled to keep from rolling her eyes. Were these two practicing some sort of standup comedy routine? "How long after you met Mr. Bishop did he propose?"

"Five weeks—"

"At our ages we don't have time for long engagements." He squeezed his wife's shoulder.

"My sweet husband passed on ten years ago, his wife seven. Needless to say, we've both been going to bed alone long enough."

A buzzing timer sent Millie rushing back to the kitchen before she could come up with a comment.

Bernie followed, closing the door behind her. "The Bishops are an adorable couple, don't you think?"

Millie stared at her as if she'd grown a third eye. "You're kidding."

"Anyone with a heart would find their love story inspirational."

"Yeah, well—" Millie removed the cinnamon buns from the oven and set the pan on the island. "Anyone with a brain would consider old fogies acting like a couple of dumbstruck teenagers beyond ridiculous."

"Hmm. Sounds as if Hilltop's chef might be a wee bit envious. In case you haven't noticed, Gordon has his eye on you."

Millie pointed her spatula toward her sous chef. "Now I know you've lost your mind."

"Maybe, maybe not." Bernie removed a bowl of yogurt from the fridge. "We'll both know I'm on to something when he invites you on a date."

Doing her best to ignore the comment, Millie began spreading vanilla icing on the buns. What if Bernie was right and Gordon asked her out? *Stop being ridiculous. He's a gentleman who doesn't act any differently toward me than he does toward Susan, Eileen, or Bernie.* Besides, she hadn't dated anyone in nearly sixty years and wouldn't have a clue how to act.

During the remainder of the morning, Millie focused on serving Hilltop's guests while enjoying comments about her culinary skills. By the time she'd cleaned up the kitchen, and Bernie had headed upstairs to prepare for new arrivals, she'd dismissed her friend's speculation as fantasy. Until her phone rang.

The early afternoon sun was warm when Erica headed down the driveway. After collecting the ranch house mail, she walked over to Hilltop's mailbox. Her eyes drifted to the red Polaris parked in Millie's driveway.

Must be another Mystery Club meeting. She removed the stack of mail then headed back up to the carport. A revving engine suddenly disrupted the peace and quiet. What was it with guys and motorcycles, even those with three wheels? Erica turned toward the sound. Two people sitting in the Polaris strapped on helmets.

Stunned, Erica backed up between the truck and her new used car while the fancy tricycle backed down Millie's driveway, then eased toward the stop sign at the end of the street. She rushed inside, tossed the mail on the kitchen counter, and headed straight to the den. "If I'm not mistaken, you're on the verge of losing your bet to Millie."

Amanda, sitting at the dining room table, looked up from her laptop. "What are you talking about?"

Erica sat across from her. "Hilltop's chef and Gordon just rode off in his fancy three-wheeled motorcycle."

Amanda's brows shot up. "Are you serious?"

"It was a sight to behold."

"Well, I'll be." Amanda's brows released. "Maybe now Millie will stop hounding me about Gary."

"We're talking about Millie. You know she's more likely to double down."

"I suppose you're right. Does she know you saw them?"

"Not as far as I know."

"Good." Amanda pushed up then headed to the kitchen.

"Where are you going?"

"To take the first step toward gaining the upper hand."

Millie strapped on the helmet then buckled her seatbelt. "How fast does this contraption go?"

"That depends." Gordon turned toward her. "How fast do you want it to go?"

"Maybe five miles above the speed limit?"

"You've got it. If the air turns too cool, I'll turn on the heater." He backed down to the street.

Millie turned her head away until they braked at the stop sign. No way she'd risk her Awesam partners thinking she and Gordon were anything more than members of the same mystery club. When they turned onto the main road, Millie settled back. Although she'd never ridden in an open top vehicle, much less one without doors, she felt more like a teenager than an old lady.

When they arrived in McCaysville, Gordon drove across the bridge to Copperhill. He found a parking spot and removed his helmet. "Sit tight. I'll help you out."

Millie huffed. "I climbed in by myself; I can manage climbing out."

"No doubt. Except—" Gordon nodded toward two women, who appeared to be well past sixty, watching them from a bench. "I don't want those ladies thinking I'm rude, crude, or socially unacceptable."

"Well now, we couldn't let that happen, could we?"

"Nope." Gordon climbed out, rounded the Polaris, and held his hand out for Millie.

She pulled off her helmet then accepted his hand and swung her legs over the side, secretly grateful for his help.

An old guy moseyed over. "Nice ride."

"Thanks." While Gordon shared details about his vehicle, Millie approached the two ladies. She grinned as if she was one of the cool girls dating the high school heartthrob. Except this wasn't a date. "Have either of you ever ridden a motorcycle?"

The woman on the left crossed one leg over the other. "You'd never catch me riding in that thing."

"Because you're an old fuddy-duddy, Mabel." The other woman peered up at Millie. "Is that good-looking man your husband?"

Millie shook her head. "He's a friend."

"You don't mind if I meet him, do you?" Without waiting for a response, the woman popped off the bench as if she'd been sitting on a spring.

"There goes old Gladys again." Mabel pumped her foot. "The town's most notorious man hunter cozying up to another unsuspecting victim."

"Not on my watch," Millie whipped around and headed straight toward Gordon. "Our fancy motorcycle has drawn a crowd."

Gladys tilted her head to one side. "You're more than casual friends, aren't you?"

"You bet we are." Millie looped her arm around Gordon's bicep. She leaned close to Gladys, her voice low. "We're members of an elite crime-busting organization, and we're here on an undercover mission."

The old man who had admired the Polaris snickered. "Seems she's got your number, Gladys."

"Our little town attracts all sorts of tourists." Gladys rolled her eyes. "Even looney tunes." She returned to the bench.

"That woman is a nuisance." The old man shook his head while shuffling away.

Millie and Gordon headed up the block. As soon as they rounded the corner, she pulled her arm away from his. "You're welcome."

Gordon laughed. "For saving me from a harmless old lady?"

"Believe me, there was nothing harmless about gold-digging Gladys."

He leaned close. "You're the most interesting woman I have ever met."

Millie's chest puffed. "You bet I am." For a brief moment, she imagined winning the bet with Amanda, until she came to her senses and dismissed the musing as ridiculous.

Chapter 17

The morning after Erica had spotted Millie riding in Gordon's Polaris Slingshot, Amanda plucked a gift bag off the kitchen counter and headed out to the carport. A cool breeze rustled the trees as she made her way across the side yard then along the inn's sidewalk. Inky, the black cat that had claimed Hilltop's front porch as its private domain, sprang off the railing the moment Amanda climbed up the steps. "I see you trying to sneak away." She brushed hair away from her cheek then unlocked the front door and stepped into the foyer, smiling at the couple ambling through the living room. "I hope you're enjoying your stay with us."

The woman nodded. "We love everything about Hilltop Inn, especially the garden."

"Our chef's masterpiece."

"Millie explained how she dedicated the garden to her best friend."

"Indeed she did." Could Millie count the number of times she'd told guests about her friendship with the inn's original owner? "Do you have plans for today?"

The woman's husband nodded. "The train ride, then shopping."

"Perfect way to spend the day in Blue Ridge." Amanda waited for the couple to leave, before heading through the den and into the kitchen. "How'd breakfast go?"

Millie spun toward her. "Same as every other day. Lots of accolades about the delicious food."

"You know, one of these days a guest is bound to complain about your breakfast menu."

"If and when that ever happens, I'll serve the old grump a bowl of bran flakes."

Amanda chuckled as she set the bag on the island. "I brought a gift."

"For me or for Bernie?"

"Selected especially for you."

Millie flung a dish towel over her shoulder. "What are you up to?"

"Are you always suspicious?" Amanda stifled a grin while climbing onto a stool. "Or only when *I* bring you a present?"

"Hmph." Millie eyed the bag for a brief moment before pushing it toward Bernie. "You open it for me."

"Why? Are you afraid?"

"It's from Amanda. What do you think?"

"You're paranoid, that's what I think." Bernie pulled out the blue tissue paper. After peeking into the bag, she pushed the gift back to Millie. "You definitely need to check this out."

Millie shot Amanda a narrow-eyed glance. "Is something going to jump out at me?"

"Can't I bring a present to my favorite chief information officer without rousing suspicion?"

Millie hesitated a moment longer before reaching in. Her lips curled into a snarl as she pulled out a silky pale blue negligee.

Amanda snapped her fingers. "Checkmate."

A flush pinkened Millie's cheeks. "You think you're so smart, don't you?"

"Did you enjoy yesterday's ride in Gordon's fancy tricycle?"

"Hold on." Bernie thumped Millie's arm. "You went for a ride in the Slingshot?"

"What's the big deal? We drove to McCaysville for lunch." Millie stuffed the gown into the bag. "In case either of you have the wrong idea, Gordon and I are nothing more than friends...without benefits, mind you."

A satisfied grin spread across Amanda's face. "Keep the gift. One of these days you'll be glad I gave it to you."

Millie propped both hands on her hips. "Our bet is a long way from being over, especially with you spending so much time with Gary."

"Only until election day." Amanda slid off the stool. Halfway to the door, she glanced over her shoulder. "Which makes me the hands-down favorite to win our bet." After rushing through the den and out the French doors, she let her eyes drift to the end of the garden's central path. In November Erica would be the second Awesam partner to share wedding vows in the gazebo. Would there be a third?

Millie grabbed the gift bag off the island and stashed it in a cabinet under the counter. "As soon as I win the bet, I'm giving this right back to Amanda."

Bernie leaned against the island, her arms crossed. "Why didn't you tell me about yesterday, and what makes you so sure you'll win the bet?"

No way she'd admit, even to Bernie, that she hadn't wanted anyone to know about the ride, or that she'd enjoyed Gordon's company far more than she'd expected. "First, yesterday was a last minute thing and no big deal."

"Are you saying Gordon just showed up in your driveway and invited you on a date?"

Millie huffed. "It wasn't a date, and I'll win because I have no interest in any sort of romantic relationship—"

"What if Gordon has other ideas?"

"Don't be ridiculous. Another reason I'm guaranteed a win is because losing to me would be a big blow to Amanda's ego."

"If you ask me, Amanda has the upper hand."

"I didn't ask. Besides, I have her exactly where I want her."

"Which is where?"

"She believes she's outsmarted me, which gives me the advantage." Millie turned away from Bernie. She had to come across as convincing. Especially after she'd invited Gordon to a movie and carhop dinner at Swan Drive In-Theater Saturday night. In her car. As a pal. To relive moments from their youth. At least that's the story she'd told herself for the past few days.

Amanda strode into the ranch house den, a satisfied smile curling her lips. Even if neither of them ended up in a romantic relationship, sparring with Millie was delightful fun. "Hands down, I'm going to win."

Erica peered up at her. "What makes you so sure?"

"Millie's face turned red when I confessed knowing about her wild ride. I'm telling you she has a crush on the ex-cop."

"Even if something is going on, she'll never admit it."

"Eventually, the truth will come out. For now, I'm off to another campaign meeting." Amanda grabbed her purse off the dining room table and hastened out the kitchen door before Erica could offer her two cents. She climbed into the truck, the last remnant of her illegal marriage to Gunter Benson. By January, she would have enough money saved to trade it in on a good used car. Amanda lowered the windows then backed down to the street. Having lived hundreds of miles away from New Orleans for nearly two years, she'd become accustomed to the crisp mountain air.

During the drive to town, she mentally shifted from Awesam's president to Keith Armstrong's campaign manager. With the election fewer than two months away, the team was racing toward the finish line. Would she miss the high-pressure drama...or spending time with Gary? Would they remain friends and meet for lunch a couple times a month, or occasionally pass each other on a downtown sidewalk? Why did it matter one way or the other? Because whether or not she wanted to admit the truth, she enjoyed Gary's company. When she reached the law office, Amanda parked beside his late model car then climbed out and walked inside.

Rosalie greeted her with a smile. "They're in the conference room. You know the way."

Amanda returned the smile. "Every step." She headed straight to the closed door and knocked once, then entered. "What's the latest?" She quickly settled across from Keith and Linda, beside Gary before he had a chance to play the role of gentleman and stand.

Keith twisted the cap off a water bottle. "After a couple of inmates threatened Crystal, the judge who agreed to hear her case had her relocated to the local jail."

"Any idea who's behind the threats?"

"Officially, no. Unofficially, you can bet our opponent wants to prevent the truth from going public." Keith propped his arms on the table. "If all goes as planned, next week's trial will result in her acquittal."

"Judge Elizabeth Davis is a good friend." Linda leaned forward. "Even though she's no fan of DA Watson, she'll be a fair and impartial jurist."

Keith faced Linda. "Everything depends on Regina's effectiveness as a defense attorney."

"There's no need to worry, darling. With Chris as second chair, they can't lose."

The hint of a smile softened Keith's features. "Spoken as a proud mother who's not at all impartial."

"For good reason." Leaning close to her husband, Linda touched his arm. "Our son takes after his brilliant father."

He placed his hand over hers. "And his talented mother."

Gary chuckled. "Should we give you two the room?"

Keith's focus remained locked on Linda. "Seems our friends are on to us old married folks."

Teetering between curiosity and envy, Amanda grabbed a bottle of water. Had Linda and Keith slipped into playful banter to lighten the mood? Or were their antics another one of Linda's ploys to force a romantic relationship between her and Gary?

"I believe we've put our campaign staff in an awkward position." A smile tugged at the corner of Linda's lips as her focus shifted from Keith to Amanda.

Could she have been any more obvious? Amanda twisted the cap off the bottle and took a sip. Had the time come to stop the nonsense, or should she wait until after they won the election?

"Back to the task at hand." Keith opened the folder lying in front of him. "Our campaign ad is scheduled to begin tomorrow..."

Definitely wait. Amanda pushed the water bottle aside while drawing on every ounce of self-restraint to ignore the undeniable effect the man sitting beside had on her.

Chapter 18

The moment Wendy turned onto the ranch house driveway, an image of Gunter's smug expression when he sat at the defense table acting as his own attorney popped into her head. Would she ever be able to eye the truck without thinking about her child's biological father? Forcing the memory into submission, Wendy climbed out and opened the rear passenger door then released Ryan from his car seat. "Are you ready to visit Nana Amanda and Aunt Erica?"

Wendy tucked her laptop under her arm then held her son's hand while they made their way past Erica's newly purchased car and into the kitchen. "We're here." She released Ryan's hand, sending him toddling straight to Amanda.

Awesam's president scooped her honorary grandson into her arms. "How's Nana Amanda's favorite little guy?"

Ryan fingered a lock of Amanda's red hair. "Nana."

"Oh, my gosh." Amanda's face lit with a glowing smile. "This is the first time you've called me Nana. Of all your grandmothers, am I your favorite?"

"Hold on a cotton-picking minute." Millie sprang to her feet then grabbed a cookie off the dining room table and held it out to Ryan. "Grammy Millie—who bakes you delicious cookies—is your favorite, right?"

"Cookie." Ryan plucked the treat from Millie's hand and took a bite.

Millie thumped Amanda's arm. "The only reason he said your name before mine is because Nana's easier to pronounce than Grammy."

Amanda tapped the tip of Ryan's nose. "We'll let Grammy Millie keep on believing that while you and I know the truth."

Erica rolled her eyes. "You two can't help yourselves, can you?"

"Season two of the Amanda and Millie sitcom uninterrupted by annoying commercials. At least they make our board meetings entertaining." Wendy set her laptop on the table before pulling out a chair. "Is Sierra excited about her first day on her new job?"

Responding to Ryan wriggling from her arms, Amanda set him down to toddle to the toy basket. "Excited and a little nervous."

Erica nodded. "Understandable given she's never worked before."

"Excuse me?" Millie scoffed while returning to her chair. "Have you forgotten that I gave Sierra her first job? Without my training she wouldn't have a clue how to show up to work on time."

"Good point." Amanda sat across from their chief operating officer. "Although you have to admit that we've all played a role in helping her prepare for today."

"Now that we've established how important we all are in Sierra's transformation—" Erica tapped her laptop screen. "It's time to call this meeting to order."

Wendy held up a finger. "Not yet." She scooted her chair closer to the table. "My stepmother reserved a room at Hilltop for next Saturday. She's had a change of heart and is bringing her sons to meet me."

"Since you've brought the subject up—" Millie leaned forward, her eyes glued on Wendy. "Gordon uncovered important information about Douglas Hewitt."

Wendy's eyebrows shot up. "Other than my father cheats on his wife and disowned his only daughter?"

"Oh yeah." Millie laced her fingers on the table. "Douglas's wife filing for divorce on the grounds of infidelity has caused a huge rift in the Hewitt family. Throw in his lawsuit, and half the females are ready to string him up and kick him out of the family business. Old Man Hewitt is sticking by his son. If you ask me, it's because the apple doesn't fall far from the tree."

Amanda crossed her arms. "How did Gordon dig up all that gossip, and what makes him think any of it is accurate?"

"I didn't ask, and he didn't reveal his sources."

Wendy's eyes remained trained on Millie. "If there's even a smidgen of truth in what you're saying, why won't anyone in Douglas's family talk to Donna?"

"Even though I don't know much about rich people—other than Eleanor and her husband—I'm guessing because they don't want their highfalutin country-club friends to know their business."

"You're kidding, right?" Amanda's tone mocked.

Millie huffed. "Believe me, Gordon knows his stuff."

"I'm sure he does. What about you?" Amanda uncrossed her arms. "If an ex-cop who lives in a different state can find out what's going on, don't you think the Hilton Head elites are clued in?"

Millie's eyes narrowed. "If that's the case, how would you answer Wendy's question?"

"Maybe the family's dissing Donna because she's an outsider."

Wendy's gaze snapped to Amanda. "Based on a comment my stepmother made, I believe you're right. Donna is the only person who married into the Hewitt clan that doesn't come from a wealthy South Carolina family."

Amanda snapped her fingers. "There you go."

Wendy's shoulders slumped. "Even if Gordon is right, the family squabble won't stop the lawsuit."

Amanda reached for a cookie. "Because your father's lawyers benefit financially from a long, drawn-out fight?"

Wendy nodded. "You nailed it."

"Now that we have the Hewitt family drama figured out—" Erica turned toward Millie. "We do, don't we?"

"I suppose." Millie shrugged. "At least until Gordon digs up more details."

"Then I suggest we get down to business."

Amanda swallowed a bite of cookie. "Today's board meeting is once again called to order by our task-oriented chief executive officer."

"Someone has to keep everything on track." Erica tapped her keyboard. "We'll begin with a review of our latest newsletter, thanks to Amanda."

Wendy's focus drifted to Ryan plopped on the floor beside Dusty. Her child was blessed to be surrounded by a quirky yet lovable extended family. Despite their bickering, Amanda and Millie respected each other and would do anything to protect the people they loved. Startled by the familiar ringtone, Wendy yanked her phone from her pocket. "It's Kayla."

She bolted from her chair then dashed to the foyer while swiping her finger across the screen. Wendy's pulse pounded in her ears at the sight of her sister's red eyes and tear-stained cheeks. "What's going on?"

"She's here."

"Who's where, honey?"

"The lady from hospice is in the living room with Mom."

Inhaling deeply then exhaling with silent precision to steady herself, Wendy stepped out to the front sidewalk. "She's there to help Mom feel better."

"I looked it up on the internet. Hospice people don't get involved until..." Kayla's voice faltered. "You know..."

A squirrel scampered across the ground chasing another up a tree. Did animals mourn when a family member passed on? "Mom needs all of us to remain positive."

"I'm trying." Kayla sniffled. "It gets a little harder every day."

"I understand." Wendy's heart ached for her sister.

"Sunday, Daddy took us to church for the first time in a long time. Zach refused to go. He says if God cared, Mom wouldn't be sick. I don't know. Maybe my brother's right."

Wendy fought back tears. How could she explain something she didn't fully understand herself? "Maybe the hospice lady taking care of Mom is God's way of letting us know he cares."

A long moment of silence. "She seems nice and smiles a lot. Riley likes her."

"Which proves she's an angel who will help our family during the days ahead."

Kayla swiped her fingers across her cheeks. "Thank you for always making me feel better."

Wendy nodded with a brave smile, blinking fast to keep tears from escaping. "That's what big sisters are for, like you are for Riley." Wendy managed to keep the rest of the conversation upbeat. When the call ended, she pocketed her phone and traipsed back inside.

Erica looked up. "Is everything okay?"

Unable to find her voice, Wendy shook her head while dropping onto her chair. All the emotion she had held at bay erupted as she buried her face in her hands and wept. In an instant her family gathered around her. The warmth of their embrace gently stitched her back together, one breath at a time.

Chapter 19

Twenty minutes before it was time to leave, Millie remained seated on her recliner, teetering between anticipation and regret. What had possessed her to invite Gordon to a drive-in theater? Back in the day, teenagers spent more time kissing than watching the movie. Did he understand that tonight wasn't a date?

Mittens sprang onto her lap, inviting a back stroke and a conversation with her feline. "Do you suppose I'm going through some sort of mid-life crisis?" Her cat meowed. "You're right, I'm way past the halfway point in my life. Would Rupert think I'm a silly old lady who's trying to relive the past? Maybe he'd be right, especially since I'm talking to a cat."

Millie shooed Mittens off her lap before traipsing to her bedroom. She opened the closet door and stood in front of the full-length mirror staring at her slim figure. Her eyes drifted to her face. A little makeup and an up-to-date hairstyle did wonders for a woman in her late seventies. Why wouldn't a man her age want to spend time alone with her? After all, her mind was sharp and she wasn't nearly as cranky as she had been before she became friends with Amanda, Erica, and Wendy.

Her eyes drifted up to Amanda's gift stashed on her closet's top shelf. The bet about which one of them would land a man to keep them warm at night first was meant to provoke Awesam's president into a relationship with Gary.

Whiskers, her tabby cat, slinked in and rubbed against Millie's leg. "I didn't expect to compete with Amanda, and I for doggone sure don't intend to start now." She pushed the closet door closed, grinning at her inclination to talk to her cats as if they understood every word she uttered.

After stepping over to her dresser, Millie wrapped her fingers around her favorite perfume. Should she or shouldn't she spritz? Makeup plus perfume would definitely send the wrong message. She yanked her hand away from the bottle before turning toward her nightstand. At least spending the evening with a former police officer meant she could leave her gun stashed in the drawer beside her bed.

A mischievous grin curled Millie's lips as she lifted her calico off the floor. "Do you suppose Gordon would be surprised or impressed if I tell him Susan Armstrong and I are pistol-packing mamas?" Whiskers escaped her grasp and raced out to the hall.

Millie chuckled while returning to the living room. Her calico sprang onto the front windowsill to keep watch while Mittens curled up under the coffee table. "You kitties behave yourselves while I'm gone." She plucked her purse and keys off the end table. Following a quick glance around, she headed straight to her garage and climbed into her twenty-three-year-old sedan.

Ten minutes after backing down to the street, Millie turned onto Gordon's driveway. Now what? Considering this wasn't a date, should she go ring his doorbell or sit tight and honk the horn? Maybe she should call or text to let him know she'd arrived? Before she could decide, Gordon strode from his front door to the passenger side and climbed in beside her. "Nice ride."

Millie tapped her fingers on the dashboard. "Pearl is old and reliable, like me."

"Interesting name for a blue car."

"Pearl was the name of my first kitten. She was snow white."

"A car named after a cat. I must say you and mechanical Pearl are both well-preserved."

Millie shot him a sideways glance. If he was flirting with her, wouldn't he have called her something more complimentary than well-preserved? "Even though you're two years older than me, so are you...well-preserved, that is."

"Age is just a number. Attitude and zest for life is what counts."

"Like two old codgers going to a drive-in?" Millie backed out of the driveway.

"I was a high-school senior the last time I watched a movie at the Swan."

"Did you actually watch, or did you spend the entire time necking with the cheerleader you were dating?"

He chuckled. "Guilty as charged."

"Like me, your former girlfriend was one of the few grads who stayed in Blue Ridge. Unfortunately she passed away a few years back."

"Yeah, I know."

Had he kept up with the cheerleader all these years, or did he check on her after moving back to town? "Did you leave Blue Ridge for college?"

He shook his head. "My parents couldn't afford to send me to school, so I enlisted in the Army for the promise of a college education."

Millie glanced at his profile. "Did you end up going to battle?"

His silence spoke volumes.

"Sorry, I didn't mean to pry."

"I spent three long years in Nam." He fell silent for a long moment. "I lost too many close friends in that senseless war." The hard edge to his voice hinted that his emotional scars ran deep.

"I'm glad you came home unharmed."

"Physically, yes. Emotionally, not so much." Another long moment of silence.

Millie braked at a stop sign and turned toward him. "Why didn't you return to Blue Ridge after you left the military?"

A flicker of pain contorted his features, gone in a heartbeat but unmistakable. "When my tour ended, a kind woman helped me fight my way back from depression and survival guilt."

"The woman you married?"

Gordon shook his head. "She was the mother of one of my buddies who didn't make it home alive. Saving vets like me helped her deal with her loss."

How many young men from their high school had lost their lives in the war? Millie drove through the intersection. "Did you end up going to college?"

"An education no longer seemed important. I figured the best way to put my new skills to use was to become a cop. Seven years after joining the force, I was promoted to detective."

"Lucky for our little club, you finally came back home." Had she come across as too enthusiastic? "After all, a good mystery club needs an experienced detective. The cop part isn't as important since most of the time, Susan and I carry our guns with us."

Gordon turned toward her, his brows raised. "How good a shot are you?"

"Doggone accurate, especially at close range."

He chuckled. "Every time I think I have you figured out, you throw me another curve ball."

I need to keep his good mood going. "You can count on me to keep your detective skills sharp."

"No doubt."

Millie turned into the Swan driveway and stopped beside the ticket booth. Her face froze, her brows nearly touching her hairline. The man staring back at her was one of the few remaining graduates from her high school class.

"Hi, Millie."

So much for keeping tonight a secret. "How's it going, Ralph?"

"Fair to middling. Who's your friend?"

She hesitated. "Gordon Davenport—"

"From our high school?"

Gordon leaned toward Millie, peering out the window. "Ralph Everson?"

"The one and only. When did you move back to town?"

"Several months ago. Did you end up marrying your high-school sweetheart?"

"I did. We just celebrated our fifty-eighth anniversary. What about you?"

"Divorced."

"Too bad."

Millie handed over the exact change. "I'm helping Gordon become reacquainted with our town's attractions."

"This is a good place to start. Welcome back to Blue Ridge, Gordon."

"Thanks."

Millie peered in her rearview mirror at the car pulling up behind them. Hoping her explanation had come across as convincing, she drove forward then found a spot in the middle of the third row. "Close enough?"

"You know—" Gordon turned toward her. "The two of us working a case would have been a more interesting cover story."

Millie cut the engine. "Why would I need a cover story?"

"To keep old Ralph from thinking you invited me on a date." His tone hinted of playfulness.

How would he react if she confirmed what he said instead of correcting it? Didn't matter, considering they were two old codgers enjoying each other's company, not a couple of teenagers sneaking off to a drive-in to do what teenagers do.

"Interesting reaction."

Millie snapped her head toward Gordon. "What reaction?"

"In my professional experience, silence usually means the subject is guilty."

No way she'd give him the satisfaction. "Seems your investigative skills are a bit rusty, Detective Davenport. Otherwise, you'd have recognized my moment of silence as acknowledgement that tonight is exactly what I told Ralph." Millie waggled her finger at him. "If you have any ideas other than watching the movie, forget it."

Gordon burst out laughing. "You really are the most fascinating woman I've ever met, and I've only scratched the surface."

Millie raised a brow. Would he consider her more fascinating if he knew she had married Rupert on the rebound from an illicit affair with a married man? "Are you planning to investigate me?"

"No need. You'll tell me what you want me to know about you."

"Hmph." One of these days she'd definitely tell him about her disreputable past, if for no other reason than to get a reaction.

Chapter 20

Days after she broke up with Tommy, returning to work had helped boost Abby's spirits but failed to move her closer to decision part two. Without a guaranteed outcome, how could she risk more disappointment, even failure? On the other hand, maybe Morgan had been right about her surrendering without a fight.

Riddled with indecision, Abby spun her wheelchair away from her desk and wheeled down the hall, past the kitchen. Their volunteer teacher was out with the flu, leaving her in charge of today's tutoring. She paused at the door to summon her best smile then maneuvered into the crisis center classroom. Time to begin the session with the two youngest students. "Is everyone ready for some fun?"

Five-year-old Bonnie, who had arrived late yesterday, sat on the floor at her mother's feet. Lucky, the crisis center's golden retriever sprawled beside her. Bonnie peered up at Abby, her eyes reflecting the pain of a child who had witnessed heart-breaking abuse—pain Abby understood all too well. Her focus drifted to Bonnie's mother, sitting on the sofa—her shoulders slumped, her left eye nearly swollen shut.

"Look what I drew." Six-year-old Mateo, who'd arrived a week earlier with his mother and baby sister, held up a drawing of his family minus the father whose uncontrolled fists had landed him here. "Do you like my picture?"

"I do." Abby wheeled closer. "You're quite the artist."

Mateo grabbed a black crayon and added a large stick figure with an angry face. "That's what Daddy looks like when he gets mad at Mommy."

Pleased the young boy had expressed his feelings instead of holding them in until they erupted in destructive behavior, Abby wheeled closer. "You know it's never okay to hit anyone."

Mateo added oversized hands to the male stick figure. "How come Daddy hits Mommy?"

Abby's mind drifted to the night all those years ago when she feared her father's beatings would end up killing her mother. Her desire to break the cycle of violence was one of the reasons she'd chosen to earn a child psychology degree and devote her life to working with women and children in crisis. "Because no one taught your daddy how to use words instead of his fists to express his anger."

Bonnie lifted off the floor then sat across from Mateo.

Abby wheeled closer to the young girl. "Would you like to draw a picture?"

She nodded.

Mateo pushed a box of crayons toward her.

Hoping Bonnie's mother would understand hope was not lost, Abby made eye contact with the woman. "When I was a little older than Bonnie, my mother and I spent time in a center like this one, but in another town. We achieved far more than survival. As will you and your daughter."

With tears welling and streaming down her face, the woman sidled beside Abby then reached out and touched her shoulder. "Thank you for understanding."

Abby reached up to touch the woman's hand. "Coming here was the first step toward a bright future for you and Bonnie." Her tone was soft and reassuring. "A few minutes ago, I saw Mateo's mother in the kitchen."

Abby pulled her hand away. "She'd enjoy becoming acquainted with you while your children and I spend some time together."

Nodding, she glanced at her child then ambled toward the door, her shoulders a little less slumped.

Abby turned her attention to creating a fun learning environment for her two young students. Ten minutes before their session ended, Mateo scooted his chair away from the table, his eyes on Abby. "Why can't you walk?"

"I was hurt in a car accident."

"Did you try to get better?"

Abby stared wide-eyed at the child. What had prompted his question? Curiosity or something more profound? "Yes, I tried."

His head tilted as if assessing her situation. "Then how come you're not all better?"

Even though he'd asked without a trace of judgement, how could a child's question hit her so hard? Maybe because at some level he understood that she hadn't fought long enough. Or that she had surrendered to fear.

"That's a really good question, Mateo." She owed him an honest answer. "Truth is, I tried for a while...then I stopped believing I could get better."

He stared at her for a long moment, then pulled a blank sheet of paper in front of him and began drawing. When finished, he carried his artwork to Abby and laid it on her lap. "This is you after you try harder."

A thickness formed in her throat as she focused on the stick figure with dark hair and a smiling face, standing on two legs. "I think..." Struggling to keep tears at bay while searching for the right words, she pressed the drawing to her chest. "I need to be brave like you."

"You don't have to be brave all the time. Just a little bit."

An involuntary smile tugged at Abby's lips. "I'm gonna keep your picture on my desk to remind me that even a little bit of bravery can make a big difference."

"Like me and Mommy leaving Daddy so he'll stop hurting her?"

"Exactly like that."

During the remainder of the afternoon, Mateo's comments played havoc with Abby's emotions. Had she given up on therapy too soon, or had she accepted reality? What if she tried again and failed? Could she take more disappointment? As soon as she finished the last tutoring session, she escaped to her office and stared at Mateo's drawing lying on her desk. How could she help children overcome the trauma in their lives if she didn't have enough courage to continue facing her own challenge head-on?

Desperate for reassurance, Abby plucked her phone off her desk and tapped a text. "Can you talk?" Seconds later she responded to Morgan's ringtone. "Thanks for calling me."

"What's going on?"

Abby relayed her interaction with Mateo.

"Now you're wondering how to react, aren't you?"

"He's a six-year-old child."

"Sometimes confirmation comes from the most unexpected sources."

Abby traced her finger over the stick figure drawing. What if Morgan was right? "I think I'm ready to start fighting again."

"I knew you'd eventually come around."

Abby stared at Mateo's drawing. "I want to keep this between the two of us until I have a better idea about the outcome."

"Your secret is safe with me."

"I know, and thank you for your encouragement."

"Any time."

Before second thoughts could override her decision, Abby ended the call and pressed her therapist's number.

Anna answered after the third ring. "Hey, Abby. I hope you're calling because you're ready to come back to therapy."

"When's your next opening?"

"Can you be here in half an hour?"

"I'll be there." Abby's eyes shifted from Mateo's stick figure drawing to Tommy's photo sitting on the corner of her desk. "I'll work hard to become the woman you deserve." She spun her wheelchair around and headed toward Pamela's office. "I need to leave for an appointment."

Her boss understood and followed Abby out to her car. After stashing the wheelchair in her trunk, Pamela leaned down and peered in the window. "Everyone's pulling for you."

"Thank you. I'll see you tomorrow morning." Abby cranked her engine and backed out of her parking space. By the time she reached her destination, the hope she'd experienced after her accident had begun to return.

A half hour before dinner, Erica responded to Abby's call and rushed out to the carport. She removed the wheelchair from her daughter's trunk then pushed it beside the open driver's door. Would her child ever be able to climb in and out of her car without someone helping her? "How'd your day go?"

"Really good." Abby maneuvered onto her chair. "What about yours?"

"Brad and I met with our contractor." Was it her imagination, or did her daughter seem more upbeat than she had in weeks? "The kitchen remodel is on schedule." Erica followed Abby to the front door.

"I can't wait to see where you and Brad are gonna live."

Should she tell Abby they'd arranged to have a ramp installed to their home's front porch? If she waited a while longer, maybe her child wouldn't need it. "Our new furniture is scheduled to arrive in a couple of weeks. It's a different style than what we had in our Asheville house."

"New life, new style." The moment Abby wheeled into the foyer, Dusty bounded over, welcoming her home with an enthusiastic tail wag. "Hey, girl. Did you miss me?" Dusty responded with a muffled bark. Abby lifted her chin, sniffing the aromas drifting from the kitchen. "Do I smell chili?"

"You do."

"Scrumlicious."

Grateful for whatever had happened to boost her daughter's morale, Erica pressed her hand to her heart while her eyes followed Abby rolling down the hall to her room. Responding to Brad's ringtone, she scurried to the den and plucked her phone off the dining room table. "The Abby we know best has come back to us."

Chapter 21

Having awakened before the rest of the household, Amanda crept from the kitchen back to her bedroom and set her coffee mug on the nightstand. Roused by a bout of nostalgia, she leaned against her headboard then lifted the thick photo album onto her lap. She ran her fingers along the word 'Memories' etched on the leather cover that held the few visual reminders of her life with Preston.

Amanda lifted the cover revealing a picture of her standing beside her handsome groom on their wedding day. The white gown she'd found at a discount store. Preston looking handsome in his rented tux. She slowly flipped through the pages stroking the photos. Their first anniversary. The shotgun house before and after they transformed the rundown property into the only home they'd owned. The first photos of baby Morgan. Their child growing through the years. Theirs had been a perfect marriage. Except for that one time.

Amanda squeezed her eyes shut as a memory she'd kept buried deep in her subconscious escaped. The huge fight she and Preston had two months before Morgan was born. The gut-wrenching moment her husband packed a bag before he stormed out the front door. For twenty-six torture-filled days she'd had no idea where he'd gone or when he would return. Then one morning he showed up at the front door begging for her forgiveness and promising never to leave her again. He never explained where he'd been, and she never asked.

Forcing the memory back into its hiding place, Amanda continued leafing through the album until she arrived at the last photo, taken three months before the drunk driver stole her soulmate from her and their daughter. That stormy afternoon her life had changed forever. Amanda's throat thickened as she laid the album aside.

Out of nowhere, an image of Paul Sullivan, aka Gunter Benson, popped into her head. Despite the fact that he was the reason she'd met Erica and Wendy and moved to Blue Ridge, marrying him had been the worst mistake she'd ever made.

Amanda sipped her coffee as her mind drifted to the present. There was no denying she and Gary Redding enjoyed each other's company. Had the time come for her to open her heart to another man? The notion triggered an eyeroll. If Gary had the slightest interest in a romantic relationship, wouldn't he have invited her on a date by now? Chances were his failed marriage left a deep scar on his heart, much like Preston's death had scarred hers.

Eager to shower before Sierra or Erica awakened, Amanda scurried to the kitchen to refill her mug then headed straight to their shared bathroom. She turned on the shower. The moment steam fogged the mirror, she stepped into the tub, breathing in the fresh scents of shampoo and body wash as hot water cascaded down her body. By the time she finished showering and returned to her room to dry her hair, the rest of the household had awakened.

Amanda stashed the photo album back in her closet, then dressed and headed to the kitchen. "Good morning."

"It is indeed." Erica dropped two slices of bread into the toaster.

Sierra ambled in with Theo propped on her right hip and a diaper bag slung over her left shoulder. "Little Pip is all ready for daycare."

Amanda refilled her coffee mug. "I'm surprised you've adopted that nickname."

"The way I see it, Pip overcame all sorts of challenges and disappointments. Kind of like me and Theo."

Abby wheeled into the narrow space with Dusty plodding behind her. "Did you read *Great Expectations*?"

"Not the whole book, just the CliffsNotes. That way if one of the students studying the book asks me a question, I won't sound like an ignoramus."

Amanda aimed her mug at the young woman. "Good for you."

Abby smiled while peering up at Sierra. "You're as smart as any of those kids."

"Thanks to you and Tommy helping me learn how to talk proper so I don't sound uneducated. Anyway, we'll see y'all later." Sierra plucked her car keys off the counter then headed out to the carport.

Erica removed the toast and placed the slices on a plate. "Sierra's transformation has been nothing short of miraculous."

"Thanks in large part to you, Mom."

"The three of us, including Millie and Tommy, played a role."

Amanda leaned back against the counter. "Speaking of Tommy, I haven't seen him around in a while."

Abby's mouth opened slightly then closed, as if she'd failed to find the right words.

Coming to her daughter's defense, Erica placed her hand on Abby's shoulder. "With all the new construction going on, I imagine he's busy with work."

Abby grabbed a power bar off the counter. "The reason you haven't seen Tommy is because we broke up." She spun her chair around and raced out of the kitchen.

Amanda stared at Erica's pinched expression. "You didn't have a clue, did you?"

Erica shook her head.

"Abby and Tommy have always seemed devoted to each other." Amanda edged beside Awesam's CEO. "What do you suppose happened?"

Erica gripped the counter edge, her eyes downcast. "What if Abby broke up with Tommy because she's lost hope of ever walking again?"

"You're talking about our Abby—the upbeat young woman who has never wavered in her belief that she'd dance at her wedding?" Amanda slid her arm around Erica's shoulders. "I can't imagine her ever giving up."

Erica swallowed. Hard. "Thank you for reminding me."

Praying she hadn't given Erica false hope, Amanda withdrew her arm. "I'm meeting Gary in twenty minutes to review our plans for the campaign's homestretch. If the judge finds in Crystal's favor, the trial should clinch Keith's win."

"Do you suppose you and Gary will continue to spend time together after the election?"

"If you're asking whether or not there are any signs of romance bubbling up, the answer is an emphatic not a one. Which makes Millie the frontrunner in our little 'snag a guy' competition."

Erica pivoted away from the counter, the hint of a grin softening her features. "Unless Gary realizes what a great catch you are."

"You know I gave my heart away years ago. Besides, I'm perfectly content remaining an independent, single woman." Hoping her tone had come across as convincing, Amanda waved over her shoulder while heading out of the kitchen. After retrieving her laptop from her room, she slipped out the front door to avoid any more questions from Erica.

During the short drive, Amanda's thoughts drifted back to the weeks after Preston had returned home. When he'd failed to explain where he'd gone, why hadn't she asked? Her fingers tightened around the steering wheel. Because she was relieved he had returned, or because she'd been too afraid to discover the truth?

By the time she parked beside Gary's car, Amanda blamed the questions on her early morning glimpse into the past. She grabbed her laptop then climbed out and rushed into the Armstrong Law Office.

As always, Rosalie greeted her with a warm smile. "Mr. Redding's in the conference room."

"Thanks." Amanda scurried down the hall, stopping three feet from the open door. Attributing her racing pulse to one too many cups of coffee, she drew in deep breaths. Moments after her heartbeat slowed, she walked into the conference room and sat across from Keith's campaign finance manager. "I have the latest poll results."

Gary grinned. "Good morning to you, too."

"Sorry, caffeine rush."

"In that case, I won't offer you another cup of coffee."

"Smart move." Amanda twisted the cap off a water bottle and took a long drink then opened her laptop. "Keith is only leading by six percentage points."

"Not surprising considering Watson's misleading television ad. Keith's ad hits the airwaves today, which will change the percentages."

"Good point." While they proceeded to review every aspect of the campaign, Amanda struggled to remain focused on the task at hand. Her mind teetered between her life in New Orleans and the man sitting across the table. What was it about the divorced bank president that kept her emotions in turmoil?

At some point, Gary leaned back, lacing his fingers behind his neck. His eyes met hers. "Is it the campaign pressure or something personal?"

Amanda's brows furrowed. "What do you mean?"

"You've been distracted from the moment you walked in."

How had he come to know her well enough to read her moods? Would he recognize a fib? Did she trust him enough to tell him the truth? Amanda broke eye contact. "This morning, for the first time in months, I opened an album displaying pictures of my first marriage." *The only marriage that mattered.* "Seeing those pictures brought back a lot of memories. Most were good. A few not so much."

Gary unlaced his fingers then leaned forward and grabbed his water bottle. "The past seems to have an uncanny way of creeping into the present." After swallowing the last drop of liquid, he swiped his hand across his mouth. His expression was unguarded, vulnerable in a way that spoke of trust. "After my wife's affair with my bank's assistant manager became public knowledge, I considered leaving Blue Ridge to avoid the humiliation. Until Keith and Linda helped me heal my wounded ego."

Drawing on the unspoken connection between them while avoiding eye contact, Amanda intertwined her fingers on the table. "After Wendy, Erica, and I discovered we were illegally married to the same man, we risked everything and moved here. Working together to create Hilltop Inn helped us reinvent our lives."

"When life takes painful turns, we discover who our real friends are." Gary reached across the table and laid his hand over hers. "I'm glad you and I have become close friends."

The tingling sensation surging through Amanda's limbs rendered her momentarily speechless. Were they destined to become more than friends? Her eyes met his. "So, am I."

142

Chapter 22

The third time Wendy changed clothes, Chris leaned against the doorframe, grinning while shaking his head. "You're welcoming your half-brothers from Hilton Head, not a couple of princes from a British royal family."

"What if they believe I'm the reason their family is falling apart?"

Chris moved close and slid his arms around her waist. "Even if they do, after they experience a few minutes of Wendy-style Southern charm, they won't stand a chance."

"I met Zach months ago, and he still doesn't consider me a legitimate family member."

"Only because he's knee-deep in family drama."

"So are Donna's sons. Which is why I'm counting on you to help entertain them."

"First Zach, now two more skeptical brothers?" Chris grinned. "Am I your secret weapon?"

"Exactly. My devastatingly handsome secret weapon."

Chris laughed while tucking a strand of hair behind her ear. "Maybe I should change my business card to read, Chris Armstrong, secret weapon lawyer."

"Who's no longer the town's most eligible bachelor." She breathed in the subtle scent of his aftershave. "Even though life was a lot less complicated when I didn't have a family, other than Mom's cancer, I wouldn't change a thing. If Cynthia hadn't walked out on me, and if I hadn't made the world's worst decision and married Gunter, our amazing son wouldn't exist and I would never have met you."

"You know I was attracted to you the day we first met in Blue Ridge Inn's dining room."

Wendy tilted her head. "My infectious Southern charm or your attraction to blondes?"

"Both. Plus your shameless flirtation after you discovered you weren't legally married."

"Maybe it was your fault for being too easy to flirt with…" Wendy trailed her finger along his chest. "And the way you treated me, Amanda, and Erica with respect."

"You were three of the strongest women I had ever met." Chris stroked her cheek. "Don't worry, angel. If I can win you over, I can handle a couple of skeptical brothers."

Ryan toddled into their bedroom with Duke padding behind.

"Seems we have company." Chris's smile broadened as he released Wendy and lifted his son into his arms. "Today we're going to meet two more of your uncles."

Wendy sat on the edge of the bed to don a pair of gold sneakers. "One day we'll need to figure out how to explain our strange family to our children."

"In today's world, our extended family isn't all that strange."

"Is your opinion based on experience or observation?"

"Both."

Duke's ears perked seconds before he raced from the room.

"Oh my gosh, they're here." Wendy's heart pounded against her ribs when she sprang to her feet and scurried through the great room.

Chris caught up with her at the front door. He smiled while brushing hair away from her cheek. "Stop and take a deep breath."

With her fingers gripping the door knob, Wendy breathed in the scent of Chris's aftershave mingling with the rich aroma of Millie's brownies. Her pulse slowed as their eyes met. "Thank you darling. I'm ready now." Summoning her warmest smile, she pulled the door open. Her half-brothers shuffled onto the porch behind their mother. Wendy embraced then released Donna. "Welcome back."

"It's good to see you and Chris again." Donna stepped aside. "Tyler, Carter, meet your sister Wendy, her husband Chris, and their son Ryan."

Wendy peered up at seventeen-year old Tyler, towering over his mother. "You favor your father."

"That's what everyone says." His blue eyes hinted of wariness.

Tentacles of doubt crept into Wendy's head. Had inviting them to their home instead of meeting them at Hilltop been a huge mistake?

Twelve-year-old Carter, who stood eye-to-eye with his mother, reached down to pet their black Lab. "What's his name?"

"Duke." Chris shifted Ryan to his right hip. "Seems he's found a new friend."

"We don't have a dog."

Ryan pointed toward his canine companion. "Doggie."

Carter peered up at his nephew. "Smart kid."

"He takes after his daddy." Her senses heightened, Wendy stepped aside, keeping a close eye on the older brother. "Come on in."

Donna crossed the threshold followed by Tyler and Duke. Carter lumbered in last and peered around the open floor plan. "Small house for a big-time lawyer." His tone screamed of arrogance.

Wendy's shoulders tightened as Donna gripped her son's forearm and shot him a stern look.

He shrugged. "Sorry, Mr. Armstrong, I didn't mean any disrespect."

"Apology accepted." Chris lowered Ryan to the floor then clasped his hand on Tyler's shoulder. "Do you play any sports?"

"Football. Wide receiver."

"No kidding? Same position I played in high school. Any idea where you're headed after you graduate?"

"Clemson. Full ride."

"Congrats."

Carter straightened, eyeing Chris. "I play soccer."

"The international version of football. Who's your favorite American player?"

While Chris escorted the boys through the great room, Carter rattled off two names launching a three-way conversation about sports.

The moment the guys stepped out to the back deck, Donna lifted Ryan into her arms. "You're blessed to have a daddy who understands how to connect with teenage boys."

Wendy's chest swelled with pride while leading the way to the great room sofa. "One of Chris's many skills."

"Connecting with his sons is one of Douglas's few positive attributes, which makes our divorce that much more painful for them."

"Do they know about their father's infidelity?"

"Just Tyler." The moment Donna settled on the sofa, Ryan wriggled from her arms. "When he asked if you were the only reason I'd filed for divorce, I had to tell him the truth."

"How did he react?"

"He stormed off to his room and slammed the door shut. After avoiding me for three days, he begged me to forgive his father and bring him back home." Donna collapsed against the back of the sofa. "It broke my heart to tell our son that even if I forgave Douglas, our marriage was damaged beyond repair. Although at some level Tyler understands, our relationship is strained."

"You're his mother." Wendy turned toward Donna and stretched her arm across the back of the sofa. "When he's ready, he'll come around."

"I pray that one day Douglas will accept responsibility for his behavior and apologize to our sons. If for no other reason than to teach them how not to treat women."

Wendy peered out the French doors at the animated conversation going on between Chris and her half-brothers. She faced Donna. Their eyes met. "How would you feel about Chris developing a relationship with Carter and Tyler to help them navigate the divorce?"

A flicker of hope seemed to burn behind Donna's stare. "Before it's too late, I want my boys to connect with the kind of man I want them to become. Which, other than meeting you, is the reason I brought them here."

While peering deep into her eyes, Wendy summoned fragile but fearless faith. "I don't know how long it will take, but I believe something miraculous will happen to heal the Hewitt family."

Donna pressed her palm to her chest. "I believe you were meant to come into our lives."

Wendy rested a hand on Donna's shoulder. "So do I."

Ryan toddled over, babbling while laying a book on Donna's thighs. "My grandson obviously agrees." She lifted him onto her lap and opened the book to the first page.

Responding to Duke laying his head on the cushion beside her, Wendy withdrew her arm from the back of the sofa. She stroked his muzzle while her mind drifted to the day she and Chris first met her father. His arrogance. His quick rejection of her. And now...the lawsuit.

After Donna read the last page, Ryan scooted off her lap. Moments later he brought her two more books and climbed onto the sofa beside her.

Moments after she finished reading the third book, Chris and the boys walked in from the deck. "Do you ladies mind if we go into town for a snack and some guy time?"

Donna peered up at Chris. "Great idea."

"Let me guess." Wendy lifted off the sofa. "You're taking them to the restaurant that serves the best pizza in Blue Ridge?"

"Yup."

Tyler propped his elbow on the fireplace mantel. "Maybe Blue Ridge isn't such a lame town after all."

Chris chuckled. "Even though we're not as fancy as Hilton Head, we're every bit as fun. Especially if you like trains and hiking trails."

Carter's eyes lit. "I've never ridden on a train."

While Chris slid his arm around the young man's shoulders and promised to treat him to a train ride, Wendy pressed her palm to her baby bulge. Her lips curled into a smile that stretched ear to ear. God had led her into the arms of the most amazing husband and father on the planet. After Chris and boys left, Wendy responded to Ryan yawning and rubbing his eyes. "Seems our little guy is ready for his afternoon nap." After carrying him to his room, she returned to the great room and settled beside her stepmother, her curiosity roused. "I've been wondering how you and Douglas met."

Donna faced the fireplace while crossing one leg over the other. "I was a freshman at Clemson, living in a cheap apartment off campus with five other girls. I worked six days a week as a waitress at a local student hangout to help pay for tuition. Douglas was two years ahead of me." She spent the next hour describing how their relationship began, developed into a romance, and ultimately fell apart. "Turns out Tyler and Carter are the only good results from our marriage."

"The same way Ryan is the only blessing from the three years I spent illegally married to a con man."

"Speaking of doomed relationships, have you heard anything from Gunter lately?"

"Fortunately no. We're hoping the message finally got through to his warped mind."

Another hour passed before Chris and the boys returned, the succulent aromas of a freshly baked pizza wafting around them. "Ordered special for you gals."

"Perfect timing." Wendy rose, patting her belly while heading to the kitchen. "My stomach's grumbled twice during the past five minutes."

Donna followed her. "My grumble was louder than yours."

The boys headed out to the deck while Chris carried Ryan from his room. He remained inside, chatting with Wendy and Donna. At some point Carter joined the adults. Tyler stayed outside until long after the afternoon had given way to nightfall.

Shortly after her oldest son emerged, Donna lifted off the sofa. "Wendy, Chris, thank you both for welcoming us into your home and your lives. We're heading home early tomorrow morning, which means I need a good night's rest."

Wendy stood to embrace her stepmother. "Promise to stay longer the next time the three of you come to our little town?"

Donna nodded. "We promise."

While Wendy gave Carter a quick hug, Tyler dashed toward the front door, making it clear what he wanted to avoid.

Struggling to mask her disappointment, Wendy clung to Chris's arm and held Ryan's hand while they escorted their guests to their vehicle. After their car disappeared down the driveway, she turned to Chris. "What'd you learn about the boys?"

"Tyler's struggling big time with the reality that his father falls way short of being his boyhood hero."

"Does he still blame me and his mom for the divorce?"

"A little less than he did this morning. He still has a way to go before accepting you as his sister and forgiving his mother."

"Any chance he'll let you continue communicating with him?"

"With a little luck and a lot of prayer."

Chapter 23

Four days after the date that wasn't a date, Millie waited for Bernie to head up the back staircase to begin her housekeeping chores before returning to the now empty dining room. She ambled to the end of the table closest to the window and gripped the back of the chair Eleanor had always occupied during her dinner parties while her husband Warren sat on the other end. She had always admired, maybe even envied the love and respect the Harringtons had for each other. Their marriage had stood in stark contrast to her and Rupert's.

Heaving a sigh, Millie shuffled between the sideboard and table, running her fingers along the chair backs. How many of the couples who gathered in this room to savor food and fellowship enjoyed relationships built on love and mutual respect?

Out of nowhere, decades old images trickled up from Millie's memory bank. She squeezed her eyes shut as the memories crystalized. The day she confronted her lover after she'd learned he was a married man. His expression when he promised to leave his wife and marry her. Ignoring his infidelity and allowing their affair to continue for seven more months. The shock wave coursing through her limbs the day after they'd spent a romantic weekend in Atlanta when he discarded her on the trash heap of broken promises.

Millie's eyes popped open. She recoiled her mouth parted in a silent gasp. Not one time in her entire life had she experienced a relationship with a man based on deep, satisfying love. Had she challenged Amanda to the SNAG bet because at a subconscious level she wanted to win?

Maybe she should talk to a friend. But who? Wendy was too young. Erica had too much going on, and Amanda was out of the question. Only one other person could possibly qualify. Millie hastened to the kitchen, grabbed her phone, and texted Bernie. Now all she had to do was wait.

Eager to stay busy, Millie turned on the oven then mixed the ingredients for a batch of oatmeal raisin cookies for tonight's mystery club meeting. Unless Gordon had discovered new information about Douglas Hewitt, they'd be forced to chat about the novel Stanley had suggested. Somehow they needed to find another real-life mystery to solve. Something intriguing. What about the innocent woman DA Watson had sent to jail? The retrial was scheduled to begin Monday. Not enough time to affect the outcome, but way more exciting than reviewing a book.

After dropping dollops of dough on a cookie sheet, Millie slid the pan into the oven and set the timer. She climbed onto a stool, booted her iPad, and opened Hilltop's reservation page. One private dinner scheduled for Saturday night—a couple celebrating their fiftieth anniversary. If she hadn't threatened to quash Awesam's rezoning efforts, would she still be spending her days complaining about everything under the sun with her cats as her only companions? In a way, Gunter Benson conning Eleanor into marrying him after Warren passed had brought Amanda, Erica and Wendy into her life and saved her from a lonely existence. Could an ex-cop introduce romance into her new world?

Startled by the timer, Millie scurried to the oven. She breathed in the mouth-watering brown sugar and vanilla scents while transferring the treats to the island. While the cookies cooled, she returned to her stool and surfed the web—another new experience since she'd met her Awesam partners.

Responding to footsteps striking the back stairs, Millie pushed her iPad aside.

Bernie ambled over. "The Bluebell, Butterfly, and Azalea suites are ready for today's check-ins." She slid onto the stool beside Millie. "What did you want to talk to me about?"

Doubt crept into Millie's head. Maybe she shouldn't have texted Bernie. But she did, so it was high time to stop hedging and start the conversation. "It's obvious Hilltop Inn has become a romantic getaway for a lot of couples. Which made me wonder...how long after you met your husband did you know he was the one?"

Bernie snapped her fingers, her eyes gleaming with realization. "I knew your trip with Gordon to McCaysville really was a date."

Millie scoffed. "It wasn't a date and neither was the Swan—"

"Hold on." Bernie's brows shot up. "When did y'all go to the drive-in?"

Heat crept up Millie's neck and attacked her cheeks. "No one knows about that night except you and Ralph Everson, unless he told his wife."

"Who's Ralph?"

"The old guy at the ticket booth. He remembered Gordon from our high school days. Anyway, that's not the point."

"What is the point?"

She'd opened the door, and Bernie was practically camped out on the welcome mat. Besides, she had become a close friend, so why not trust her with the truth? "I don't know if the way I feel when I'm with Gordon is caused by pent-up romantic feelings or gas."

"Well, I declare." Bernie giggled. "This is the first time I've heard infatuation compared with gastrointestinal distress."

Millie drummed her fingers. "Are you or aren't you going to answer my question?"

"Which question?"

"The only one I asked." Millie glared at her friend. "Forget it—"

"Oh yeah. The question about when I knew Eddie was the one." A dreamy-eyed expression softened Bernie's features. "It happened during our third date in a movie theater. We were the only two people in our row. That's the night he held my hand for the first time. Then halfway through the film he leaned close and kissed my cheek. I turned toward him. Our eyes met, then closed." Bernie pressed her hand to her chest. "When we kissed, the way my heart beat so fast, I thought it might explode... and that's the moment I knew."

Millie smirked. "Sounds more like a bad case of heartburn than love."

"Bless your cynical little heart, Mildred Cunningham. You're absolutely right about McCaysville and the drive-in not being dates." Breaking eye contact, Bernie reached for a cookie. "Because you don't have a romantic bone in your body."

Millie recoiled, stunned.

"In case you're wondering—" Bernie broke eye contact. "Your condition isn't incurable."

Millie planted her right hand on her hip. "Are you suggesting a big dose of penicillin?"

"More like a splash of sexy perfume and a healthy dose of subtle flirtation." Bernie flashed a devilish grin. "Get a little mystery going, you know? After all, you and Gordon are members of an exclusive mystery club."

"I'm a senior citizen." Millie lifted her hand off her hip. "Not some googly-eyed teenager."

Bernie took a bite out of her cookie. "Maybe you should stop acting like an old lady and realize you can still manage a little eyelash batting."

"The last time I batted my lashes, one of them stuck in my eye. I spent ten minutes trying to flush it out."

"Aha. Somewhere deep inside you there does exist a little spark of romance. All you need is an incentive to turn it into a roaring flame. Which, if you're not too stubborn to face reality, you've already set in motion."

"My bet with Amanda is about *her* winning, not me."

"Sure it is. I'll see you tonight." Bernie climbed off her stool. Halfway to the door, she halted and spun around. "By the way, you winning the bet would be a victory for all of us old ladies." She turned and walked out.

Millie's eyes rolled at a cardinal landing on the windowsill then pecking at the kitchen window. "If you think you're going to sway me with your bright red feathers, forget it. Great—" She hastened to the counter. "Now I'm talking to birds." After tapping the window to shoo the pesky bird away, Millie packed the cookies in a container then headed out to the rear patio and across the side yard to her back door.

Inside, Millie laid the cookies on the counter while glancing around her new kitchen, thanks to the lightning strike that had set her house on fire. She strode through the dining room to her newly furnished living room. Except for the ornate coffee table with a glass inlay—the one salvageable piece of furniture—she'd changed her décor from formal and stuffy to casual and comfortable.

Millie dropped onto her recliner. The day her new furniture arrived, she had bragged to Amanda and Erica that being financially independent meant not having to invite a lonely old codger to share her bed because she needed the money. Back then, the comment had been a joke meant to shock her friends. Millie leaned back, raised her footrest, and closed her eyes. Maybe her words hadn't been a joke after all.

Chapter 24

The third time since Mateo presented Abby with his artwork, she parked in front of the therapy clinic with her fingers curled tightly around the steering wheel. Would today's session pave the way to recovery or lead to more failure and disappointment? Other than Morgan, no one had a clue about her recommitment. In a town as small as Blue Ridge, how long before someone close to her discovered her secret?

Dismissing the thought, Abby peeled her fingers off the steering wheel then released the trunk and pushed her door open. She grabbed her phone off the passenger seat and texted her therapist. "I'm here."

Anna responded with a thumbs-up moments before she rushed out to reposition the wheelchair from Abby's trunk to the driver's side.

"I'm excited about today."

Abby couldn't help but smile at her therapist's upbeat tone. "Are you trying to cheer me up before the torture session?"

Anna's grin widened. "Comes with the territory."

"Required training to earn a physical therapy degree?"

Anna nodded. "Especially important for my more challenging patients."

"What you call challenging, I call realistic."

"Now that you're back, I suggest a big dose of optimism." Before Abby could respond, Anna rushed to hold the front door open.

After moving her body into her chair, she maneuvered up the ramp. At the front door, she peered up at Anna with a poor excuse of a grin. "Good point about being positive."

"I know." Anna stepped aside.

Abby wheeled through the reception area into the large open space filled with all sorts of rehab equipment. She halted. Her breath caught in her throat as she stared at the harness suspended over a pair of waist-high parallel bars.

Gripping the wheelchair handles, Anna pushed Abby close to the bars. "Today we'll begin retraining your legs to do what God intended them to do."

"How do you know that contraption will work for me?"

"Faith plus experience." Anna leaned down and set the wheelchair brakes. "Are you ready to begin?"

"Wait." Abby closed her eyes as images from the last day she'd been able to walk came roaring back. She had dashed out the back door and climbed behind the wheel. Close to town, she'd braked at a stop sign before easing forward. A shiver cascaded up her spine at the memory of crushing metal and breaking glass. She pressed her hand to her neck as more images surfaced. Waking up in the hospital with a brace securing her head. Tommy sitting beside her, holding her hand. Forgiving Jimmy after discovering he had driven the other car.

Her eyes popped open as the full measure of reality weighed heavy on her shoulders. She peered up at the contraption suspended from the ceiling. A full recovery would have a profound impact on everyone she loved. Besides, Anna wouldn't put her through the motions if she wasn't ready to take the next phase, would she? "Okay, I'm ready now."

"All right then." Anna removed the wheelchair footrests and placed Abby's feet on the mat between the parallel bars. "Grip the bars while we lift you off your chair."

Drawing on the upper arm strength she'd developed post-accident, Abby wrapped her fingers around the cool metal and pulled her body off her seat. With the help of another therapist, Anna strapped Abby into the harness then pressed a remote button triggering a pulley that slowly lifted her to a full standing position.

Delighted to be upright for the first time in months, Abby wiggled her toes while peering at her straightened knees. Was it her imagination, or could she actually feel the floor beneath her sneaker-clad feet?

"While I move you along the mat, you need to concentrate on the movement."

"You want me to trick my brain into believing I'm controlling the steps, don't you?"

Anna smiled. "Exactly. Training 101."

Abby tuned out the sights and sounds around her while focusing every ounce of energy on the task at hand. When they arrived at the end of the mat, Anna turned her to face the opposite direction. During the five round trips, she concentrated while imagining a wheelchair-free future. If she worked hard enough, would she be able to walk to the gazebo at the end of the path in Millie's English country garden on her mother and Brad's wedding day? What about Tommy? Could they hold hands while hiking down a familiar trail or strolling to their favorite downtown restaurant?

When the exercise finished, Abby kept an iron grip on the bars while Anna removed the harness and lowered her into her wheelchair. She looked up at her therapist. "How long before my brain tells my feet to move without your help?"

"No one can say for sure. However, your positive attitude and determination will make a huge difference."

"Thanks to one six-year-old kid who doesn't believe I tried hard enough." The moment she wiggled all ten toes, a flush rushed to her cheeks, and her mouth curved in a way that suggested maybe—just maybe—one day soon life would return to normal.

Chapter 25

After arranging appetizers and libations on the buffet, Millie placed six chairs on one side of the dining room table before glancing at her watch. She had five minutes to spare—plenty of time for one last check before the mystery club gang arrived. She hastened to her bedroom and stood in front of the mirror on the back of her closet door reassessing her black jeans and red long-sleeved tunic. Casual meets sophisticated. Perfect.

Startled by the doorbell, Millie breathed deeply to slow her pulse while making her way down the hall and into the foyer. Summoning her warmest smile, she pulled the door open as the ladies' designated driver backed down to the street. "One of these days, Keith should stay and join us."

"I doubt my son would enjoy spending the evening with us old folks." Susan eyed Millie from head to toe. "Love the outfit." She leaned close, sniffing. "And the perfume."

Millie propped one hand on her hip. "Have you suddenly become some sort of fashion expert?"

"I'm just saying you make a good impression."

"Seems you would benefit from a little liquid refreshment." Millie's tone mocked. "Libations and appetizers are in the dining room."

Susan grinned. "Seems our hostess is a bit sensitive about her outfit."

"I don't know about you—" Eileen linked arms with Susan. "But I'm ready for a glass of wine." She led Keith's mother from the foyer through the living room then on to the dining room.

Bernie remained beside Millie, an amused expression crinkling the skin around her eyes. "Let me guess," she whispered. "Your fancy outfit means you're in flirtation mode."

Millie lowered her hand, while her eyes narrowed to a slit. She pushed the door closed. "What did you tell Susan and Eileen?"

"I can't believe you asked me that question." Bernie planted her hands on her hips, Millie style. "You're my friend, so I would never betray your trust. Although—" Bernie hesitated as she lowered her hands to her sides. "I didn't need to say anything—"

Millie arched a brow. "Meaning what?"

"Susan and Eileen have drawn their own conclusions about Gordon having a big-time crush on you." Bernie leaned closer. "Maybe they're on to something."

Millie scowled while tapping her foot. "If you ask me, those two are acting like a couple of gossipy teenyboppers."

"Or, maybe what I said about a romance between you and Gordon being a victory for all of us old ladies is resonating with them."

"Hold onto your chickens…" The roar of the Polaris engine announcing Gordon and Stanley's arrival released a fluttering sensation in Millie's chest. Rocked by conflicting emotions, she backed away from the door. "You stay here and let the guys in—"

"Won't me answering the door seem a little strange?"

"Strange or not, you're on door duty." Millie escaped to the living room, then slowed her pace, swallowing hard to stop the fluttering sensation attacking her chest. She dismissed the sensation as indigestion, then squared her shoulders and turned the corner to the dining room.

Susan fingered the wine bottle label before filling her glass. She sipped. "Excellent choice. You're becoming quite the wine connoisseur."

"I'm the chef in a first-class inn. What else would you expect?"

"Good point." Susan turned and aimed her glass toward the six chairs. "What's with the crazy setup?"

"Tonight we have another big case to solve."

Gordon ambled in and set his laptop in the middle of the table. "Millie's idea of a mystery club goes way beyond discussing books."

Stanley grabbed a beer from the chiller. "Who do you suggest we investigate this time?"

"Crystal Bullock." Millie headed to the buffet. "She's the innocent victim who spent years behind bars because of DA Watson's incompetence."

Susan eyed Millie. "Are you aware that her case is scheduled for a retrial next week?"

"Of course, I'm aware. You're not suggesting we don't investigate, are you?"

"You understand that Vincent is already on the case?"

Gordon uncapped a beer bottle. "I assume Vincent is the future DA's private investigator."

Susan nodded. "One of the best in Georgia."

Eileen plucked a mini sandwich off a platter. "Are we giving up on reviewing books altogether or just for tonight?"

"Well now." Millie filled a glass with red wine. "That depends on how many potential new cases pop up."

Gordon chuckled. "I'm guessing we're all more intrigued with undercover investigations than discussing fictional characters."

"I have to admit you're right." Susan held up a finger. "However, we all need to understand that most of our snooping around is strictly for our own amusement."

Stanley pulled out a chair. "Maybe we should change our name to Old Codgers Snooping-around Gang."

"Forget old codgers." Eileen sat beside Stanley. "We're senior citizens on a secret mission."

"Give us enough time, and we'll write our own novel." Bernie settled on an empty chair and set her wineglass on the table.

"Now that we've all agreed on tonight's activity—" Millie eyed Gordon while pointing to the chair in front of the laptop. "Time for you to take your seat and get our mission underway."

"I'm on it." Gordon dropped onto the chair and opened his laptop.

Millie didn't fail to notice Susan's rush to sit on the other side of Bernie, leaving the chair beside Gordon vacant. Could she have been any more obvious? Had Gordon noticed? Millie hesitated for a brief moment then rounded the table and dropped onto the chair, aware that mere inches separated her and the ex-cop. Why had she placed the chairs so close together? So everyone could see the screen, that's why.

"Here we go." Gordon typed Crystal's name, then scrolled through the list of potential sites. "This is a good place to begin." He pulled up a newspaper article reviewing the woman's arrest and trial. After reading the summary aloud, he leaned back. "That reporter obviously had doubts about the verdict."

Millie nodded. "If you ask me, Richard Watson belongs in jail, not Crystal Bullock."

Gordon chuckled while nudging Millie's arm. "You'd make a good witness for the prosecution."

"One fact is becoming crystal clear." Susan leaned forward, peering around Bernie. "Millie's unbridled curiosity combined with your experience as a detective make you two one heck of a team."

Hoping to stop the heat attacking her neck from spreading to her cheeks, Millie cleared her throat.

"Excellent observation, Susan." Gordon's tone hinted of playfulness. "In fact we should attend Crystal's trial as well-informed observers."

Millie nodded. "Great idea."

"Sorry." Susan lifted off her chair and headed to the buffet table. "I'm babysitting my granddaughter next week."

Eileen joined her. "I've already volunteered to work at the food bank. What about you, Bernie."

"Monday's my day to serve breakfast to Hilltop's guests." Bernie scooted away from the table. "Which leaves you, Stanley."

He shook his head. "No way I'm spending a day listening to lawyers duke it out."

"Well then—" Gordon faced Millie. "Seems you and I will need to give the rest of the gang a full report during our next meeting."

Millie's eyes drifted from Susan's satisfied smile to Bernie's wide-eyed expression. Should she set them straight or have a little fun at their expense? Better to have fun. She turned toward Gordon, a sly grin tugging at the corners of her mouth. "If our friends were any more obvious, they'd be waving pom-poms and chanting 'Go Team Gordie.'"

Gordon stared at her for a split second before releasing a full-throated laugh. "What do you say we give the gang a show?"

"Hmm." Millie tilted her head. "What do you have in mind?"

"Nothing too shocking. We don't want to send any of our friends to the emergency room." He planted a kiss square on her lips. "That'll keep them guessing."

Stunned, Millie stared at him, her eyes round as saucers. "Now what?"

He winked.

Play along, that's what. "Careful, Detective Davenport. Next time our friends might expect fireworks."

"Well now." Susan's tone hinted of humor. "Seems our club's co-leaders are on to us."

Stanley's brows raised. "On to what?"

"Pay attention." Susan patted his arm. "You'll figure it out."

"I never did understand women." Stanley shook his head then grabbed another beer and returned to his seat. "Have we finished digging up details?"

"Not by a long shot." Gordon tapped his keyboard while the rest of the gang returned to their seats. "Take a look at this."

While the mystery club members settled back into investigative mode, responding to each new detail with lively conversation, Millie delighted in the satisfaction that she and Gordon had outwitted their friends.

Chapter 26

Ten minutes before the retrial was scheduled to begin, Amanda and Gary entered the courtroom and sat in the last row. Regina, Chris, and Crystal sat at the defense table quietly chatting. Amanda nodded toward the middle-aged woman sitting beside a young man at the prosecution table. "Do you know either of them?"

"Just her. Assistant DA Judith Alexander. She was part of the team before Watson was elected."

"I wonder how she'll react after the election if Keith wins?"

"You mean when, and it depends on how loyal she is to her current boss."

"Or if she's as corrupt as he is."

The courtroom door swung open. Amanda gawked at Millie as she and Gordon entered and settled beside them. "Is solving Crystal Bullock's case your mystery club's latest quest?"

Millie set her purse on the floor. "We're just here to satisfy our curiosity."

Gordon peered around Millie. "During my years as a detective, I spent countless hours testifying both for and against defendants."

Gary leaned forward. "Given your experience, how do you predict today's trial will turn out?"

"Based on our cohorts' investigation, in the defendant's favor."

"This is like a real live version of *Law and Order*." Millie's tone hinted of excitement.

Amanda snickered, leaning close to her. "How many times have you been in a real courtroom?"

"Twice. The first time to dispute a speeding ticket."

"How fast were you going?"

"The sheriff claimed his radar clocked me at twelve miles over the limit."

"And?"

Millie shrugged. "I paid the fine."

Amanda snickered. "Difficult to beat recorded evidence."

"Yeah, well..." Millie pointed to a well-dressed elderly woman heading up the aisle to the row directly behind the defense table. "Anyone know who she is?"

Amanda nodded. "Gladys Zander. She's the woman involved in prison ministry who brought Crystal's case to our attention."

The bailiff stood. "All rise for Her Honor, Judge Elizabeth Davis."

The judge entered then settled at the bench. "Please be seated. Who's representing the defendant?"

"I am, Your Honor. Regina Reeves with Chris Armstrong as second chair."

"Welcome to Blue Ridge, Counselor." The judge turned toward the prosecution. "You may proceed with your opening statement."

After ADA Alexander declared that evidence would prove the defendant had been correctly convicted for the crime, Regina countered by claiming that newly discovered facts would prove her client had been falsely imprisoned. When she finished, the judge leaned back. "Call your first witness, Counselor."

ADA Alexander stood. "We call Deputy Logan Baker."

The burly sheriff lumbered into the courtroom as if he owned the building. He swore to tell the truth then settled in the witness box.

After establishing his credentials, Alexander moved closer. "Were you the first officer to respond to the 911 call?"

"I was."

"Tell us what happened when you arrived at the scene."

He leaned back, his shoulders squared, his chin high. "I found Mr. Victor—he owned the liquor store—dead on the floor behind the counter from what appeared to be a gunshot wound to the chest. The cash register was empty, indicating a robbery gone bad."

"Did you find a weapon?"

"Yes, the following day under a thick bush in the town's park. Same caliber bullet as the one that killed Mr. Victor."

"What led the authorities to suspect Ms. Bullock?"

"Her reputation as a homeless drug addict and the victim's complaint a couple of weeks earlier that Ms. Bullock had attempted to steal a bottle of booze."

"Did the owner press charges?"

"No." Baker shrugged. "Guess he felt sorry for her."

"Where was the defendant when you arrested her?"

"Passed out on the bench beside the bush where the gun was hidden."

"How did Ms. Bullock react when you arrested her?"

"Mostly confused, probably from a hangover."

Regina stood. "Move to strike."

The judge nodded. "So noted. Please continue, Counselor."

Alexander stepped back from the witness stand. "When you arrested the defendant, did you read her Miranda Rights?"

The deputy hesitated. "I always read suspects their rights."

"Is that a yes or a no?"

"Yeah, I read them to her."

Millie leaned close to Amanda, whispering. "Did you notice how his shoulders drooped a little? He's telling a big fat whopper."

Amanda smirked. "Now you're a body-language expert?"

"An important skill for a chief information officer, don't you think?"

Amanda rolled her eyes.

Regina backed away from the witness and leaned against the prosecution table. "How did the defendant act when you questioned her about her involvement in the shooting?"

"Again..." The deputy glanced at the judge. "Mostly confused."

Following two additional questions, Alexander returned to her seat.

Regina lifted off her chair and quickly closed the distance to the deputy. "Did the forensic team find the defendant's fingerprints on the murder weapon?"

Deputy Baker cleared his throat. "The gun had been wiped clean."

"What about gunpowder residue on her hands?"

"Negative."

"Was the victim's blood on her clothing?"

He shook his head. "Didn't find any."

"I see. What made you think Ms. Bullock was confused while being questioned?"

Baker shrugged. "She swayed back and forth and blinked a lot."

"Is it possible she was in shock after being handcuffed and hauled off to jail?"

"I don't know." He fidgeted. "Maybe."

"Did the investigation continue after Ms. Bullock's arrest?"

"No."

"Given the lack of evidence against my client, why did your department drop the case?"

"We followed directions."

"From whom?"

The deputy shifted his weight.

"Do you need me to repeat the question, Deputy Baker?"

"No ma'am." He cleared his throat. "District Attorney Watson told the department to charge Ms. Bullock with murder."

"How soon after Ms. Bullock's arrest did her trial take place?"

Baker hesitated. "About three weeks."

"It was seventeen days to be exact, wasn't it?"

"Best I can recall."

Regina turned toward the prosecution table. "Do trials normally take place that soon after an arrest, or only when the district attorney is two months from a hotly contested election?"

"Objection."

"Withdrawn. I have no more questions." Regina returned to her seat.

Judge Davis leaned forward. "Do you have another witness, Counselor?"

ADA Alexander conferred with the young man sitting beside her. He shook his head. She faced the bench. "No, Your Honor."

"All right." The judge turned toward the defense. "Are you ready to proceed, Counselor?"

"Yes, Your Honor. We call Jeremy Wagner to the stand."

Millie nudged Amanda. "He's that reporter."

"Yeah, I know."

"How?"

"Crystal told us about him when Gary, Regina, and I visited her in prison."

After the gentleman was sworn in and seated, Regina stood. "How long have you been a reporter, Mr. Wagner?"

"For thirty years."

"During your career, how many criminal cases have you investigated and written about?"

"At least a dozen."

Regina strode to the defense table. After Chris handed her a newspaper, she returned to the witness stand. "What prompted you to write an article declaring Ms. Bullock's innocence after her trial?"

"In addition to the fact that no evidence had been found to connect her to the crime, the DA failed to call a key witness."

"What witness?" Regina handed copies of the article to the judge and to the prosecution.

"A man everyone called Flash, who wandered around town taking pictures with disposable cameras."

"What happened to confirm your belief in the defendant's innocence?"

"Flash took a picture of Ms. Bullock asleep on a park bench at the time of the crime."

"Objection. Hearsay."

"Overruled."

"How were you able to ascertain when the photo was taken?"

"The clock tower in the background."

Regina returned to the defense table. Chris handed her a sheet of paper. She carried it to the witness stand and held it up in front of the reporter. "Is this a photocopy of the picture in question?"

"It is."

"Why don't you have the original?"

"I mailed it first class—signature required—to DA Watson five days before Ms. Bullock's trial."

"Has anyone from the district attorney's office ever contacted you or responded to your inquiries?"

"No ma'am."

"Where is Flash now?"

"He passed away a couple of years ago."

"Thank you, Mr. Wagner." Regina passed the photo to Judge Davis and ADA Alexander before returning to her seat.

The judge faced the prosecution. "Do you wish to cross, Counselor?"

"No, Your Honor."

"You may step down, Mr. Wagner. Does the defense have additional witnesses?"

"Yes. We call Crystal Bullock."

The defendant, wearing a pale blue suit, walked to the front of the courtroom. After the bailiff swore her in, she stepped onto the witness stand and settled on the chair.

Regina approached. "Explain to the court why you frequently slept on park benches."

"Two years earlier, I was hurt in a bad wreck that totaled my car and left me with three broken ribs, a shattered femur, and a concussion, plus lots of cuts and bruises. Six months later I was hooked on pain pills. When the prescription ran out, I medicated with drugs and alcohol. That's how I lost my job and my apartment."

"Did you have family members or friends to turn to for help?"

"No one. I was on my own."

"Walk us through the morning you were arrested."

"Like most mornings, I woke up dazed from a hangover." Crystal's voice was soft, yet steady. "A big man wearing a badge and a gun glared down at me. He asked where I'd been two nights ago. I thought he wanted to arrest me for turning tricks—that's how I survived. When I told him I couldn't remember, he yanked me off the bench and handcuffed me."

"Did he read you your rights?"

Crystal shook her head. "Not that I remember."

"What happened next?"

"The deputy drove me to the sheriff's office and left me alone in a little room with a table and two chairs. The next hour is kind of a blur, until he came in and asked what I knew about the liquor store owner's death. I had no idea what he was talking about."

"How would you describe your reaction?"

"Shocked. Confused. By the time I realized he was accusing me of murder, I was so scared I could barely remember my name. At some point I told him I was innocent. He continued accusing me until I asked for an attorney. That's when he locked me behind bars. A couple days later, a lawyer showed up and told me my best bet was to accept a plea of manslaughter. I refused. Fifteen days later I was in a courtroom, accused of second-degree murder. When the jury returned with a guilty verdict, I knew that my attorney was either incompetent or he'd been paid off."

"Objection, Your Honor. Calls for speculation."

"So noted, Counselor. Sustained."

Regina moved closer to Crystal. "When did you become aware that a photo proving your innocence exists?"

Shielding her mouth with her hand, Amanda leaned close to Millie. "Here it comes. The final nail in DA Watson's campaign."

Crystal glanced up at the judge for a brief moment. "A couple of months after the trial, that reporter, Jeremy Wagner, visited me in jail. He brought me a copy of the article he wrote as well as that picture of me asleep on the park bench. After he left, I wrote the first letter to the district attorney."

Regina stepped back. "Richard Watson?"

"Yes."

"Did he respond?"

"Not one time." Crystal's tone hinted of disgust.

"Do you still have the photo or the article?"

Crystal shook her head. "Both disappeared from my cell shortly after Mr. Wagner's visit."

Regina paused, seemingly to allow the statement to resonate. "One final question. Do you believe DA Watson took you to trial because he was behind in the polls and needed to secure a win?"

"Objection, Your Honor."

"Withdrawn." Regina returned to her seat.

After the ADA declined to cross, Judge Davis peered down at the defendant. "You may step down, Ms. Bullock." Following closing statements, Judge Davis leaned forward. "I'll review all the information provided by both sides as well as the transcript from Ms. Bullock's first trial and return a verdict at nine o'clock tomorrow morning." She exited the courtroom.

After ADA Alexander and her cohort rushed out the main door, Amanda and Gary met Gladys in the aisle. "Are you as hopeful as Gary and I are about Judge Davis's verdict?"

"If I were a betting woman, I'd lay odds that tomorrow justice will be served and Crystal Bullock will be a free woman."

Chapter 27

Before dawn crept over the horizon, Erica carried a platter of chocolate chip pancakes and crisp bacon to the den and set it on the dining room table.

"Saturday breakfast on Tuesday?" Abby wheeled her chair up to the table with Dusty padding beside her. "Is today a special occasion?"

"Every day I spend with you is special, sweetheart." Erica sat beside her daughter. "Especially since in a few weeks, you and I will begin living apart for the first time in our lives."

"Good news is you'll only be a few miles away." Abby transferred pancakes and bacon to her plate.

Amanda carried her coffee mug from the kitchen. "Given your mom's occupation, and considering this is Awesam's corporate headquarters, she'll be here often."

"True." Erica stared at her empty plate while her mind drifted to the three-story house she and Brad would soon call home. If she hadn't been reluctant to live in the single-story house he'd shared with his wife, Abby could move in with them.

Dressed and ready for work, Sierra walked out of her room carrying Theo. "Saturday breakfast on Tuesday?" She lowered her son into his swing. "What's the occasion?"

"Mother and daughter are dealing with empty-nest syndrome." Amanda pulled a chair away from the table. "Except Erica's the one leaving."

Sierra sat between Erica and Amanda. "Would you believe I've never been to a wedding?"

"Mom and Brad's will be the second in the gazebo since it opened." Abby doused her pancakes with syrup. "Both with Awesam family members."

Sierra plated a pancake. "You should advertise Hilltop Inn as a wedding venue."

"We do on our website." Amanda cut a piece of pancake. "Thus far, no results."

Erica swallowed a bite of bacon. "Speaking of results, if Judge Davis releases Crystal from prison, she'll need a safe place to stay."

"We have a couple of vacant bedrooms at the crisis center." Abby swirled a forkful of pancake in a puddle of syrup. "Assuming she wants to remain in Blue Ridge, she could stay there until she can afford a place of her own."

Amanda faced Abby. "You realize she's an alcoholic and a drug addict."

"Except she's been behind bars—"

"According to Keith, prisons are hotbeds for illegal drugs."

Abby slipped Dusty a piece of bacon. "Another reason the crisis center could serve as a safe halfway house for her."

Erica eyed her daughter. "Will your boss go along with the idea?"

"Pamela has a big heart, so yeah, she will."

"All right, then." Amanda grabbed her coffee mug. "I'll talk to Crystal after the verdict."

Sierra swallowed a bite of pancake. "My baby's gonna grow up knowing not to smoke, take drugs, or do anything against the law. He's gonna get a good education and be one of the good guys who people respect. Except—" Her eyes clouded over, as if she was struggling with a heavy burden. "Will he hate me when he learns that I gave him away the day he was born?" Her tone hinted of anxiety.

Erica placed her hand on Sierra's arm. "When Theo's old enough to understand, you'll explain that you took him to a safe place then came back into his life because you love him with all your heart."

"Mom's right. Know what else?" Abby's tone was confident, reassuring. "You and Theo will always be part of our extended family."

"I love you all so much." Tears pooled and streamed down Sierra's cheeks. "How can I ever repay you for everything you've done for me and Little Pip?"

Amanda turned toward her. "You already have, honey, by rejecting your mother's victim lifestyle and becoming the amazing woman God intended you to be."

Sierra dabbed at her cheeks. "Maybe I can find a way to help my little sisters understand their potential so one day they'll have the courage to break free."

Abby snapped her fingers. "That's how to pay it forward."

Erica's eyes drifted from Sierra to her daughter as a flicker of faith filled her with renewed hope. Her child would not spend the rest of her life in a wheelchair.

Amanda's lungs expanded with deep, satisfied breaths as she tuned out the conversation. When she, Erica, and Wendy chose not to become victims of Gunter Benson's betrayal, they had no idea how many lives they would touch. *Had the time come to take a chance on a romantic relationship once again?*

By the time she walked into the courthouse, Amanda had made one all-important decision. If Gary made the first move, she would open her heart to the possibility of new love. Besides, it would be fun to win the bet with Millie.

Gary, smelling of shower gel and shampoo, met her outside the courtroom. "Chris and Regina showed up a few minutes ago."

"How'd they seem?"

"Guardedly confident." He held the door open, then followed Amanda to the row directly behind the defense table.

Amanda nodded toward the empty prosecution table. "Do you suppose Watson will fire his ADA if she loses?"

Chris turned toward them, shaking his head. "He's too smart a politician." His voice lowered. "You can bet he'll blame her for the loss, then repackage himself as a good guy for keeping her on his staff."

Regina pivoted toward them. "ADA Alexander played it safe yesterday by presenting her case with just enough effort to avoid coming across as skeptical."

Gary nodded. "Chances are she suspects that, come November, she'll have a new boss."

Gladys Zander slid into the row beside them, her face flush. "I've known Judge Davis going on thirty years. I'm confident she'll make the right decision."

ADA Alexander strode up the aisle, her expression hinting she'd rather be anywhere else. After setting down her briefcase and dropping onto a chair, she faced her opposition and gave a slight nod.

Gary leaned close to Amanda. "She knows something."

Moments after a deputy escorted Crystal, wearing the same suit she'd worn yesterday, into the courtroom, the bailiff called the court to order.

Judge Davis resumed her position at the bench, her shoulders squared. "During my tenure as a judge, I've observed ineffective defenses and overzealous prosecutions. But never a flagrant violation of an individual's rights to a fair trial...until I reviewed every aspect of this case." She paused, her eyes seemingly focused on the defendant. "Ms. Bullock, I believe a great injustice has been committed against you. While I'm unable to give the years you spent behind bars back to you, I am vacating your conviction and granting you the freedom you deserve. Furthermore, no one would find fault if you chose to right the wrong through the legal system."

Amanda's eyebrows shot up. Was Judge Davis suggesting the defendant sue Richard Watson or the district attorney's office? She stiffened. Had saving Crystal created a future nightmare for Keith?

Tears flowed down Crystal's cheeks when she stood to embrace Regina, then Chris. She turned to face Amanda, Gary, and Gladys. "Thank you for believing in me."

ADA Alexander rose then stepped across the space separating the defense side of the courtroom from the prosecution. "I'm sorry for the injustice you've endured, Ms. Bullock. Yesterday your defense team served you well." She paused for a brief moment, her focus shifting to Chris. "Please tell your father that I wish him all the best in his campaign, Mr. Armstrong."

"I will."

The assistant district attorney turned toward the aisle and headed straight to the exit.

"Smart woman." Regina faced Chris. "She knows this case has the potential to unseat her boss."

"For years I've imagined one day being set free." Crystal dropped onto her chair, a downcast expression clouding her face. "Now that it's happened, I have no idea where to go or what to do."

"I can help." Amanda stepped around the barrier and held her hand out to the woman who was no longer a convicted felon. "Will you trust me to take you to a safe place where you can stay while you decide your next steps?"

Crystal hesitated, peering up at Amanda. "That day you visited me in prison, I was grateful a professional woman like you would take the time to hear my story." She accepted Amanda's hand while lifting off her chair. "Which is why I trust you."

"Good." Amanda looped her arm around Crystal's elbow then they stepped into the aisle and headed to the exit. "During our drive, I'm going to tell you a story about the victory sorority sisters. After they were conned by a man they trusted and lost everything, they refused to become victims."

Crystal's eyes widened. "You're one of them, aren't you?"

"Yes." A soft smile formed as Amanda opened the door. "Along with Chris's wife, Wendy, and Erica, who is a few weeks from marrying her soulmate. Against all odds, we took control of our lives. Now you, my friend, have been given a chance to take control of yours."

Chapter 28

Wendy stood in the doorway gazing at Ryan asleep in his crib converted to a youth bed, her heart overflowing with love. Her eyes drifted to the photo dimly lit by the night lamp on his dresser. Cynthia holding their little guy in her arms, a visual reminder of how much his mother favored his maternal grandmother. Wendy pressed her hand to her belly, her focus drifting back to her son. Would his little sister look more like her or his daddy?

Chris slipped up behind Wendy and wrapped his arms around her chest. "In a few weeks, we'll have a son and a daughter to love."

She leaned against him, savoring the warmth of his embrace. "I was confident my first baby was a girl, until the ultrasound proved otherwise. Now we'll have the perfect family." Wendy's shoulders stiffened as Kayla's ringtone chimed from the kitchen.

"I'll bring your phone to you." Chris released her and dashed down the hall.

Wendy pressed her hand to her chest, praying her sister wasn't calling with devastating news. The moment Chris returned, Wendy forced a tight smile. She accepted the phone and held it in front of her face. "Hey, how'd your history test go?"

"B plus."

"Good for you."

"Mom helped me study the best she could." Kayla paused, a pained expression wrinkling her brow. "As much as Riley and I try to cheer her up, every day she slips away a little more."

Choking back tears, Wendy shuffled across the hall to the nursery. She turned on the crystal chandelier illuminating the light blue ceiling accentuated by fluffy white clouds. What would give her mother the strength to hold on long enough to cradle her granddaughter in her arms? Wendy pressed her hand to her baby bulge while her eyes drifted to the pink and white stripes accenting the wall behind the white crib. Cynthia needed to know how much she was loved and that her memory would live on. "I know what to do. Before I explain, I need to talk to Chris. I'll call you back shortly." Wendy ended the call before rushing from the nursery to the great room.

Chris peered up from the sofa. "Is everything okay?"

Teetering between hope and heartbreak, Wendy laid her phone on the end table then dropped onto the sofa as if her legs could no longer support her. "Mom's losing ground faster than we expected." She pulled a knee onto the cushion and turned toward Chris. Her eyes searched his. "I have an idea I hope will give her the will to hang on long enough to meet her granddaughter."

Without hesitation, Chris reached for her hand. "I'm listening."

Her words poured out in a rush, thick with emotion. "What do you think?"

Chris kissed her cheek, his lips lingering with unspoken tenderness. "You have the heart of an angel." His voice was low, almost reverent.

Wendy blinked, a lump forming in her throat. "You approve, don't you?"

He nodded, his eyes glistening as he placed his hand gently on her belly. "Our little gal has the most amazing mother."

Wendy swallowed the lump rising in her throat while laying her hand over his. Their fingers laced together. "As well as the most remarkable daddy, husband, and son-in-law on the planet."

Chris chuckled softly. "Now that we've confirmed how much we admire each other—" His smile warmed. "Are you ready to share the news with Kayla and Cynthia?"

She grabbed her phone while nestling closer to Chris, letting his love calm her fluttering heart. "I'm ready." She tapped Kayla's number then activated FaceTime.

Kayla answered, her face appearing on the screen. "What's going on?"

"Is Mom awake?"

"I'm sitting beside her in the living room."

"Activate the speaker because Chris and I have exciting news to share with the two of you."

"Okay." Kayla turned her phone toward her mother. "It's Wendy and Chris."

Wendy held the phone out allowing the screen to frame her face and Chris's. "Hey, Mom."

Chris smiled. "Hi."

"You both look wonderful." Cynthia's voice was weak, threaded with the weight of her decline. "How's my grandson?"

"As amazing as ever."

"And my granddaughter?"

"Oh my goodness." Wendy's face lit as she placed her hand over her belly. "Our little gal responded to your question with a good kick."

"She's strong like her mother." A faint twinkle emerged in Cynthia's tired eyes.

"And her grandmother." Wendy's voice tightened with emotion. "This summer when you and I were sitting on your back deck, you told me you always knew your mother was happy when she called you sweet Cindy Marie."

Cynthia's eyes grew misty. "One of the few happy memories I have of her."

Wendy's gaze flicked to Chris. He nodded, silently encouraging her. Wendy's heart pounded loudly, echoing in her ears. She turned back toward the phone. "In a few weeks…" Her voice quivered with emotion. "When you meet your granddaughter for the first time, you'll be gazing into a beautiful baby named after her maternal grandmother."

Cynthia's mouth fell open. Her eyes welled up, glimmering with hope. "Are you saying what I think you're saying?"

Wendy smiled through the tears gathering in her eyes. "Chris and I are naming your second grandchild Cindy Marie."

Tears flowed freely down Cynthia's cheeks, unashamed and pure. "You have given me the perfect gift." Her voice filled with gratitude and love. "I will find a way to deserve this gift I will carry in my heart forever."

Wendy's throat tightened, and tears spilled over. "You're already worthy of having your granddaughter named after you, Mom." Chris slipped his arm around her shoulders, pulling her close while they shared the moment of grace poured out to the woman who had abandoned her firstborn child all those years ago.

Cynthia sniffled while dabbing her cheeks. "The day I meet my precious granddaughter, I will thank you and Chris properly."

Wendy tilted her head skyward, rejoicing in the peace washing over her like warm sunshine on a beautiful spring morning. In that moment she understood beyond the shadow of a doubt that she would embrace her mother again before she slipped from earth to her eternal home.

Chapter 29

After struggling for half an hour to focus on work, Abby lifted Tommy's photo off her desk and pressed it to her chest. She closed her eyes, remembering the last words he had spoken to her. *Call me when you're ready to stop feeling sorry for yourself and return to being who you really are. When you understand that no matter how far you run, I will never stop loving you.* The words echoed in her memory, sharp yet tender.

She hadn't heard a word from him since that day he climbed out of her car and walked away. Her eyes popped open as realization arrested her thoughts. What if during the weeks they'd spent apart, Tommy had fallen out of love with her?

Her hands trembled as she pulled the photo away from her chest, her eyes searching his warm smile. Following her accident, he had remained steadfast and patient, never once wavering in his love. If she lost him, it would be her fault for pushing him away. The weight of that truth settled heavy on her shoulders.

She stared at her phone lying beside her laptop. One call wouldn't hurt. Unless... What if he didn't answer? Worse, what if he answered, and his tone no longer held even a trace of affection? Her heart ached as she set his photo on the desk then wheeled out of her office.

Halfway down the hall she stopped beside the kitchen's open door. Crystal stood at the counter, her back turned toward Abby. "Are you okay?" The woman who had been granted her freedom two days earlier jumped as if someone had struck her. "Sorry, I didn't mean to startle you."

Crystal spun around, her face pale. "Living with dangerous criminals requires constant vigilance, especially when one's back is turned. It'll take time to adjust to my new reality." She exhaled then settled on a chair and set a glass of water on the table.

"I know what you mean." Abby wheeled inside. "My family helped me adjust to my new reality after an accident damaged my spine."

"You're lucky to have people in your life who care about you."

Sensing the former inmate's need to trust someone, Abby maneuvered closer. "The women staying here and our staff—we're like family."

Crystal remained silent for a long moment. "A week before my eighteenth birthday, my parents and brother were killed in a car wreck. My entire family...gone in one terrible instant."

"I can only imagine how devastated you were."

"If I hadn't had a big disagreement with my mother..." Crystal tucked her chin to her chest, shrinking in on herself. "For a long time, I wished I had been in that car."

Unsure how a woman released from prison forty-eight hours earlier would respond to touch, Abby laced her fingers on her lap. "Survivor guilt is a powerful emotion."

"I drifted into deep depression, until I met Daniel. He was ten years older than me and seemed like a good guy." Crystal lifted her chin. "We'd been married less than a year the first time he hit me. I didn't have a job or any place to go...so I stayed with him."

Abby kept her eyes gently fixed on Crystal's face. "The abuse didn't stop, did it?"

She shook her head. "Not until he was arrested for manslaughter."

"My mother endured my father's beatings for years before we escaped to a woman's shelter, much like this one. Now she's a successful business woman, weeks away from marrying a wonderful man who adores her."

Crystal's eyes appeared heavy with unshed tears. "I can't remember the last time I had control of my life." She looked away, her expression screaming of self-doubt.

Hoping Crystal wouldn't recoil, Abby reached across the corner of the table and touched her arm with her fingertips. "You took control the moment you began fighting for your freedom. When you're ready to take the next step, we'll help you find a job."

Silence wrapped around them like a fragile cocoon. Crystal's features slowly softened, her body appearing to unclench ever so slightly. A spark of something—hope, maybe—glinted behind her tears. "Thank you..." Her voice cracked. "For caring."

Mateo's mother stepped in, then halted, her gaze shifting from Crystal to Abby. "Am I interrupting?"

"Not at all." Sensing Crystal needed a friend, Abby offered a soft smile and withdrew her fingers. "I'll leave you ladies to become better acquaint-ed." Her lungs expanded with deep, satisfied breaths as she wheeled out of the kitchen and turned toward her office. Halfway down the hall, the front doorbell rang. She pivoted, then headed straight to the reception area. Following a moment of hesitation, she pressed the intercom. "Can I help you?"

"It's me."

Her breath hitched. That voice. Unmistakable. Abby buzzed him in.

The door eased open. Tommy stepped inside, gently shutting the door behind him, as if he knew the drill. "Hey."

Abby peered up at him, her heart beating in her chest like rolling thun-der. "Hey."

He handed her a bouquet of flowers. "Can we talk?"

Her throat tightened. She nodded, barely trusting her voice. "Come with me."

Tommy followed her down the hall and into her office. He closed the door before walking around her and settling on the loveseat.

Abby laid the flowers on her desk, her fingers lingering on a petal. Avoiding eye contact, she whispered, "How have you been doing?"

"I've stayed busy." He nodded toward her desk. "You kept my picture."

Should she admit how much she missed him? What if his feelings for her had changed?

"Earlier today I ran into Anna at Walmart."

Abby blinked, stealing a quick glance at Tommy's pinched brow.

"Why didn't you call and tell me you'd gone back to therapy?"

Abby swallowed hard, desperate to unscramble the conflicting thoughts playing havoc with her emotions. "That day when I broke up with you I had no idea if I'd ever walk again. Even though I'm working hard to heal, I still don't know if I'll ever have a normal life."

Tommy scooted to the edge of the cushion. "What's normal is the two of us facing together whatever the future has for us. Loving and supporting each other." He reached for her hand, his knees brushing against hers. "If keeping my picture on your desk means you're still in love with me—"

"During these past weeks...I've missed you more than you can imagine." Her voice trembled. "I love you with all my heart."

Tommy stood, his eyes never leaving hers. Sliding one arm around her shoulders, the other under her knees, he lifted her out of her wheelchair.

Abby leaned into him, her arms wrapped around his neck as he lowered onto the loveseat. Drawing on his strength, she closed her eyes and focused every ounce of energy on sending a message from her brain to her foot. Her eyes popped open. "Oh my gosh." Her cheeks flushed with excitement. "Watch my right foot…"

Tommy leaned forward, peering down.

Abby squeezed her eyes closed, concentrating. Her toes curled upward, lifting her foot. "I'm not imagining what's happening, am I?"

Tommy shook his head. "Your foot lifted."

Abby pressed her face to Tommy's, their tears mingling as they flowed down their cheeks. In that moment every doubt vanished. "One day, I will walk again." Her voice emboldened, her tone laced with confidence.

"Today, the girl who captured my heart has returned."

Chapter 30

Erica turned onto the paved driveway leading to the log cabin-style house on a wooded lot then parked in front of the double car garage on the lower level.

Amanda opened the passenger door and stepped onto the concrete. "Talk about a dramatic contrast between this house and the one in Asheville."

Erica rounded the front of her car. "A total change from my life with Gunter." She led the way to the backyard and up the stairs to the covered deck spanning the full length of the house.

"The perfect place to enjoy the changing scenery. A fireplace on one end to keep you and Brad warm in the winter." Amanda pointed toward the other end of the deck. "And a grill for every season." She ambled to the railing overlooking the wooded backyard sloping down to the railroad tracks.

Erica moved beside her. "There's a deck half this size off the main bedroom."

Amanda pivoted away from the railing. "You're going to love living here."

"Wait until you see the inside." Erica skirted the outdoor sofa left by the previous owners and opened the French doors.

Amanda followed her into the newly renovated great room anchored on one end by a stone fireplace and a kitchen on the other.

Erica nodded toward the smooth wall painted pale beige. "Do you like the color?"

"Perfect choice to accentuate the paneled ceiling." Amanda moseyed to the kitchen. "So are the olive green cabinets."

"Before the three of us moved here, Wendy lived in a high-rise condo on the beach, and Abby and I lived in a sprawling ranch house in the burbs. How would you describe the Louisiana house you and Morgan shared with Gunter?"

"Typical New Orleans style in an upscale neighborhood. Lots of antiques. Some real, most fake like the owner."

"Appropriate. What do you suppose Gary's home is like?"

Amanda ran her finger along the island's granite countertop. "He's a bank president whose adult beverage of choice is beer. Your guess is as good as mine."

Erica ambled over. "Maybe I should invite Gary to join you, Brad, and me for dinner."

"To do what?"

"Become better acquainted? Especially since Awesam's business account is in his bank."

"Slick move, Sherlock."

The doorbell chimed. Erica glanced over her shoulder while heading toward the front door. "You didn't reject my idea."

"Because I know you're fishing."

"With bait but no hook." Erica pulled the door open.

The burly man tilted his head toward the truck parked in the driveway. "Furniture delivery, ma'am."

Erica propped the door open then returned to the kitchen. A half hour later, she thanked the guys and closed the door. She moved in front of the fireplace facing the new tan sectional sofa and wood-framed glass top coffee table centered around a dark red and beige ornately patterned area rug. "What do you think?"

Amanda held up her hand, her forefinger and thumb forming a circle. "Casual, with the perfect touch of elegance."

"The rest of the furniture is scheduled for delivery next week."

"A special home created by a beautiful couple." Amanda eased beside her. "I'm as happy for you and Brad as I was for Wendy and Chris."

Erica looped her arm around Amanda's elbow. "What's the real reason you didn't reject my dinner invitation suggestion?"

"Let's just say if—and that's one giant if—Gary were to invite me to dinner that isn't related to campaign business, I wouldn't turn him down."

Erica snapped her fingers. "Then you do have feelings for him?"

Amanda rolled her eyes. "Now you sound like Millie."

"Speaking of Millie. Since she's on inn duty this afternoon, why don't we head to town so you can help me shop for accessories?"

"You're the decorating expert."

"And you have a good eye for detail. So, what do you say we spend a couple of hours boosting the local economy?"

"On your dime?. Sounds like fun." Amanda linked arms with Erica. "Lead the way, Sherlock."

Abby drove up the ranch house driveway, eased past Sierra's car, and parked beside the truck. With her mom's car nowhere in sight, she pressed Amanda's number. The call went to voicemail. Would coming home an hour earlier than normal leave her stranded? Hoping Sierra's phone was turned on, Abby called her.

She answered after the third ring. "Hey."

"I'm in the carport—"

"I'm on my way."

Releasing a huge breath, Abby popped the trunk.

Sierra rushed out the kitchen door. Moments later she positioned the wheelchair beside the open driver's door.

"I'm glad you're here."

"Me too. I'll unlock the front door." Sierra dashed inside.

Abby lifted her body onto the chair, wheeled out of the carport, then maneuvered across the sidewalk to the front porch. Dusty bounded out, her tail setting her backside in motion. Abby stroked her dog's head. "I'm happy to see you too." She rolled into the foyer.

Sierra stepped aside, her eyes perked up. "I've been wanting to catch you alone, so the two of us can talk privately."

Abby peered up at her, her head tilted. "About work or something personal?"

"Personal." Sierra pushed the door closed then strode to the den and settled on a club chair.

Roused by curiosity, Abby followed, stopping beside Theo in his swing, clutching a ring of toy keys. "What's going on?"

Sierra pulled an envelope from her pocket and handed it to Abby. "This came in the mail today."

Abby eyed the Chattanooga postmark and return address without a name. "From your mother?"

Sierra shook her head. "Read the note."

Abby removed and unfolded the sheet of paper. *"Dear Sierra. It's not much. I'll send more later. Dereck"*

Abby's eyes widened. "Did he send you money?"

Sierra handed Abby a seventy-five-dollar money order. "We've sort of been communicating."

"What do you mean by sort of?"

"Texts. One phone call. Even though Dereck is Theo's father, I doubt your mother and Amanda would approve. Millie definitely wouldn't. Especially since he and his brother showed up here to demand I go back to Chattanooga with them."

"After Millie threatened to have him arrested if he didn't leave you alone. Who reached out first, you or him?"

"He did. Mostly to find out how Theo and I are doing."

"At least that shows he cares." Abby returned the money order. "Are you going to cash the check?"

"Do you think I should?"

"I can't think of a reason why you wouldn't. By the way, in my opinion you should tell Mom and Amanda about the check."

"What about me communicating with Dereck?"

"That's up to you." Abby paused. Sierra had confided in her, so why not do the same? "Tommy showed up at the crisis center today."

"Oh my goodness." Sierra's eyes lit. "You're back together, aren't you?"

"We are." Abby hesitated.

Sierra blinked. "There's more, isn't there?"

Abby nodded. "A couple of weeks ago, I started therapy again. Other than Tommy and my therapist, you're the only person who knows."

"Why haven't you told your mother?"

"I didn't want to give her false hope. Then today, this happened. Watch my right foot."

Sierra leaned forward.

Abby closed her eyes, concentrating on her toes.

"Oh my gosh." Sierra's tone was laced with excitement. "Your toes lifted off the footrest. Now you have to tell your mom."

"I will, as soon as she comes home."

Sierra stood and pulled her ringing phone from her back pocket. "It's my mother. I haven't talked to her since that day she drove here from Chattanooga." She swiped her finger across the screen and activated the speaker. "Is everything okay?"

"What? No hello, or nice of you to call?" Ms. Wellington's tone screamed of sarcasm.

"Sorry." Sierra slumped against the back of the chair. "Hi, Mom."

"That's better. Guess you don't know 'bout cops raiding the Hackett brothers' trailer last night and hauling Jay off to jail. Stupid kid had illegal drugs and a wad of cash in his bedroom."

Sierra's back stiffened, the color draining from her face. "What about Dereck?"

"He wasn't home. Rumor around here is Jay's the one the cops were after, not Dereck. Far as I know, he ain't been arrested."

Sierra swallowed, her shoulders curled forward. "Thank you for letting me know."

Her mother remained silent for a long moment. "I ain't too stubborn to admit you was smart not to bring your baby back here."

Sierra stared at the phone, her jaw slack. "I...um...have a good paying job as an office assistant at the local high school."

Another long moment of silence. "I'm proud you're gonna make something of yourself."

Sierra pressed her palm to her chest, her eyes welling with tears. "Those are the sweetest words you've ever spoken to me, Mom."

"Thank those ladies you're living with for being a good influence on you."

"I will." Sierra dabbed at tears spilling down her cheeks. "I love you, Mom."

"I ain't done much to deserve your love, but I'll work on it. Not enough to get a job, mind you, but enough so you'll let me visit my grandson from time to time. Enough with the mushy stuff. I'll call you when I hear any news about Theo's daddy."

"Thank you." The moment the call ended, a flicker of light crossed Sierra's face, as if the past few minutes had caught her off guard. "If Dereck isn't in jail, and if he turns his life around, maybe one day I'll trust him enough to allow him to visit his son."

Abby's mind drifted to the day she had last come face-to-face with her father in Hilltop Inn's dining room. She'd cringed at his shocked expression the moment he realized of all the towns and hotels in the south, Jennifer, his fiancée had reserved a room in an inn owned by his ex-wife. The next morning Abby and her mother accompanied her to confront Jack Nelson about his abuse. Abby's last image of her father was his back as he stormed out of the dining room after Jennifer refused to leave with him.

Footsteps struck the kitchen floor.

Erica strode into the den, followed by Amanda. "You're home early, sweetheart." Erica set her purse on the dining room table then moved closer. "Is everything okay?"

"Come join me and Sierra." Dismissing the painful memory, Abby wheeled close to the sofa. "We have a lot of news to share with you two."

Chapter 31

After escorting a newly arriving young couple to the Dogwood Suite, Amanda returned to the main floor to wait for the last scheduled check-in. She ambled to the inn's living room window overlooking the front lawn. Inky, the stray black cat that had adopted Hilltop's porch as its domain, sprawled on the railing licking its paw. As much as she disliked felines, most guests seemed to appreciate the inn's self-appointed mascot.

Amanda turned away from the window and moseyed to the bookstand displaying the inn's scrapbook. Her eyes drifted up to the engraved plaque declaring their chef as the first winner of Hilltop Inn's Holiday Dessert Competition. This year the event would be legitimate, with Millie serving as one of the judges instead of inserting herself as the winner.

Responding to the front door chime, Amanda rushed to the foyer and pulled the door open. "Welcome to Hilltop Inn, Mr. and Mrs. Jansen, and happy fortieth anniversary. I'm Amanda, one of the owners."

The woman crossed the threshold, her face beaming. "Your inn came highly recommended by our closest friends who stayed here last spring."

Mr. Jansen carried two suitcases into the foyer. "My beautiful bride has been looking forward to this trip for months."

"We're delighted you've chosen to celebrate with us." Amanda motioned toward the desk. "Please sign our guest book."

While her husband complied, Mrs. Jansen peered into the living room. "Our friends also told us about Hilltop's history—how you transformed this abandoned house into a luxury inn."

Amanda lifted a key off the desk then stepped beside the woman. "A labor of love. About your stay..." After finishing the spiel she had repeated with each new arrival, Amanda led the way through the den and unlocked the door to the Rainbow Suite. "You're staying in the original owner's room." She stepped inside, headed to the French doors leading to the back patio, and pulled back the curtains. "This is Hilltop's best view."

Mrs. Jansen followed her. "What a gorgeous garden and fountain. The gazebo is the perfect touch."

Amanda smiled. "All designed by our chef and dedicated to Eleanor Harrington."

Mr. Jansen slid his arm around his wife's shoulders. "Perfect place for a morning stroll, darling."

A twinge of envy tugged on Amanda's heartstrings as she stepped away from the couple and laid the keys on the nightstand. "Please let us know if there's anything we can do to make your stay perfect." She eased out of the room, closing the door behind her. Had the sensation been triggered by this morning's unexpected phone call?

Amanda returned to the foyer and closed the guest book then headed out to the porch and down the steps to the sidewalk. A gentle breeze rustled leaves as she crossed the side yard to the ranch house carport. She stepped into the kitchen and tossed the inn keys in the bowl on the counter then grabbed a bottle of water from the fridge. After breathing deeply and slowly releasing the air, Amanda walked into the den. "The new arrivals are all checked in."

Erica tapped her keyboard. "Mrs. Jenson scheduled a massage for eleven tomorrow morning."

"Good for her." Amanda sat across the dining room table from Awesam's CEO. "Are you still floating on a cloud over Abby's news?"

Erica's eyes held the soft glow of prayers answered. "One day, not too far in the future, my daughter will walk again."

"Without a doubt." Amanda uncapped her water and took a drink. *Time to stop stalling.* "Gary's picking me up in thirty minutes."

"Another campaign-planning meeting?"

"Not exactly."

"Oh my gosh." Erica pressed her palms together. "You two are going on a date."

"Don't go jumping to conclusions—"

"Unless Gary discusses Awesam's bank account, tonight will definitely qualify as a date."

"Whatever dinner turns into, don't breathe a word to Millie."

Erica zipped her fingers across her lips. "Not a peep...especially if you promise to give me the details after he brings you home."

Amanda tilted her head. "Are you stooping to blackmail?"

"More like a little encouragement. Are you going to change into a sexy outfit?"

"And come across as a blooming idiot if it's not a date? Not a chance." Amanda pushed away from the table then headed straight to her room. After peeling out of her jeans, she opened her closet door. What would she wear if she knew for certain that tonight was a date? Slacks and a jacket? Skirt and a sweater? Maybe something a little more appealing. She pulled out a teal sheath. Good color for a redhead.

Amanda slipped into the dress that accentuated her curves. She stood in front of her mirror, smiling. *Not bad for a forty-five year old.* After choosing gold earrings, she stared at her favorite perfume. Should she or shouldn't she? "Stop hedging already." She spritzed then returned to the den and turned in a slow circle. "What do you think?"

"With that outfit, if tonight doesn't start out as a date, it will definitely end up as one." Erica lifted her phone off the table. "Abby's home." She rushed out to the carport, returning through the front door.

Abby followed her mother into the den. "Wow, Amanda, great outfit." She wheeled closer. "Have you called Morgan?"

"To tell her what? That I'm going to dinner with Keith's campaign finance manager?"

Abby giggled. "When Gary sees you in that dress, he'll be hooked."

Erica peered out the office window. "The fish you're minutes from reeling in has arrived."

"If you don't mind—" Amanda crossed her arms. "I prefer to answer the door without you two lurking in the background like a couple of ogling teenagers."

"Not to worry, Abby and I will be discreet." Moments after Erica followed her daughter to the den, the doorbell chimed.

Her palms dampening, Amanda summoned her best smile and opened the door. "Hi."

Gary, wearing a sports jacket and open-collar shirt grinned. "Wow. You look incredible."

Sensing her cheeks were seconds from turning a bright shade of pink, Amanda cleared her throat. "So do you."

He held out his arm, his expression making it clear tonight had nothing to do with Keith's campaign.

Amanda stepped onto the porch, pulled the door closed, and looped her hand around his bicep. "Where are we going?"

"To one of my favorite restaurants."

Half past eleven, Amanda stepped into the foyer and quietly closed the door, leaning against it for a heartbeat if only to hold onto the night a moment longer.

She'd barely taken a step when Erica rushed in from the den.

"You're still awake?"

Erica studied Amanda's face. "Based on your expression, it's clear tonight began and ended as an official first date."

Amanda gave a slow nod. Her lips tugged into a soft smile. "You're right."

With a grin, Erica looped her hand around Amanda's elbow and steered her toward the den. "I have to hear every detail."

Amanda settled on the sofa beside her, kicked off her shoes, and propped her feet on the coffee table. "The evening began at the restaurant's bar."

"Let me guess. A beer for Gary and wine for you?"

Amanda nodded, her smile widening. "During dinner we talked...really talked and laughed. After sharing a dessert, we strolled to the park. Gary wrapped his jacket around my shoulders."

Erica faced Amanda with her arm stretched across the back of the sofa. "He held your hand, didn't he?"

Amanda leaned her head back, her eyes fluttering closed for a moment as the memory washed over her. "My hand felt warm and safe in his, as if we'd known each other for years." Her voice softened. "When he walked me to the door a few minutes ago, his kiss was gentle and sweet."

"Gary obviously adores you."

Amanda held up her ringless left hand, her fingers splayed. "Tonight I realized that in her own convoluted way, Millie was right. I don't want to spend the rest of my life going to bed alone."

"Nor should you. Now for the number-one question. Is Gary the one?"

Amanda closed her eyes, summoning heart-warming memories of Preston. Waking up beside the love of her life in their New Orleans shotgun house. Holding hands while they strolled along the Mississippi River. Would she ever love another man as much as she had loved him? The image dissolved, and a new picture formed. Amanda opened her eyes. "Gary's a good man, with a good heart...and I enjoy his company."

Erica leaned closer. She touched Amanda's shoulder. "You're comparing him to your first love, aren't you?"

"Time will tell if tonight was the beginning of a serious relationship." Amanda's voice was barely above a whisper. "Or simply two single people enjoying each other's company."

"I understand. Especially since it took me a long time to admit I'd fallen in love with Brad." Erica yawned. "Now that I'm all caught up, I'm ready for a good night's rest." She stood and circled the coffee table. "Sleep well."

"You too." Amanda remained in the den well past midnight summoning memories of her life with Preston, until the twenty six days he had disappeared resurfaced. Had she been too afraid to hear the truth to ask where he'd gone? And why after all these years, with no chance of ever learning what happened, had the question popped up?

Amanda awakened to sunlight peeking around the edges of the blinds. She glanced at her bedside clock. Nine-ten. How could she have slept so late? She swung her legs to the floor. Because too many memories had kept her awake until the wee hours, that's how. If she had thought to set her alarm, she'd have more than twenty minutes to shower and dress. Amanda rushed to the kitchen, prepared her morning caffeine fix, then headed straight to the bathroom. Showing up late for her scheduled meeting with Millie would raise all sorts of suspicions.

With less than a minute to spare, Amanda squared her shoulders and strode into Hilltop Inn's kitchen. "Good morning." Had her sing-song tone come across a bit too jovial?

Millie spun away from the counter, her brow wrinkled. "What has you in such a good mood? Did something happen between you and Gary?"

Definitely too cheerful. "A better question. Why are *you* so cranky?"

Bernie turned away from the sink, drying her hands with a paper towel. "Because the inevitable finally happened. One of our guests complained about Millie's quiche."

"That man's a cantankerous old goat." Millie scoffed. "I should know; I was married to one."

"Let me guess." Amanda climbed onto a stool. "You retaliated by serving our guest a healthy dose of bran?"

"Actually." Bernie edged closer to Millie. "She kept her cool and scrambled him some eggs."

"No kidding?" Amanda chuckled. "What happened to the chef we've all learned to tolerate?"

Millie waggled her finger at Amanda. "Why did you ignore my question about you and Gary?"

She couldn't possibly know about last night, could she? "What makes you think anything has changed between me and Keith's campaign finance manager?"

"Your hair's wet, which means you just showered. Which also means you slept late this morning because you were up late last night."

Amanda gawked at Millie, then burst out laughing. "You're taking your role as the leader of a mystery club way too seriously, don't you think?"

"You can't show up all cheery and expect Awesam's chief information officer not to be at least a little suspicious."

"Has it occurred to you that I'm excited about planning a wedding shower for Erica?"

"Hmph."

Bernie shook her head. "Now that everything's back to normal, what do you say we get on with our meeting?"

"Great idea, Bernie." Amanda tapped her finger to her chin. "I'm thinking a linen and lingerie shower."

"A Sunday brunch in Hilltop's dining room." Millie skirted the island, settling on a stool beside Amanda. "Catered by me."

"Good idea." Eager to keep the conversation from drifting back to Gary, Amanda faced Millie. "Should we or shouldn't we surprise Erica?"

"A surprise party is a lot more fun. Now, about the menu..."

An hour after she'd walked into Hilltop's kitchen, Amanda returned to the ranch house, pleased she'd prevented Millie from asking any more questions she had no intention of answering.

Chapter 32

Showered and dressed before dawn, Amanda pulled a blue sweatshirt jacket from a dresser drawer then headed to the kitchen. "Good morning."

"Hi." Sierra closed the fridge and turned to her, Theo balanced on her hip gripping a sippy cup. "Do you have breakfast duty?"

Amanda nodded. "Bernie's day off. How's your job going?"

"Really good. Back when I found out I was pregnant and became a dropout, I never imagined that one day I'd end up working in a high school."

"Life is full of unexpected twists and turns. Three years ago I had no idea I'd ever leave New Orleans."

"Do you miss living there?"

"I did. Until I returned for Morgan's wedding and discovered the little shotgun house her father and I called home had been demolished."

"By a hurricane?"

Amanda shook her head while slipping into her jacket. "A developer had razed every house on a square block to build condos. So-called progress destroyed our home but not my memories. Anyway, time to help Millie serve Hilltop's guests before I head off to this afternoon's campaign-planning meeting."

"I'll leave as soon as I pack Theo's diaper bag."

"Have a wonderful day." Amanda grabbed a key from the bowl then exited to the carport. Cold air nipped her cheeks as she closed the distance to Hilltop's front porch. After unlocking the door and stepping inside, she followed the aroma of freshly brewed coffee through the living room and dining room to the kitchen. "Good morning. In addition to cinnamon buns, what's on today's menu?"

Millie cracked an egg into a bowl. "Sausage and mushroom frittata, hashbrowns."

"Sounds delish."

Millie added two more eggs. "What else would you expect from an award-winning chef?"

"I don't know. Maybe a little humility?"

"Big waste of time, if you ask me."

Amanda poured a cup of coffee, stirring in creamer and sweetener. Time to throw Hilltop's chef a giant curveball. "Know what I think?"

"I don't have a clue." Millie grabbed a whisk. "Although I'm sure you're dying to tell me."

"Despite your grumbling, you're an incredibly talented woman with a kind heart."

Millie shot Amanda an incredulous look. "What are you up to?"

Mission accomplished. "Are you averse to all compliments, or only those from me?"

"What's come over you since the last time you filled in for Bernie?"

"Nothing." Amanda's eyes remained trained on Millie as she took a sip of coffee. "I just want to play nice for a change."

"Well, thank you for the nice words." Millie aimed her spatula at Amanda. "I still believe you're up to something."

Amanda set her cup on the island. "You can't help yourself, can you?"

"Hmph."

Tickled by Millie's response, Amanda hummed while carrying plates to the dining room. After setting the table, she settled into the morning routine until the first guests arrived. By nine o'clock she and Millie had greeted and served ten guests.

Ten minutes after nine, a middle-aged couple ambled in. "Good morning, everyone."

Amid the chatter, Amanda placed coffee cups on the table in front of the newcomers. Why did they look familiar?

The woman peered up at Amanda, smiling. "We saw you and that good-looking man in the restaurant last night. Is he your husband?"

Amanda forced a tight smile, her eyes flicking toward the open kitchen door. "He's a business partner and a close friend. I hope you enjoyed your dinner."

"We did, most likely as much as you and your friend seemed to enjoy your meal and each other."

Hoping Millie hadn't heard the exchange, Amanda stepped away from the table and headed toward the kitchen.

Millie brushed past her. After serving the new arrivals their breakfast, Millie returned to the kitchen, closing the door behind her as if sealing off a crime scene. "Now everything makes sense." She moved closer. "You and Gary were on a date last night, weren't you?"

Amanda turned away to refill her coffee cup. Should she trust Millie and admit the truth or fake a coffee spill and split?

"You don't have to respond; your silence gives you away." Millie eased beside her. "Everyone knew he'd eventually ask you out."

No way Millie would believe an outright denial. Avoiding eye contact, Amanda shrugged. "Gary and I simply enjoyed a meal—"

"Aha." Millie snapped her fingers. "He kissed you, didn't he?"

Amanda gawked at Millie. "Talk about jumping to conclusions—"

"You can't fool me. I see that little twinkle in your eyes."

Amanda scoffed. "It was a first date, detective."

"That much I already know. Next question, when's your second date?"

Amanda tilted her head, a brow raised. "What makes you think there's a second?

"You're a beautiful, successful woman, and Gary Redding's a red-blooded American man. Why wouldn't he ask you out again?"

Amanda released a long sigh. "You're not going to stop hounding me, are you, detective?"

"That's how crackerjack gum shoes operate." Millie folded her arms, a triumphant sparkle in her eyes. "We prod until the truth spills out faster than lemonade pouring from an overturned pitcher."

"All right, Officer Cunningham, I'll spill, but only if you agree to give me the real scoop about you and Gordon."

"Managing a political campaign has turned you into a tough negotiator."

"Doggone right." Amanda mirrored Millie's stance. "Do we or don't we have a deal?"

"You go first."

Amanda aimed her palm at Millie. "Not until you answer my question."

"Yes." Millie tapped her foot. "We have a deal."

"All right then." Amanda rounded the island and climbed onto a stool. "Gary and I are going to the Swan drive-in Saturday night. Your turn."

Millie unfolded her arms. "A couple of days after our ride to Mc-Caysville, Gordon and I watched a movie at the Swan."

"No kidding?" A sly grin tugged at Amanda's lips. "You know what this means, don't you?"

"Our competition has turned into a dramatic double feature, without the popcorn." Millie's head tilted left. "How many people know about last night?"

"As far as I know, other than you and everyone in Hilltop's dining room, just Erica and Abby. What about your drive-in date?"

"You, Bernie, the guy at the ticket booth and the cute young carhop who brought us food. Although she doesn't count because she had no idea who either one of us were." Millie plated a slice of frittata and pushed it across the island.

Amanda picked up a fork. "Is this my reward?"

"It's a new recipe."

Amanda tasted. "Deliciously boast worthy."

Millie reached across her chest and tapped her own shoulder. "Another well-deserved compliment from Awesam's president."

"One fact is undeniable. No one could ever accuse you of suffering from a lack of self-confidence."

Millie hesitated, as if suddenly at a loss for words. She broke eye contact. Her chin dipped. "I owe a lot to you, Erica, and Wendy for trusting me enough to be part of Awesam's team."

"You know you're more than a team member, Millie." Amanda climbed off her stool, walked around the island, and slid her arm around her shoulders. "You're family."

"Careful, or you might make me tear up. Although—" Millie patted Amanda's hand. "An emotional response would add to my naturally charming personality."

Amanda burst out laughing. "You're a trip, Chef Millie." She pulled her arm away and grabbed the coffeepot. "What do you say we check on our guests."

"I'm right behind you."

Hours after finishing her Hilltop Inn duty, Amanda parked on Keith and Linda Armstrong's driveway behind Gary's car. She lifted her laptop off the passenger seat, climbed out, and made her way to the front porch. How long ago had Gary showed up? A few minutes? Half an hour? If he'd mentioned their dinner date, she'd know the second Linda answered the door. If he hadn't, should she mention it? Amanda hesitated a moment longer then pressed the doorbell.

The door opened. "Glad you're here. The guys are downstairs."

Amanda stepped inside, probing Linda's expression. "Playing pool?"

"Talking football. The number-one topic every autumn."

Gary obviously hadn't breathed a word, at least not yet. Amanda's pulse accelerated while she followed Linda down to the terrace level. Always the gentleman, Gary, sitting across the pedestal table from Keith, stood the moment Amanda walked into the room. He smiled. Their eyes met and lingered, releasing a deliciously warm sensation. Amanda blinked. Had their hosts noticed?

Linda moved behind Keith, placing her hands on his shoulders. "Seems our talented campaign managers are especially delighted to see each other."

Gary winked at Amanda, sending heat creeping from her neck to her cheeks.

"Oh my gosh." Linda's eyes widened. "You two have been on a date, haven't you?"

"What do you think?" Gary pulled a chair out for Amanda. "Should we give Linda an update on her matchmaking efforts or keep her guessing?"

Amanda's brows shot up. Her question of whether or not Gary had known about the ploy was answered. "Well now." She lowered onto the chair and set her laptop on the table. "Considering that Millie and every Hilltop guest knows, we might as well confess."

Linda sat across from Amanda, grinning. "It took you two a long time to realize you're a good match."

Keith faced Gary, chuckling. "All this time I thought my wife wanted you on our team strictly for your financial expertise."

Linda leaned close to her husband, patting his arm. "The fact that Gary's a handsome, charming bachelor made him the perfect candidate for both roles, darling."

Amanda laced her fingers on the table. At the moment she couldn't agree more.

Chapter 33

Erica carried four water bottles from the kitchen to the dining room table. "I still don't know how to interpret Sierra's decision to communicate with Dereck."

Amanda pulled out a chair. "Good news is he lives two hours away, and his brother convinced the police he had nothing to do with the drugs they found in their trailer."

Erica settled across from Amanda. "Unless Jay's covering for him."

"Based on what I observed about the way Jay dominated when they were here, I believe Dereck's a victim, not an accomplice."

"For Sierra's sake, I hope you're right. Speaking of victims, Abby called earlier. Gladys Zander has invited Crystal to live with her until she's able to support herself on her own."

Amanda folded her arms on the table. "This little town is full of good people."

Millie breezed in from the carport, empty-handed.

Erica peered up at her. "This is the first time you haven't brought sweets to our meeting."

"I've been too busy preparing for tonight's big event to bake cookies. By the way—" Millie settled between them. "Bernie's unavailable, which means I'll need you both to help me serve."

Erica uncapped a water bottle. "What time?"

"Meet me in Hilltop's dining room at five o'clock."

Wendy ambled in without Ryan and laid a sheet of paper on the table. She pressed her fingers to her lower back before easing onto a chair. "Chris dropped me off. He'll pick me up after I welcome today's guests."

Erica leaned toward Wendy. "Are you sure you're up to check-in duty?"

"Positive. Today's the last time I'll be able to share those responsibilities for a while. Besides, Millie volunteered to help with the upstairs check-ins." Wendy eyed Millie. "By the way, I know all about your date with Gordon, and Amanda's date with Gary, so we can get down to business before my little gal sends me scurrying to the bathroom." Wendy tapped the spreadsheet she'd brought. "Starting with a financial update." Twenty minutes after arriving, she scurried to the hall.

Amanda leaned back. "I'd forgotten what those final days of pregnancy were like, not being able to sleep through the night without multiple trips to the bathroom."

"When you reach my age. you'll need to keep a night light on to find your way to the bathroom in the wee hours of the morning." Millie giggled. "No pun intended."

Amanda aimed her water bottle at her. "Good one, Millie."

Wendy returned, her hands stretched underneath her baby bulge. "I'm more than ready to welcome Ryan's little sister into this world, so I can stop waddling around like an overfed duck."

Amanda turned toward Wendy. "What's the latest about your due date?"

"According to Allison, next week is spot on." Wendy lowered onto the chair. "It's convenient having an ob/gyn in the family. Especially since she's Chris's sister."

Determined to keep the meeting on task, Erica glanced at her watch. "Our first guests are likely to arrive any time now. Which means we need to move on to the next agenda item. Our second annual Holiday Dessert Competition."

Ten minutes into the discussion. Wendy grabbed the ringing phone off the table. "Hilltop Inn. May I help you?" She listened, then nodded. "We'll meet you on the front porch in two minutes."

Millie stood and pulled a key from her pocket. "I assume it's time for us to head next door."

Wendy nodded. "Our first guests have arrived."

After pocketing her phone, Wendy gripped the edge of the table and pushed off her chair. She followed Millie through the kitchen and out the back door then retrieved the gift bag she'd stashed in the back of the truck. "As far as I can tell, Erica doesn't have a clue about tonight's surprise party."

"This is one event we've all managed to keep under wraps."

"Unlike your motorcycle ride with Gordon?"

Millie scoffed. "It's a three-wheeled Polaris without doors, and yes."

"I think it's cool how you two are proving it's never too late for a little romance."

"At our ages, a little is all we need."

"Are you kidding? You're the hottest senior citizen I've ever met." Wendy nudged Millie's arm. "By the way, how old are you?"

"Let's just say I'm not that far from entering my ninth decade."

"You're pushing eighty?

"Getting closer every day."

"Impressive." Wendy gripped the handrail while climbing onto the porch, smiling at the new arrivals. "Welcome to Hilltop Inn. I'm Wendy, one of the owners, and this is Millie, our award-winning chef and business partner. We're delighted you've chosen to stay with us."

Millie's chest puffed as she unlocked the front door, then stood aside while the couple carried their bags into the foyer. "Please sign our guest book."

Leaving their chef to handle check-in duties, Wendy ambled into the living room. She set the gift bag on the coffee table before easing onto the sofa facing the fireplace. Her eyes closed as memories bubbled up of her surprise combination wedding and baby shower hosted by Keith, Linda, and Susan Armstrong. A kick popped her eyes open and sent her hand to her belly. "Good one, Cindy," she whispered. "Your grandmother would be proud."

Bernie ambled in from the dining room. "Does Erica have any inkling about the shower?"

"Not that I could tell."

She sat beside Wendy. "Are you giving her lingerie or linens?"

"Both. A frilly teddy and fancy hand towels for her powder room. What about you?"

"Bath towels. Wait until you see what Millie's giving her."

"Something practical?"

"Hardly." Bernie leaned close. "A sexy nightie that would make a lady of the evening blush."

Wendy laughed. "You've gotta love Millie's sense of mischief."

"One fact is undeniable. There's never a dull moment around her."

Five minutes before five, Erica lifted off the den sofa and headed to the office. "Are you ready to report for duty?"

Amanda pushed her chair away from the desk. "As ready as I'll ever be to take orders from Hilltop's cantankerous chef."

"She's always on her best behavior around guests."

"Unless one of them does something to arouse her suspicion."

"That hasn't happened in a while." Erica led the way to the kitchen. She grabbed the inn's key then stepped out to the carport. "Do you have any idea what sort of party we're serving?"

Amanda shrugged. "Millie said something about a ladies night out."

"With or without libation?"

"She didn't say."

Erica breathed in the cool evening air as they made their way across the side yard, along the inn's front sidewalk to the porch, then into the foyer. "Why do you suppose Millie wants us to meet her in the dining room instead of the kitchen?"

"Your guess is as good as mine." Amanda led the way through the living room. She paused in front of the dining room's double pocket doors. "Are you ready?"

Erica moved beside her. "For what?"

Amanda gripped the pulls, easing the doors apart. Voices shouting 'surprise' disrupted the silence as ten ladies applauded and cheered. Amanda leaned close. "Welcome to your special evening."

Erica's heart raced as she pressed her palm to her chest and scanned ten pairs of eyes focused on her. Linda, Susan, Eileen, and Allison smiled from one end of the table, Abby and Sierra from the other. Millie, Bernie, and Wendy stood in front of the sideboard. Erica's eyes drifted to gifts spread across the table. "No one has ever given me a shower."

Lauren moved to her side. "When a woman is weeks from marrying her soulmate, she deserves a party."

Abby wheeled beside Erica, lifting her hand. "We couldn't be happier for you and Brad, Mom."

Erica laced her fingers with her daughter's. "I'm blessed beyond words to have a beautiful family and close friends."

Millie stepped aside revealing flutes filled with Champagne lined up on the sideboard. "Time to toast the next bride to exchange vows in Hilltop's gazebo, and if all goes well, not the last." She distributed the glasses, then raised hers. "We all wish you and Brad a lifetime of happiness."

After Amanda and Lauren clinked their flutes to hers, Erica released Abby's hand then sipped the effervescent wine, reveling in the moment. Two years ago she could have never imagined her heart dancing with so much joy.

Chapter 34

Six days after Erica's surprise shower, Wendy winced while pressing her phone's stopwatch, counting the seconds. The contraction stopped. She recorded the time and duration on a pad of paper. "Fifty seconds, five minutes after the last one. Based on Allison's instructions, we need to go to the hospital if I have six more during the next thirty minutes."

Chris settled beside her. "Mom's on her way over."

Wendy handed Chris the phone. "You time the next one." She leaned back. "Donna called this morning,"

"Anything new going on with your stepmother?"

"She started working part-time in a friend's bookstore to stay busy and keep her mind off the lawsuit. I still can't believe my father is suing his only daughter and his wife. Especially since his infidelity is the reason their marriage is toast."

"Some men refuse to admit their failures."

Wendy nodded. "Appropriate description of Gunter."

"That name hasn't come up in a while."

"The word failure combined with my pain brought the con man to mind."

Duke padded over and plopped his head on the cushion beside Wendy. She patted his head. "Are you my comfort animal?" His tail slapped the floor. "I'll take your tail wag as a yes." Wendy winced. "Here comes another one."

Chris tapped her phone.

She straightened her back and closed her eyes, focusing on deep, rhythmic breathing to control the pain. When the contraction stopped, she nudged Chris. "How long?"

"Sixty-one seconds." Chris added to the list. "Five minutes since the last one."

"Two more, and I'll definitely be in labor."

Chris gently grasped Wendy's hand. "When's the last time I told you how much I love you, angel?"

"An hour ago when you raced home." Wendy turned toward him. "I can't wait for our little gal to meet her daddy."

His eyes met hers. "The day I met you was the second luckiest day in my life."

Wendy tilted her head. "What was the first?"

"The night I proposed on that balcony overlooking the Atlantic, and you said yes."

Wendy smiled. "What would you have thought if years ago someone had told you that one day you'd propose to a seven-month pregnant woman after only knowing her for five months?"

He chuckled. "That they'd had one too many drinks or smoked too many funny cigarettes."

"When I was a little girl, after Mom left me, I dreamed of growing up, marrying a handsome prince, and living in a castle. Even better, I married a handsome, brilliant lawyer and live in a home filled with love."

Chris lifted Wendy's hand to his lips and kissed her fingertips. Wendy closed her eyes, smiling, until the next contraction began four minutes after the last. Seconds after it ended, the doorbell chimed, sending Duke racing to the front door.

"I hope that's Linda because it's time to go to the hospital."

Chris scrambled to open the door. "Perfect timing."

Fifteen minutes and three contractions after Linda arrived, Allison met Wendy and Chris at the hospital entrance. "Seems the newest Armstrong member is eager to meet her family." She helped lower Wendy into a wheelchair.

"Our little gal isn't as eager as her mother is for an epidural."

"One epidural coming up."

An hour and ten minutes after Allison steered Wendy into a birthing room, she laid the newborn on her mother's chest. "Meet your beautiful daughter."

"She's perfect." Chris wiped Wendy's damp forehead with a cloth. "Just like her mother."

Wendy stroked her infant's cheek, her smile bursting forth uncontrollably. "Welcome to our family, sweet Cindy Marie. It's time to meet your maternal grandmother."

Allison covered the infant with a warm blanket while Chris pulled his phone from his pocket, tapped a number, then pressed FaceTime. The moment Cynthia's face appeared, he aimed the phone toward Wendy and the child they had created. "Meet your granddaughter."

"She's beautiful." Cynthia's face appeared drawn, the circles under her eyes darker than yesterday. Her voice was barely above a whisper. "I can't wait to hold her in my arms."

Struggling to keep tears at bay, Wendy understood that her mother was fading fast. "We'll bring her to Nashville soon."

"I'll hold on until then."

When the call ended, Allison lifted her niece into her brother's arms before cradling Wendy's hand in hers. "Pediatricians don't recommend an infant travels for at least two months."

"I doubt my mother has three weeks, much less two months." Wendy's voice faltered. "I promised I'd take a picture of her holding her granddaughter in her arms."

Nurse Polly moved beside Allison, her eyes filled with compassion. "Where is your mother, and is she still living in her home?"

"Nashville, and yes. After eighteen years apart, Mom and I have reestablished a relationship. If cancer takes her from me before..." The tears Wendy had held back broke free. "I can't bear the thought of breaking my promise."

"One thing I've learned as a neonatal nurse is sometimes exceptions are called for." Polly squeezed Wendy's hand. "If your baby is thriving after two weeks, and if no one else in your mother's home is ill, God will send his angels to provide the protection she needs to make the trip."

"Thank you." While Allison and Polly turned their attention to post-birth tasks, peace flowed over Wendy like warm sunshine spilling through clouds after a storm. In that moment she understood beyond the shadow of a doubt that her mother would live long enough to cradle her namesake in her arms.

Chris dabbed Wendy's forehead with a cool cloth, his eyes welling. "I love you more than words can possibly express."

She pressed her palm to his cheek. "My heart is so filled with love for you and our babies it might burst."

Thirty-six hours after welcoming their daughter into the world, Wendy peered out the passenger window as Chris drove up their driveway and eased past Erica's and Linda's cars.

"Your welcome-home committee has arrived."

Wendy smiled. "It's time for our little gal to meet more of our amazing family."

After parking in the garage, Chris helped Wendy step from the passenger side then released the baby carrier from the rear seat. Thrilled to be home, she followed him as he carried their daughter and her duffle into the kitchen.

Erica hovered close, followed by Amanda and Millie. "We can't wait to welcome the newest member of our little family."

Chris set the duffle and carrier on the counter. Wendy peeled the blanket away from their sleeping daughter. "Meet Cindy Marie Armstrong."

Amanda slid her arm around Wendy's shoulders. "She's beautiful, just like her mother."

Erica pressed her hand to her chest. "There's nothing more precious than a new life."

Millie leaned close. "Well done, Wendy and Chris."

Linda lifted Ryan off the floor and placed him in Chris's arms. Wendy released their daughter from the carrier and held her close to her big brother. "Meet your little sister, baby Cindy."

Ryan fingered the pink blanket. "Baby."

Linda snapped a photo with her phone, capturing the moment. "Our family has been blessed with three beautiful grandchildren, until Allison and Mark decide to have a second child."

Chris chuckled. "Given my sister's competitive nature as well her excitement when she delivered her niece, I doubt you'll have to wait too long."

"Speaking of sisters." Wendy pulled her ringing phone from the duffle and tapped the screen. She pressed the phone to her ear while walking toward her bedroom. "Hey, Kayla. How's Mom?"

"Not so good." Kayla's voice came in a hoarse whisper. "Dad's barely hanging on. Zach hardly says a word to any of us."

"How are you doing?"

"I've gotta stay strong for everyone."

Wendy sat on the edge of the bed, her heart heavy. A fifteen-year-old should be laughing with friends, not bearing the burden of keeping her family from falling apart.

"If you don't come soon..." Kayla's voice faded away.

"We'll drive over twelve days from now." Wendy closed her eyes, sending up a silent prayer that she hadn't made a commitment she couldn't keep.

Chapter 35

Six hours after Nurse Polly examined two-week-old Cindy Marie, Chris turned onto the Gilmores' driveway. Wendy's heart rose and fell in rapid bursts. Would her mother have enough strength to hold her granddaughter in her arms?

Chris leaned across the console and touched her hand. "Do you need a few minutes?"

Wendy shook her head. "I've had the last four hours to prepare. A few more minutes won't make any difference." She nodded toward Riley rushing out the front door and dashing across the lawn. "Besides, a member of our welcoming committee is on her way over."

"So I see." Seconds after Chris climbed out, Riley circled to the driver's side and peered up at him. "I wanna walk my nephew inside."

Chris patted her head. "Ryan's eager to spend time with you."

"Can he say Aunt Riley?"

"Not yet." Chris opened the rear door then released his son from the car seat.

Riley gave Ryan a hug before gripping his hand and leading him toward the front door.

Wendy stepped onto the pavement, grateful for the cloudless sky and autumn sunshine warming her cheeks. She turned toward Chris rounding the SUV. He opened the back door then lifted the baby carrier off the seat.

Wendy's heart warmed as she tucked the blanket around their sleeping infant. "Are you ready to meet Glamma Cynthia?"

Chris chuckled. "Your mother picked the strangest grandmother name."

"Linda had already claimed Grandma, and Millie Grammy." Wendy fingered one of the four matching bracelets Cynthia had bought during her visit to Blue Ridge. If only her mother had chosen a name easy enough for a toddler to say.

"Are you ready to go inside?"

Wendy breathed deeply, willing the flood of emotion to pass. "I am now." She clung to Chris's arm while they made their way to the front porch.

Kayla, wearing the matching bracelet, held the front door open. After embracing Wendy, she peeked into the carrier. "Riley and Ryan are in the den. Carol, Mom's hospice nurse, helped her get ready before she left. She'll come back after supper." Kayla nodded toward the living room. "Mom's waiting for you."

Summoning a brave smile, Wendy followed her sister into the room. "Hi, Mom."

Cynthia, wearing makeup and a white yoga suit that hung loosely on her thin frame, peered up from the sofa. A pink streak highlighted her blonde hair. She slowly lifted her arm encircled with the matching bracelet. "I'm glad you're here."

Kayla dropped onto a chair while Wendy settled beside her mother, grasping her frail hand. "Are you ready to meet your granddaughter?"

"More than ready." Her voice, though weak, shimmered with delight.

After lowering the baby carrier onto the piano bench, Chris lifted his daughter and placed her in his mother-in-law's arms. "Meet your granddaughter."

A smile curled Cynthia's lips. "She's the perfect image of her beautiful mother." Her granddaughter opened her eyes. "Hello, sweet Cindy Marie, I'm Glamma Cynthia."

"Perfect time for a picture." Chris removed his phone from his belt clip and took a series of photos.

Cynthia stroked her granddaughter's tiny fingers. "In the future when you look at a picture of us, you'll know your Glamma is watching over you from heaven."

Struggling to fight off tears, Wendy caught her lower lip between her teeth.

Chris cleared his throat. "How about a picture of three generations?"

Wendy released her lip while scooting closer to her mother. She looked up at Chris.

He smiled. "Beautiful." He aimed his phone then tapped the screen. "Now one with you, Kayla."

She moved beside Wendy. "We need to take lots of pictures before you leave."

Wendy patted her knee. "Dozens and dozens."

Cindy Marie's face scrunched seconds before she emitted a cry, her chin wobbling.

"I believe all this picture taking has made my grandbaby hungry."

"So it seems." Wendy lifted her child from her mother's arms.

Chris stepped closer to the sofa. "How about I take pictures of you, Ryan and Riley, to give your mother and Wendy time to visit?"

Kayla leaned forward, her face turned toward her mother.

Cynthia nodded. "Go ahead, sweetheart. I'll be fine."

"You sure?"

"Positive."

Wendy nudged Kayla's arm. "We'll call if we need you."

Kayla hesitated before following Chris to the foyer and around the corner.

Relishing the opportunity to share an intimate moment with her mother, Wendy unbuttoned her blouse then positioned her baby for her afternoon nourishment.

Forty minutes after Chris and Kayla walked out of the living room, Wendy carried her sleeping infant into the den. "Mom drifted off to sleep a few minutes ago."

Kayla looked up from the sofa. "She can barely stay awake longer than an hour."

"Daddy says Mom's getting ready to go to heaven." Riley lifted off the floor then snuggled beside Kayla. "He also says she won't be sick anymore."

A door opened, followed by a pair of footsteps and the succulent aromas of tomato, cheese, and sausage wafting from the kitchen.

"Yay. Daddy and Zach brought us pizza." Riley rushed into the kitchen. "Mom's asleep in the living room." She clutched her father's and her brother's hands. "Come see Ryan's baby sister."

Chris stood, greeting Brent when Riley led the guys into the den. "It's good to see you both."

Zach pulled his hand away from his sister's, his eyes focused on Chris. "You been playing that video game I taught you?"

Chris shook his head. "Helping Wendy care for a toddler and a newborn, I haven't had much time. However, if you're willing, I'm up to a challenge while we're here."

Zach shrugged. "Whatever."

Riley pulled Brent close to the sofa. He hiked his hip on the sofa arm beside Wendy. His shoulders slumped. Circles darkened the skin under his eyes. "Thank you for making the trip. Meeting her granddaughter means more to Cynthia than you can imagine."

Wendy pressed her palm to her chest. "Before she fell asleep, Mom shared some stories about our first five years together. Stories I'll one day share with her grandchildren."

"During the past few weeks, when she's had the energy, she talked about our life together." Brent's tone was tight. "I think she's storing up memories."

Wendy touched Brent's arm. "We all are."

He swallowed. Hard. "Let's eat before the pizzas turn cold."

Riley's eyes widened. "Do you want me to wake Mom up?"

Brent shook his head. "She'll wake up when she's ready. We'll eat in here so we won't disturb her."

Kayla grasped her sister's hand, leading her toward the kitchen. "Let's go help Dad."

Chris scooped Ryan into his arms while Wendy carried their baby out of the den. She paused in the foyer, peering into the living room. Cynthia remained stretched out on the sofa, her eyes closed, her breathing steady. Careful not to wake her, Wendy tiptoed into the room. She placed Cindy Marie in her carrier then carried her back to the den.

An hour and a half after the family began eating picnic-style, Cynthia shuffled into the den. Brent rushed to assist her. Riley followed her dad and held her mother's hand. Chris and Kayla lifted off the sofa to make room for her. Zach sat cross-legged on the floor playing a video game on his phone.

A wistful smile softened Cynthia's features as Brent helped her settle on the sofa beside Wendy. As if nudged by angels, Ryan toddled over and climbed onto her lap. She stroked his cheek. "Always remember how much Glamma loves you."

Her grandson fingered the pink streak in her hair. "Glamma."

Tears flowed down his grandmother's cheeks. "Thank you, sweet boy—" she whispered. "For giving me a precious gift."

Reveling in Cynthia's sudden burst of energy, the family gathered around her, laughing and sharing stories. With Chris's nudging, Zach set his phone aside and joined in the conversation. By nine o'clock, Ryan had fallen asleep curled up on the floor beside a stuffed dog, and Cynthia's energy had given out.

Brent pulled Chris aside. Moments later they walked out of the den followed by Zach.

Cynthia grasped Wendy's hand. "Today, surrounded by all the people I love, has filled me with unspeakable joy. Now, I'm tired. You, Chris, and my grandbabies will sleep in our room—"

"Oh no, we couldn't take your room."

"I haven't had the strength to climb the stairs for a while, which is why Brent and I have been sleeping down here on the sofa bed. Don't worry about germs. We've had the house thoroughly cleaned, so every room is safe for my granddaughter."

Struggling to hold back tears, Wendy squeezed her mother's hand. "Tomorrow I want us to make more memories."

Silence fell over the room as Cynthia pressed her other hand on top of Wendy's then leaned her head back and closed her eyes. Kayla cuddled beside her mother. Riley sat at Cynthia's feet, her head resting on her lap. Wendy swallowed the fist-sized lump forming in her throat while closing her eyes to cherish the moment.

A gentle tap on her shoulder forced Wendy's eyes open. She peered up at Chris.

"The main bedroom is all set up for us."

Wendy leaned close to her mother. "I love you."

Cynthia's eyelids lifted. Their eyes met. She drew in a shallow breath. "I love you with all my heart. Goodnight, my darling Wendy." Her eyes closed.

Wendy kissed her mother's cheek. "Goodnight, Mom."

Hours after climbing into the king-sized bed with their daughter in the portable crib and Ryan curled between her and Chris, Wendy yielded to exhaustion. She slipped into a dreamless sleep—until a knock broke the silence. Her eyes popped open. The bedside clock glowed two a.m. Chris rushed to open the door.

"You two need to come down to the den." Brent's words came in a trembling rush. "Quickly."

Wendy's heart beat wildly in her chest. Her fingers trembled as she tucked pillows securely around Ryan. Her touch lingered on his cheek for a moment. She slid into her robe and gripped Chris's arm fearing her knees might buckle. They stepped out to the hall. The stairs blurred beneath her feet.

In the den, Kayla and Riley stood holding hands on one end of the sofa bed, their faces pinched with emotion. Zach stood on the other side, his arms dangling by his side. Brent sat on the edge of the bed holding his wife's hand. His eyes flicked to Wendy, heavy with unspoken truth, then returned to Cynthia. "We're all here, sweetheart."

Cynthia's head rested on a pillow. Her eyes fluttered open. She scanned the faces peering down at her, each glance deliberate. "From the moment I first learned of my illness..." Her voice came across as fragile, yet steady. "I've prayed to spend my last hours surrounded by everyone I love. Laughing. Enjoying every moment. Holding my granddaughter in my arms. Hearing my grandson call me Glamma." Her breathing was shallow.

"Today my heart overflowed with love." A serene, almost angelic expression brightened Cynthia's features. "Tonight...I'm ready to go to my eternal home, knowing you will all take care of each other."

Tears broke loose from Riley's eyes, streaking down her cheeks. "I don't want you to go, Mommy."

Cynthia's lips curved upward. "Come here, sweet girl."

Riley climbed onto the bed and nestled against her mother's chest, her lips quivering.

With visible effort, Cynthia lifted her arm and placed her hand on her youngest child's shoulder. "I want you to be happy for me." Each word seemed a gift of precious breath. "Soon I will fall into a deep sleep. When I wake up in heaven, I'll hear angels singing. My cancer will be gone. I'll spend my days smiling...dancing...loving you..." Her voice softened to a tender whisper. Her eyes closed. "Watching over you, my precious daughter."

Riley's lips stopped quivering.

A surreal calm filled the room as if an army of angels had floated down from heaven and wrapped their arms around Cynthia's family.

Kayla lowered to her knees. She grasped her mother's hand and began singing.

Listening to the tender words, Wendy understood. She laced fingers with Chris. Her sister was singing the song she and her father had written to honor her mother. Cynthia's eyes remained closed. Her lips curved into a gentle smile. Moments after Kayla sang the last refrain, her mother drew in one last breath before drifting into eternity.

Chapter 36

Wendy gazed out the bay window at the early afternoon sun shining on the Gilmores' manicured front lawn. Eighteen months earlier, after Armstrong Law Firm's private investigator located Cynthia, she and Amanda showed up unannounced at her front door. That day her mother's rejection had broken her heart all over again.

She turned away from the window, lowered onto the piano bench, and ran her fingers across the smooth keys. Her eyes drifted to the new addition among the array of family photos displayed on the white baby grand. A photo of grandmother and grandson sat beside the picture of her, Chris, and Ryan. A family she hadn't known existed eighteen months earlier had become an important part of her life.

Brent ambled in. "Gilmore's Bar and Restaurant is all set up."

Wendy peered up at him. "I was a little surprised by Mom's instruction to host a celebration of life party instead of a funeral."

"Hanging out at our place of business with friends and our band helped ease her disappointment over a failed singing career. These last few months, she realized how much she loved being a mother and a grandmother." Brent paused. "A week ago, Cynthia gave me seven letters sealed in envelopes along with specific instructions on when to give them to each family member. I opened mine last night. Her children and grandchildren are set for future birthdays."

Brent moved closer. "Except the one she wrote to you." He handed it over. "She wants you to open yours today. If Cynthia's words are as emotional as those she wrote to me, you'll need time alone to read your letter." Brent turned and walked out.

Wendy stared at her name followed by a heart for a long moment before she moved to the foyer, then upstairs to the main bedroom. After gently closing the door, she settled on the chair beside her daughter sleeping in the portable crib. She peeled back the flap and removed a folded sheet of pink stationery along with two photos—one taken on her one-month birthday. The other of Cynthia, her arm around Wendy, a cake with five candles on the table in front of them. Her hand trembled as she laid the photos on her lap then unfolded the handwritten letter.

My Dearest Darling Wendy,

There are events that profoundly impact our lives which, at the time they occur, are often beyond our understanding. During the past few months, I have identified those occasions relevant to each of the most important people in my life. For you, there are three that stand out above all the others.

The first was the day, driven by blind ambition, I abandoned you. Every time guilt threatened to overwhelm me, I pulled out the photo taken on your fifth birthday. Seeing your beautiful blue eyes, your precious smile, I imagined you living with a loving family, playing, laughing. Over the years the guilt disappeared, and the photo became a distant memory.

Until the second event—when eighteen years later you showed up at my home. A beautiful, young woman, pregnant with my grandchild. Rejecting you was the only way I believed I could survive the guilt that instantly overwhelmed me. The remorse for all those years I missed watching you grow up.

Everything changed the day I learned I was terminally ill. At that moment I understood that God was giving me time to make up for all the hurt

I inflicted on you. The afternoon Brent took me to Gilmore's to meet you, I had no idea how you would respond. Now it is nearly impossible to describe the joy I experienced from the third event—the moment you forgave me for abandoning you all those years ago.

The time we have spent together following that day—discovering how much you and Chris love each other and your child—filled me with indescribable joy. I understood that despite all the challenges and heartbreak you faced, you have grown into the incredible woman I should have aspired to become. You gave me the courage to spend my last days fulfilling the most important roles in my life—wife, mother, and grandmother.

Today, I hope you are comforted knowing how your love changed my life forever. I love you with all my heart, my darling Wendy. One day, after you have lived a long and beautiful life, I will again gather you in my arms and welcome you to your eternal home. Until then, whenever you need a little whisper of hope, read this letter and remember how much I treasured the times we shared as mother and daughter.

Love forever,

Mom

Wendy clutched the letter to her chest, smiling through the torrent of flowing tears. Every peak and valley that had shaped her life had brought her to this moment of joy mingling with sorrow over losing her mother.

The door eased open. Chris stepped inside. "Brent told me about Cynthia's letter."

Wendy held it out to him while swiping her fingers across her cheeks.

He sat on the edge of the bed, reading, his eyes reddening. "Your mother's words are a beautiful tribute to her firstborn child."

Wendy handed Chris the photos. "These are the only pictures I have from my first five years."

Chris held the photo of Wendy as an infant close to their baby's face. "Cynthia was right when she claimed her granddaughter is the perfect image of her beautiful mother."

Wendy moved beside him. "When I made the decision to ask Vincent to find Cynthia, I had no idea how much joy and heartache awaited."

Chris slid his arm around her shoulders. "I hope the joy outweighs the heartache."

She leaned into him. "Immeasurably." A gentle knock disrupted the moment, prompting her to open the door.

Brent tilted his head toward the stairs. "Cynthia's hospice nurse is here."

Wendy froze, her chest tightened. They'd never left Ryan with a stranger, much less their newborn.

Chris moved beside her. "If you're uncomfortable leaving our babies with someone you don't know, I'll stay here while you attend the celebration."

She blinked. "I'll decide after I meet her." She drew in a deep breath then slowly made her way down to the foyer.

The attractive, middle-aged woman's face lit with a warm smile. "Hi, I'm Carol." She extended her hand.

Their eyes met as Wendy accepted.

Carol gently squeezed her hand. "I imagine you're reluctant to leave your precious babies in the care of a stranger. I would be as well." She released Wendy's hand. "Hopefully the fact that I'm a former neonatal critical-care nurse will help ease your mind."

Riley walked in holding Ryan's hand. "Hi, Miss Carol."

"Hi, honey. This handsome boy must be Ryan."

"Uh-huh. He's my nephew." Riley placed Ryan's hand in Carol's. Babbling, he peered up at the stranger.

"I agree." Carol's smile widened as she lifted Ryan into her arms. "Your Aunt Riley is a special young lady. You and I will have lots of fun while your mommy and daddy celebrate your grammy's life."

Chris eased beside Wendy. His eyes met hers, his question unspoken.

She nodded then faced Carol. "Come meet the newest member of our family."

Twenty minutes after leaving their little guy and gal in the care of a woman who had earned their trust, they arrived in front of Gilmore's Bar and Restaurant in a limo. The driver rushed to open the rear door. Wendy and Chris stepped out, followed by her half siblings. Kayla held Riley's hand as they closed the distance to the entrance. In an unexpected display of chivalry, Zach rushed ahead and held the door open. Wendy stepped inside. Dozens of guests mingled in the space warmed by brick walls and a newly installed coffered ceiling.

Brent, donned in cowboy boots, jeans, and a plaid shirt, greeted them. "Everything is set up the way Cynthia instructed, including what I'm wearing."

"This was always Mom's happy place." Kayla nodded toward the young man playing the baby grand piano centered on the raised stage. "He's gonna play all of her favorite songs."

Two more guests walked in, drawing Brent's attention.

Riley pulled away from Kayla and rushed toward guests gathered at a long table displaying an array of family photos and memorabilia.

Wendy followed, her eyes settling on two side-by-side photos—one of Cynthia and Ryan, the other of Cynthia and her granddaughter.

"Me and Kayla set this up. Do you think Mom's watching us from heaven?"

Wendy eased her arm around Riley's shoulders. "She's watching with a big smile, proud of her girls."

The woman standing beside Riley shifted her focus from the display to Wendy. "You must be Cynthia's sister."

Riley shook her head. "Wendy's *my* big sister."

The woman's brows raised. "I've known Cynthia for years." Her eyes fixed on Wendy. "I had no idea she had three daughters."

How many guests would have the same reaction? "For good reason. Mom and I have only recently become reacquainted."

"Considering how much you look like her, don't be surprised if people stare at you."

Chris ambled over. "Kayla's ready for us to join her and Zach."

Within seconds of walking away from the display, Wendy discovered guests were too engaged in conversation to notice her, Riley, and Chris weaving their way through the crowd. After seating her at the family table adjacent to the stage, Chris settled beside her. Riley sat across from them, between Kayla and Zach. Four mocktails and two beers along with a platter of appetizers were on the table.

Kayla plucked a bacon-wrapped date off the platter. "These are all of Mom's favorites." Zach opted for a pizza bite while Riley sipped her mocktail.

The pianist stopped playing. Brent climbed onto the stage and stepped up to the microphone. The crowd quieted. "My family and I thank you for joining us to celebrate the life of a woman we all loved." He paused. "If you have a happy story about Cynthia you'd like to share, feel free to come up to the mike." He stepped aside.

A woman stepped onto the stage, introducing herself as Cynthia's best friend. Following her heartwarming comments about the weekends they'd spent at her vacation home, another person stepped up. Then another and another.

Watching her siblings respond to more than a dozen uplifting stories about their mother, Wendy understood the brilliance of Cynthia's request to host a party in their restaurant in lieu of a funeral. Following two days of the family shedding tears, praying, and sharing memories in private, they were creating warm memories while bidding their mother farewell with smiles and laughter. Wendy lifted her chin, smiling toward the ceiling. *Well done, Mom.*

Chapter 37

Amanda along with Millie supervised the placement of dozens of white padded folding chairs on the English country garden paths and the inn's patio. "We couldn't ask for more perfect weather. Clear blue sky." She glanced at her phone. "Sixty-eight degrees predicted for seven o'clock."

Millie pointed to the enormous white tent extending from the gazebo to Hilltop's back wall. "Ends up Erica didn't need this."

"True, although it does create a lovely atmosphere. Especially all those miniature lights strung across the tent."

The French doors leading to the Rainbow Suite swung open. The guest who had checked in the day before stepped onto the patio. "What a romantic setting. Would the bride and groom mind if my husband and I attend the ceremony?"

Amanda turned toward her. "They'd be honored." After the woman returned to her suite, Amanda strolled up the center walkway, stopping beside the three-tier bronze fountain.

Millie followed her. "How many dates have you and Gary been on?"

Amanda stooped and dipped her fingers in the pool of cool water. "I should ask the same question about you and Gordon."

Millie thumped Amanda's arm. "You're not going to answer, are you?"

"Excellent assumption, detective." Amanda nodded toward a bluebird landing on the gazebo's white wrought-iron railing. "Our first guest." The bird took flight.

"I'm your second."

Amanda spun toward Morgan heading toward them. "I'm delighted you're here, honey." She embraced her daughter.

"I wouldn't miss another Awesam wedding. Kevin's sorry he couldn't come. He's working all weekend." Morgan released Amanda. "Does Erica have any inkling about Abby's big surprise?"

"No, but Brad's clued in."

Millie plucked a leaf off the path. "Somehow we have to keep Erica from tearing up and ruining her makeup."

One of the men hired to set up the tent and chairs headed toward them. "Do you need any changes before we leave?"

Amanda glanced around. "Everything looks great. Thank you."

"You're welcome. We'll return tomorrow to tear down."

When they left, Millie turned to Amanda. "Now that we're ready out here, I need to head back inside and help Bernie with final preparations for the reception."

"We'll see you soon." Amanda linked arms with Morgan while they headed to the ranch house. "Tonight Erica and Brad are staying at Blue Ridge Inn before leaving for Maui tomorrow."

"Where she first met you and Wendy. How's your relationship with Gary going?"

"We're enjoying each other's company—"

"Along with a healthy dose of romance, I hope."

Amanda's thoughts drifted to their last kiss. "We have our moments."

"If sometime in the future he proposes, will you say yes?"

"Don't you think you're getting a little ahead of yourself?"

Morgan shrugged. "I'm just saying he'd be crazy to let you go." She held the kitchen door open, then followed her inside and on to the den.

Abby wheeled in from the hall, her face beaming. "I'm glad you're here to help."

Morgan bent to hug Abby. "We have a lot of catching up to do before I head back home tomorrow." She straightened. "Including the latest on your therapy."

"Until then, Anna and Tommy are meeting me in Hilltop's massage room an hour before the wedding to help me get ready." She explained. "I can't wait to surprise Mom."

Sierra stepped out of her room, quietly closing the door behind her before hugging Morgan.

"How's little Pip?"

"Growing like crazy. Three high school seniors are coming over to babysit him and Wendy's little ones."

Amanda leaned back against the sofa. "I'm surprised Wendy agreed to leave their baby with a sitter."

"Only because one of the sitters' mother is Allison's physician's assistant." Sierra pressed her palms together. "Today is my first wedding. If a man ever proposes, I want to keep the family tradition going and marry him in the gazebo."

The back door opened followed by footsteps. Erica walked in fresh from the beauty salon. "What do you think?" She turned in a slow circle revealing delicate white flowers woven into braids encircling her head then cascading along with the rest of her dark hair down her back.

"Oh my gosh, Mom." Abby wheeled closer. "Your hair, your make-up—everything's perfect."

Wendy, carrying her daughter, walked in through the kitchen, along with Chris, who held on to Ryan's hand. "Time for the Victory Sorority Sisters plus three to celebrate."

Sierra's head tilted. "What kind of sorority?"

Chris set the diaper bag on an end table. "An alliance that replaced the Exclusive Wive's Club after Amanda, Wendy, and Erica declared victory over one big-time loser named Gunter."

Fifteen minutes before the ceremony was scheduled to begin, Erica lifted a card off the dresser. "Yesterday, I received this congratulations card from Bobby, Brad's oldest son. He's on an aircraft carrier somewhere halfway across the globe. Anyway, he wrote 'Thank you for making Dad happy again.'"

"What a sweet message." Amanda lifted the wedding gown off the bed.

"I know." Erica stepped into an elegant floor-length, fitted white gown flared at the hem.

Wendy pulled the zipper up, then stepped back. "Fabulous dress."

Amanda nodded. "As elegant as the bride."

Erica faced her sorority sisters, forming a tight circle. "Thank you for being here with me."

Amanda squeezed her hand. "We'll always be there for each other."

"Through every peak and valley." Wendy lifted the bridal bouquet off the dresser. "Are you ready to become one with your groom?"

A radiant smile lit Erica's face. "More than ready." She stole one last glance in the mirror before heading out of her room and down the hall. Outside, she lifted her dress while crossing the side yard to the inn's front sidewalk.

"By the way," Amanda looped her arm around Erica's elbow as they climbed onto the porch then into Hilltop's foyer. "There's been a change. Abby and Jimmy are replacing Lauren and Carl as your maid of honor and best man."

Erica's brow pinched then released. "Abby didn't want her wheelchair to be a distraction. What made her change her mind?"

"You'll see." Wendy's smile brimmed with excitement as she led the way through the den.

Millie waited for them at the French doors, her eyes sparkling. "Look who's waiting for you."

Erica stared for a heartbeat, frozen in place. Her pastor stood in the center of the gazebo. Brad, handsome in a black tuxedo, stood beside his son to the right of the steps. On the left side, Abby stood tall, gripping a cane, beautiful in a royal blue gown. Erica pressed her hand to her chest. "How—"

"Special leg braces." Amanda leaned close, her voice tender. "Tommy's sitting two feet from her for security."

"It's time." Millie pulled the French doors open, signaling the DJ to begin the wedding march.

Wendy slipped the bouquet into Erica's hands.

The music swelled, then the crowd rose and turned toward her. Erica stepped across the threshold under twinkling lights, her heart overflowing with pure joy. Each step across the patio seemed like a miracle. Her gaze lifted from Abby's beaming face to her groom waiting at the end of the path. Brad's eyes locked on hers, shining with love. In that moment, surrounded by family and friends, time seemed to stand still. Her world was whole. Her heart was home.

Abby gripped her cane with one hand while holding the bridal bouquet with the other, her chest rising in deeply satisfied breaths. Hearing her mother exchange heartwarming vows with the man who loved her unconditionally made her own heart sing. Especially after all the heartache her mother had endured. The moment the bride and groom were introduced as Mr. and Mrs. Barkley, Abby could barely contain her joy. Her mother's eyes met hers, her smile speaking volumes—the bond between mother and daughter was stronger than ever.

As planned, after the newlyweds strolled down the path and across the patio, the pastor invited the guests to join the couple for a reception inside Hilltop Inn, eliminating the expectation that she and Jimmy would follow.

Tommy slid his arm around Abby's waist, his strength helping to support her. "I'm guessing you'll take your first steps by the time your mom and Brad return from their honeymoon."

Ashley linked arms with her boyfriend, Jimmy. "I can't begin to tell you how happy Jimmy and I were when we heard you'd be able to stand beside your mother."

Jimmy nodded, his eyes focused on Abby. "Knowing you'll walk again, plus the fact that me putting you in a wheelchair didn't destroy Dad and your mother's relationship, helps lift a huge weight off my shoulders."

Abby smiled at the young man who today had become her stepbrother. "Our lives will only get better from here."

Ashley smiled. "Abby's right, sweetie."

Sierra rushed over accompanied by Morgan. "I'm loving everything about this wedding." She crossed her hands on her chest. "The big white tent. The sparkly lights. You standing up for your mom."

Anna retrieved Abby's wheelchair from behind the garage the Awesam team had transformed into Hilltop's spa.

Morgan moved closer to Abby. "What do you say all us young folks go enjoy the reception, especially since Millie's one of the best chefs in Blue Ridge. Or according to her, the entire South."

"I'm all in." Tommy helped lower Abby into her chair then pushed her down the path and into Hilltop.

An hour after the reception began, guests mingled in the living room, in the den, and under the tent. Responding to her mother's request to gather the Awesam team, Abby waited for Morgan to open the front door then maneuvered to the far end of the porch under the glow of a newly installed outdoor chandelier. Morgan helped Abby lift out of her wheelchair. Standing for the second time today, Abby gripped the railing.

Wendy, Millie, and Amanda joined them, the latter setting a Champagne bottle and six flutes on a glass-topped wrought-iron table.

The bride breezed out as if floating on a cloud. "I didn't want tonight to end before spending a few minutes alone with the five most important women in my life."

Amanda poured the Champagne. Glasses clinked. Six women sipped, strengthening a bond few would ever understand.

Chapter 38

Ten minutes before the polls were scheduled to close, Amanda sat beside Linda at the Armstrongs' kitchen island sipping a glass of chardonnay. She nodded toward their candidate and his finance manager relaxing on the great room sofa. "All indications are Keith will win by a healthy margin."

Linda wrapped her fingers around her wineglass stem. "Which means, after all these years in private practice, my husband will need to transition from helping clients to prosecuting lawbreakers."

"Do you ever wish he hadn't decided to run?"

"Yes and no. Yes, because I understand what he's giving up, especially working with Chris. However, no, because our friends and neighbors deserve an honest DA. Keith is hoping to groom one of the attorneys in the DA's office to follow in his footsteps before the next election."

"So he can retire?"

"I doubt he'll ever retire, at least not full-time. He'll return to practicing law in the firm his father established. Enough talk about careers and politics. How's everything going with you and Gary?"

Amanda swirled the golden liquid in her wineglass. "After the disaster with Gunter, I didn't know if I'd ever trust another man with my heart, until Gary and I began seeing each other socially. Like Preston, he's one of the good guys."

"Keith and I have been close friends with Gary for years. You're the first woman he's trusted since his wife betrayed him."

"Maybe because I'm an outsider."

"You stopped being an outsider the day you and your partners opened Hilltop Inn." Linda nudged Amanda. "Gary loves you for who you are."

A soft smile tugged at Amanda's lips. Maybe, just maybe, she'd follow in Wendy and Erica's footsteps and at some point in the future marry again.

Keith meandered over and pulled two beer bottles from the fridge. "Polls are now officially closed."

Gary followed, accepting a beer from Keith. He twisted off the cap then clinked his bottle to Amanda's glass. "Which means we're about to celebrate a campaign brilliantly managed by a bank vice president and a luxury inn owner."

"Hey, don't forget a super-efficient recording secretary," Linda's tone playfully mocked.

Keith chuckled. "Seems my staff has forgotten that winning requires a talented candidate."

"Who's also a shameless pool shark." Gary nudged his friend's arm. "While we wait for results, I'll challenge you to a game."

"You're on."

While the guys headed toward the stairs, Linda climbed off her stool. "We might as well join them."

Amanda followed her down to the terrace level that for months had served as campaign central. Before the night ended, the space would transition back to a game room, where friends gathered to have fun and enjoy each other's company. In the high-ceilinged room that opened to a patio beneath the deck, she and Linda settled on two of four club chairs encircling a round coffee table. Amanda focused her attention on Gary racking the cue balls. So much beyond his handsome face and muscular body intrigued her. His playful sense of humor. How he engaged in meaningful conversation. The tingling sensation that surged through her every time he gathered her in his arms and kissed her.

"Our guys love the competition."

Amanda blinked, her focus shifting to Linda. Her friend's smile, the way she said 'our guys', hinted that she somehow understood Amanda's thoughts. "So it seems."

"Have you heard from Erica since she and Brad flew to Hawaii?"

"A text to the Awesam team telling us they're having a wonderful time, with photos to prove it."

"Hilltop's garden is the perfect venue for romantic weddings."

Could she be any more obvious? Time to change the subject. "How do you plan to spend all the spare time you'll have now that the campaign is coming to an end?"

Amanda and Linda continued chatting until Keith plucked his ringing phone off the table.

"This is the call we've been waiting for." He swiped his finger across the screen, activating the speaker. "What's the verdict?"

"Congratulations, DA Armstrong. You have soundly defeated Richard Watson."

Gary clasped his hand on Keith's shoulder. "Congratulations, buddy."

Linda rushed to embrace her husband. "You're going to be a wonderful district attorney, darling."

"Without your support, victory would not have been possible. What do you say we rerack and celebrate with the four of us playing."

Linda released Keith. "Great idea. Are you game, Amanda?"

"There's only one issue." Amanda set her wine glass on the coffee table then moved close to Gary. "I've never played pool."

"Not a problem." Gary slid his arm around her shoulders while handing her a pool cue. "I'll teach you."

"How can I refuse such a generous offer?" Delighting in his touch while ignoring Linda's grin, she wrapped her fingers around the grip. While celebrating victory, Amanda imagined spending many more enjoyable evenings with the man who had taken one step closer to capturing her heart.

Chapter 39

Amanda grabbed a down jacket from the closet then stepped out of her room and headed down the hall. She paused beside the bedroom Erica had occupied from the day she, Wendy, and Abby moved into the ranch house until her wedding. Dusty padded into the space, sniffing. "You miss her, don't you, girl? She'll come to visit after returning from her honeymoon tomorrow." Abby's canine companion returned to her side, responding with a tail wag. Amanda patted her head. "Time for me to head next door for check-in duty."

After continuing to the kitchen, grabbing a key off the counter, and donning her jacket, Amanda stepped out to the carport. The bitter mid-November cold front that had moved in yesterday sent a chill through her while she scurried to Hilltop's front porch then into the foyer. She peeled off her jacket and strode through the den to the kitchen.

Millie sat at the island tapping her iPad keyboard.

"I'm surprised you're still here."

"Two couples hung out in the dining room, talking and drinking coffee until an hour ago. What's going on with you, now that the political campaign is over?"

Amanda poured a cup of coffee. "Unplugging was more difficult than I had imagined."

"Sounds as if you need a new challenge." Millie pushed her iPad aside. "Our Mystery Club is meeting tonight. You're welcome to join us."

"Are you discussing a book?" Amanda settled beside Millie. "Or are you investigating some random case?"

"A book, until something more interesting comes along. Do you or don't you want to join in the fun?"

"I would, except Gary's cooking dinner for us tonight."

Millie raised a brow. "At his house?"

"He didn't rent space in a restaurant kitchen, so yeah, at his house."

"Are you planning to stay the night?"

Amanda stared wide-eyed. "Don't you think that question is way too personal?"

"Well, are you or aren't you?"

"For your information—" Amanda aimed her thumb toward the ranch house. "I'm planning to sleep next door, alone in my bed. Now, how about we change the subject to what's going on with you and Gordon."

Millie shrugged. "Let's just say I haven't had an occasion to wear that sexy nightie you gave me."

Amanda laughed. "One of these days, one of us is destined to win the 'snag a guy for Amanda' bet."

"You know, we could end up in a draw."

"Not likely, but maybe." The front doorbell chimed. Amanda slid off her stool. "Are you expecting a delivery?"

Millie shook her head. "Today's only check-in must have arrived early." She followed her through the den to the foyer.

Amanda summoned her best innkeeper smile then pulled the door open.

A young woman with long dark hair, gripping a suitcase handle, stared at her.

"You must be Savannah Landry. Welcome to Hilltop Inn. I'm Amanda, one of the owners. This is Millie, our award-winning chef."

The pretty young woman with expressive brown eyes stepped across the threshold.

Millie moved closer. "Where's home?"

"New Orleans."

"Same place Amanda hails from. Maybe you know some of the same people."

"New Orleans is a big city, Millie. Not a small town like Blue Ridge." Amanda motioned toward the desk. "After you sign our guest book, Ms. Landry, I'll tell you about our inn."

Millie followed their new guest as she eased to the desk and wrote her name. "Is this your first trip to Blue Ridge?"

Savannah nodded.

"We're honored you've chosen to stay with us." After launching into the spiel she repeated with each new arrival, Amanda lifted a key off the desk. "The Dogwood Suite is one of our loveliest." She led the way up the stairs, stopping at the landing. Was Millie tagging along to find out why a pretty young woman checked into a romantic inn alone?

Amanda led the way along the hall that spanned the full length of the second floor to the last room on the left. She unlocked the door, her hand lingering on the knob for a moment longer than necessary before pushing the door open.

Savannah pulled her suitcase into the room then moved to the window overlooking the front lawn. She stood perfectly still, as if bracing herself.

Amanda laid the key on the dresser, forcing a polite smile. "Please let us know if there is anything we can do to make your stay perfect."

"Before you leave..." Savannah's voice faltered as she turned away from the window. "Do you have time to talk?"

Amanda tilted her head. "Would you like more information about Hilltop or our town?"

"No. Do you mind closing the door?"

Amanda hesitated, a silent alarm rising in her chest.

"So we can talk in private."

An odd request. At least she seemed harmless. Amanda closed the door knowing full well Awesam's chief information officer wouldn't budge an inch. She moved closer to the young woman. "What's on your mind?"

Savannah sank onto the edge of the bed, her hands clenched tightly on her lap. "My mother—her name's Jacqueline Landry—passed away a month ago."

A pang of sympathy eased the tension gripping Amanda's shoulders "I'm so sorry. I was about your age when I lost my mother."

"We lived in an apartment a couple blocks off Canal Street. Mom never married and never had any other children."

Amanda remained standing, her arms stiff at her sides. What would compel this young woman to lay bare her life to a stranger?

"I never knew anything about my father..." Savannah's voice trembled. "Until after Mom died." She picked at a fingernail. "I came here because...you're the only family I have left."

Icy tentacles of dread crept up Amanda's spine. "How old are you?"

"Twenty-two. Same age as your daughter." Savannah lifted her chin. Her eyes locked on Amanda's with settled certainty. "You need to know that Preston Smith...was my father."

The world seemed to spin out of control. A ringing filled Amanda's ears as twenty-six missing days flashed like lightning across her mind. The man she had loved with all her heart—her soulmate—would never have cheated on her, would he? Her pulse pounded in her ears. "I have no idea who you are, or what you really want."

"I—"

"Stop." Amanda aimed her palms as if to ward off another blow. "No more." She rushed to the door, yanked it open, then she stumbled out to the hall.

Millie tapped her foot, her arms tight across her chest. "You can count on our mystery club to find out what sort of scam that innocent-looking woman is trying to pull."

Amanda pressed her back against the wall, gulping air to steady herself. Praying Savannah Landry was a con artist. Terrified she wasn't. She forced words past her dry throat. "I hope your invitation is still open...because I'm coming to that meeting."

In one last move, Amanda pushed off the wall and forced herself to walk away. If the woman who had checked into the Dogwood Suite was telling the truth, her life would never be the same.

Thank you for reading Whispers of Hope, Blue Ridge series book seven. The story continues in Fragile Hearts. Is Savannah Landry who she claims to be, or is she a con artist? Find out when Fragile Hearts publishes in February 2026.

While waiting, if you would like to read a completed series and haven't read my Willow Falls series, check out book The Secret of Willow Inn, book one in the four-book series.

If you aren't already one of my newsletter friends, I invite you to become one: https://www.subscribepage.com/pat-nichols-newsletter

Afterword

Every author travels their own writing journey. Mine began when I wrote my first manuscript at the ripe young age of sixty nine. Four years and three books later, I became a published author. Now while writing book number sixteen, I'm continuing to prove it's never too late to follow your dreams. I am grateful for the wonderful people who are traveling this journey with me.

My editor and dear friend, Sherri Stewart, who's also a multi-published author, has edited twelve of my books. She knows my characters as well as I do. Elaina Lee has designed all sixteen of my current covers.

My beta readers, Pat Davis, Carlene Dunn, Bev Feldkamp, Kitty Metzger, Kathy Warner, CJ Bruce, Zanase Duncan, and Lynn Worley give me excellent feedback from readers' perspectives. My Word Weaver friends provide feedback from authors' perspectives. My dedicated launch team members are the first to read and post reviews. My newsletter friends and readers' loyalty always make my heart sing.

A special thanks to my high-school-sweetheart husband, Tim, for smiling when I talk about my characters as if they lived outside my head. I'm grateful to my entire family for their encouragement and patience when I share my newest plot twist.

Above all I'm grateful to God for His amazing grace, His Son, my savior, and the gift of eternal life.

www.ingramcontent.com/pod-product-compliance
Lightning Source LLC
Chambersburg PA
CBHW030431160726
47991CB00005B/1682